The
BELLES
of
WATERLOO

The
BELLES
of
WATERLOO

ALICE CHURCH

UNIVERSE

This edition published by Universe
Unicorn Publishing Group
Charleston Studio
Meadow Business Centre
Lewes BN8 5RW

www.unicornpublishing.org

10 9 8 7 6 5 4 3 2 1

ISBN 978-1-914414-23-7

Inside cover: © Chronicle / Alamy Stock Photo
Cover design by Felicity Price-Smith
Typesetting by Vivian Head

Printed in the UK

Historical note

The characters in this book all existed in real life, and the majority of the story is told as it really happened. Each chapter begins with an extract of a letter written by one of the Capels to the family matriarch, the Dowager Countess of Uxbridge, except the first which is written by Lady Uxbridge to one of her grandsons. The original spelling and punctuation has been left as in the original transcripts.

A note on titles

Readers will notice a discrepancy in the title of Lady Caroline Capel and that of her husband, the Hon. John Capel.

John Capel was the younger son of the 4th Earl of Essex, and the half-brother of the 5th Earl. His wife, Caroline, was the daughter of the 1st Earl of Uxbridge, a close friend of King George III. Lady Caroline claimed her title from her father, whereas John Capel, being the younger son of an earl, could not.

*To Charlie and Freddie, for completing
my own search for happiness*

PART I

∽⚬∾

MAY 1814

Preface

It all began with London coming alive to celebrate the end of Napoleon's reign of tyranny. 'The Ogre' was finally defeated and the English were revelling in their victory. Houses were decorated with banners and bunting; the city was a riot of colour. Celebratory parades and balls were being planned by the dozen. Yet in one house the mood was about to take a sombre turn.

Lady Caroline knew the situation was serious and that the news couldn't be kept from her children any longer, but she was determined that the true reason they had to leave London so quickly would remain a secret. It wasn't something she wanted her children exposed to, and in any case only her three eldest daughters were likely to put up a fight; the other eight children were too young to fully understand.

The weather that morning had been rather grey and dank, a fitting backdrop for the news Lady Caroline was to impart. Her three eldest daughters Harriet, Georgy and Maria, sat on the sofa in front of her.

'Girls, it has been decided that we are to leave London and move to Brussels, and we must make a start right away.'

In her mind she had imagined their responses, and they were exactly as she had predicted. Harriet merely stared as she processed the information, Georgy gasped dramatically and Maria immediately set her brow in a determined frown of discontent. Lady Caroline, stoic yet not impervious to the tantrums of her children, calmly continued from her position of safety on the opposite sofa.

'I'm sure we will be very happy there. You know Brussels is just as established a town as London, with shops, theatres and ballrooms in exactly the same number and to the same standard...'

She rambled on in this vein for some time, but the frosty reception to her news didn't thaw. It was Maria who broke the silence and the questioning commenced.

'Well, I must say I don't like the idea one bit,' she said. 'We shall have to leave behind all our friends, our family. What sort of people shall we find in Brussels in any case?'

'I can't even recall where Brussels is!' said Georgy, who was looking crosser by the second. Lady Caroline made a mental note to scold the governess about the girls' poor geography.

'Shall there even *be* dances?' Georgy continued.

'Plenty,' Lady Caroline replied. 'Less crowded than London, too, so you girls can shine all the more brightly.'

'What will Grandmama say? She'll be horrified at the idea of our leaving!' said Harriet.

'But you can write and tell her about all your adventures, and hopefully one day she'll visit us herself.' Before any girl could parry her, Lady Caroline continued, 'You know, much of the British army is stationed in Brussels at the moment.' She said it lightly, watching for their reaction.

Their expressions brightened.

'The militia?' said Georgy.

'No, the regular army; the Duke of Wellington is said to be interested in the area strategically.'

Lady Caroline allowed a moment for the information to sink in. The girls glanced at each other. The next youngest of her daughters, Louisa, was sitting on the floor at their feet, doll in hand, looking confused by the changing expressions on the faces of her elder sisters. Even Harriet, sensible and book-minded as she was, looked mollified at the prospect of living in such proximity to the army.

'Then will Uncle be there?' This was Lady Caroline's brother, and a great family favourite.

'I should think eventually, yes.' Before they could ask another question, Lady Caroline cut in.

'Really, girls, I cannot reason why you're not more excited. Just think of the fun you shall have! You will all be married by Christmas, I am sure!'

Sadly, this comment didn't have quite the impact she had hoped for.

'I really don't see why we have to move to a different country in order to find suitable husbands,' snorted Maria. *If only she knew*, Lady Caroline thought. Maria's colour was rising as she went on, 'Surely we are better known here. We have friends from Mayfair to Chelsea. I, for one, would rather we stay here in London, *where we belong*.' Great emphasis was placed on those last three words.

'Maria,' Lady Caroline sighed. 'It's just not as simple as that any more.'

'But why not?'

'There are things that you must just accept, and this is one of them.'

'We three are no longer children like the others. What is it that causes us to leave with such haste? Is it something to do with Papa?'

Lady Caroline began to have a sinking feeling that Maria knew more of their situation than she had realised. Lady Caroline had never been very good at lying and as the children got older, she found it harder and harder. She felt her colour rise and her response was more bluster than reassurance.

'Really, Maria, how can you say such a thing! Of course it isn't. Your papa says we are to go, and so we go. As we are leaving now it should mean we get the pick of the houses. Your father is trying to secure one that faces the royal park. It will be quite a step up, I assure you.'

Now it was Georgy's turn. 'If we are to leave London, why must it be done with such haste? Could we not stay in London a little longer and join the celebrations?'

Lady Caroline was losing patience. 'Girls, the decision has been made and the sooner you accept it, the better. You're always talking of adventure; well, here is one for you! Now you had better go upstairs and start thinking about packing. Your father will be home for supper and we must have progress to report to him.'

The girls reluctantly went upstairs. The first battle had been won.

∞◦∞

'Home for supper? When has father ever made it home for supper of late?' grumbled Maria, minutes after she, Harriet and Georgy had stomped up the stairs to their rooms. She was so cross her palms were hot and damp. 'Whatever has happened to require us to move with such haste?'

'Mama is clearly worried, but doesn't want to tell us what the true reason is... but I suppose we can guess.' Georgy looked awkwardly across at the other two. There was a pause. Indeed, they all had a sense of the true cause of their abrupt removal from London, but it wasn't something they usually spoke about.

Maria sighed. 'So you've both heard the rumours? I suppose I wish they could just be spite and hearsay.'

'I've heard people commenting on Papa's gambling, yes,' replied Harriet, with caution. 'I hoped it was just, as you say, a rumour, and after all, so many of our family and friends gamble, don't they?'

'Yes, and many do so beyond their means. But I think we had less means than most to begin with.' Maria's anger was replaced by more complicated emotions that felt nearer to shame. 'Do you think that's why we have to leave so suddenly? To escape creditors?' The word was a horror to her.

'I think I've already seen such people outside on the street, but when they tried to speak to me, I ran inside. This was a few days ago,' said Georgy hesitantly. 'Awful men, they were. It begins to make sense, now.'

Georgy's eyes widened. 'So I suppose there really is no money left?'

'That would appear to be the reality of it.' Maria wrapped her arms around herself. 'I've often thought that Grandmama hints in her letters how much she helps Papa, and I suppose that has been money all along.'

'And I suppose this also means...'

'No money for dowries,' Georgy finished Harriet's sentence, her eyes downcast.

'Well, yes. I suppose not.' Maria said.

They were quiet for a time. It wasn't a pleasant thing to talk of, money, or indeed the very acute lack of its presence in their lives. It was even less pleasant to talk of the money that was needed for them each to make a good marriage. Yet the reality of the situation was becoming more apparent to them with each tick of the clock on the mantel.

'So, we are to move to Brussels. Do you suppose it will be an adventure, like Mama says?' said Georgy.

'We can surely make it an adventure if we want it to be.' Maria hoped she sounded surer than she felt. Truth be told, she felt painfully disappointed that her father had got them into this situation. Why could he not control himself? He had always presented himself as a mild, kind-hearted figure, so unlike the cold, ill-mannered fathers with whom many of her friends had to contend. But in this way he had failed them, and for that Maria wondered if she would ever really forgive him. Their lives, once so clearly set out before them, now seemed bleak. Without dowries, how could they ever make good marriages and keep houses of their own?

The sad fact was that, due to John Capel's gambling, the family was flat broke. The debts had been growing for years, and was an unspoken canker in the marriage between John Capel and Lady Caroline. Without the financial provisions made by both their families, they would all have ended up in debtors' prison many years ago. The damage permeated every aspect of their lives, including their credibility in the higher circles of society, the kind of circles that by rights they should be mixing in and marrying into. Everyone knew of Capel's gambling problem. It was whispered about at the dinners, balls and banquets they attended, the parlour rooms in which they played bridge and the picnics to which they took the children. Many people felt sorry for Lady Caroline and her growing number of children, but pity wouldn't pay the bills or keep the creditors at bay.

Capel's addiction to the 'Green Table' wasn't at all unusual for the time. Many men entertained themselves in this way and some, indeed, lost and won great fortunes, but without a fortune to start with, Capel had gambled with the position and security of his family. Lady Caroline had little means of protecting her children other than by securing funds from her mother. This kept the bailiffs from the door. In the end, Brussels looked like the solution to all their problems, providing cheap living, a smaller number of families to compete with socially and a chance to remove Capel from the gaming tables to which he was always drawn back, despite his best promises.

With the threat of bailiffs and debtors' prison more likely by the day, Capel was insistent that they leave London as soon as peace with France had been declared. They were headed to the newly created Kingdom of the Netherlands, where soldiers were still looting, stealing and getting into all kinds of trouble since the fall of Napoleon. Capel was undeterred, and the family began to pack up their lives, knowing further argument was futile.

CHAPTER I

Heroes in the Parlour

'To think a Month ago the Monster might have had the Kingdom of France, and that he is now reduced to the State of Pauper, fills the mind with astonishment.'

The Dowager Countess of Uxbridge to Arthur Capel

As their carriages trundled through the city a few days later, they saw coloured banners streaming from house to house and Londoners rushing around the streets making last-minute preparations for the now imminent celebration balls. It seemed such a waste to be missing them. Maria looked out of the window, one of her younger siblings, Horatia, sitting on her lap. She felt glum beyond words.

Their journey would be a long and uncomfortable one with little hope of respite, especially as a lack of funds meant they could only afford two carriages. Both were packed to the gunnels with the two parents, eleven children, five servants and all their possessions.

Joyful London fell behind them and they trundled towards the coast. Hours and days of travel stretched before them, and Maria wondered how she might make the best of moving to Brussels. She could hardly feel excited at the prospect of living in a foreign country of which she had no knowledge, where she knew nobody and didn't even speak the common tongue. She couldn't see how Brussels could ever compare to London and all the fun she'd had to look forward to there now that she was coming of age and would be allowed to go to evening parties and soirées. She felt thoroughly depressed by the whole affair.

Perhaps the knowledge of their financial collapse would follow them to Brussels? If English families were there, how could it not? The idea haunted Maria. She thought of her friends and peers whispering behind gloved hands. She thought of young men once wanting to add their names to her dance card now moving on to another. Time and time again she thought of her father and disappointment hung heavy around her shoulders like a winter cloak. Luckily, he was in the other carriage with their mother, so she didn't have to look at him. How could he have driven them to this? She sighed, leaning her forehead against the cold windowpane, and closed her eyes.

⌘

Of the eleven Capel children, the eldest was Harriet, serious and artistic, at twenty-one years of age. Second came Georgiana, always called Georgy, at nineteen. Georgy had a warm-hearted, open manner, with charm and gaiety that led to strong friendships as well as flirtations that sometimes caused trouble. She was similar in character to Maria, the third eldest. Maria was a lover of adventure, although she was often held back from by the protestations of her parents and eldest sister.

Georgy was more concerned with falling in love with one

of the handsome visitors that came to take supper than with going on adventures, while Harriet, as befits the eldest of a large family with often absent parents, took on the mothering role with a kind earnestness. This often saw her stopping Maria from running wild through the streets of London, sometimes in the company of the boys who helped out in the kitchens, or from playing practical jokes on their papa, which saw him roaring round the house, wrongly assuming the culprit was their brother Arthur.

Despite their differences, the three eldest Capel daughters were the closest of friends. This caused much dismay to Louisa and Horatia, the two sisters who came next and who often felt left out. The three eldest had bonded together for mutual support and comfort as their family quickly increased in number. For after Louisa and Horatia another child came, and luckily for Lady Caroline she was finally delivered of a boy. Arthur had grown into a hardworking and spirited eleven-year-old, but to his great sadness he was to be left behind in England for schooling at Eton, an expense covered by his step-uncle, the current Earl of Essex.

After Arthur came little Janey, then Algernon, who hadn't yet reached his seventh birthday. The nursery was kept busy by the arrival of Mary, then Amelia; and, finally, baby Adolphus, who was the apple of everyone's eye at just under a year in age. Their large family was far from unusual for their time and class, and although hectic, Maria wouldn't have had it any other way. Although she sometimes felt crushed in the midst of so many children battling for the attention of their mother and father, they had somehow muddled through life in

London and were on the whole as close and connected as she could wish. Certainly there was never a dull moment, unless you wanted there to be one, in which case you would have to find a secret corner of the house in which to have it, hiding from the little ones who always wanted to either complain or play a game with you.

Lady Caroline had high hopes for Brussels and was anxious to get her tribe there as soon as possible. Her focus centred on her eldest daughters, now of marriageable age. Harriet, Georgy and Maria had all turned out to be beautiful and confident young ladies who gave her great pride. Despite the financial problems that had dogged them for years, the Capel girls had been brought up with all the accomplishments that society demanded of them. They could sing, dance and draw admirably.

Harriet's intelligence shone through when speaking to people three times her age, and she was an accomplished pianist and needlewoman. Georgy loved to dance and was the life and soul of every party. Maria had a quick wit and easy manner; she made friends easily and never lost them. All three loved to laugh, and wrote songs and plays to entertain their family, dragging the little ones in to perform minor roles and dressing the babies until they vaguely resembled whatever character or animal they wanted to represent.

If Capel had been the eldest rather than the second son of the 4th Earl of Essex, they would have had a fortune with which to provide dowries for Maria and her sisters, but this was not to be their lot. Lacking the personal motivation and courage to secure an occupation for himself, Capel had led an unfulfilled and unprofitable life. His lack of daily occupation took him more often than not to the gambling clubs of St James's, to Brooks's or White's, and when trying to conceal his habit from his peers and wife, to the gambling dens of Soho. He drowned his insecurities with whisky and games of whist that lasted until the sun rose and blurry thoughts of Lady Caroline's anger drew him home. Brussels was to be a chance for a fresh start, a place where they could put the troubles of England behind them and make new lives for themselves.

∽∾∾

A little over a week after they had left London, Maria stood in the parlour of the Ship Inn in Dover, where they had rented rooms while awaiting passage to Brussels. Although the journey from London had been as tortuous as expected, the days they had spent in the busy coastal town had more than made up for their discomfort.

While exploring Dover, Harriet, Georgy and Maria had seen people of all nations and ranks celebrating Napoleon's downfall. Foreigners wearing strange fashions and speaking unknown tongues roamed the streets and filled the taverns; their shouts created cacophonies of joyful noise. Rockets were fired and gun salutes roared out seemingly at random. Forgetting their disappointment at having to leave London, the Capel sisters were thrilled to be part of such excitement.

Today, Maria and her siblings were lined up in their Sunday best, ready to greet some eminent guests who their father had brought to meet them. Their lodgings were situated alongside the main thoroughfare of the town, so Maria had an excellent view of the excitement in the street, where she could see the rabble running about like madmen. One or two had looked through the glass and seen who was in their parlour, so a crowd had gathered and begun hammering at the windows and door, demanding entry to their party.

Maria felt quite safe inside the parlour, despite the increasing noise outside. Turning to the window she saw a boy, not much older than herself, his face crushed against the windowpane, his arm pressed to it at an odd angle. Dozens more bodies pushed against the rattling pane.

Maria fought back a laugh. Everyone inside the parlour was avoiding any acknowledgement of the riotous behaviour just a hair's breadth away on the street. Maria glanced at her mother and saw a rosy flush across her cheeks, a family trait and a tell-tale sign of excitement. She lifted a hand to her own cheek and felt that it, too, was warm. Just at that moment, the King of Prussia grasped her other hand and greeted her in a thick accent. He was one of a whole host of tall and imposing men waiting to meet her, each wearing the formal attire of his respective nation, assorted medals jostling for position on dress uniforms.

Next, General Blücher shook her hand vigorously, with a warm smile. He smelt of whisky and the road. Blücher was adored by the Prussian troops he commanded, and was a firm favourite in the Capel household, too. Maria grinned, hardly able to believe that she was finally meeting the famous Prussian field marshal. He moved on to the younger Capel children, bending down and kissing each on the cheek. His extravagant whiskers must have tickled because they giggled and blushed, too.

Blücher looked as old and battle-worn as Maria had imagined. He was a legendary military leader, known to be difficult and cantankerous, but admired for his dogged determination on and off the battlefield. Now he stood in their grotty little parlour, conversing good-naturedly in German with their papa. Maria could tell her father was struggling to keep up; he was nodding earnestly in agreement with whatever Blücher was saying, and saying as little as possible himself. His German was quite limited and Blücher's accent extremely strong.

Maria had now been introduced to a king, an emperor, a prince and four generals. It was quite overwhelming. She didn't catch all their names the first time, and would have to ask her mother for the spellings later. Her grandmother, the Dowager Lady Uxbridge, would want to hear about them all.

What a stroke of luck that the Capels should be making the crossing to France at the same time as these men were journeying to London to join the celebrations of Napoleon's abdication and exile. Maria could feel the palms of her hands, clasped behind her back, were clammy. They had met men like Blücher before, of course; they had even met the Duke of Wellington once or twice, but to greet such a group of notable individuals all at once and at such an important and victorious moment for Britain was something else altogether.

Maria caught Georgy's eye; she looked as excited as Maria felt. On her other side, Harriet was conversing with Prince Hardenburgh, nodding and smiling like their father. Georgy grinned slyly and Maria stifled a giggle.

'Do you think any of them are unmarried?' Georgy whispered, out of the corner of her mouth.

Maria wanted to laugh even more. Their mother gave them a warning look and both looked away sheepishly. Meanwhile, the drumming on the glass grew ever more insistent. Turning again, Maria saw the boy she'd noticed earlier had disappeared, perhaps pushed below the frame.

Of course, more than any of the other dignitaries, it was General Blücher who the crowd had really come for. He was more famous than the emperors and princes put together. In England, he was a war hero to match only their own Duke of Wellington.

Suddenly the noise from the drumming and shouting could be contained no longer and one of the panes of glass smashed, causing everybody, military heroes and royalty included, to jump out of his or her skin. Once one gave way, others followed, and hands pushed through the panes. Shouts and cries burst in on them, the sudden increase in volume alarming and thrilling in equal measure, and Maria could see blood on the hands that stretched towards Blücher, beseeching him to join them in their celebrations.

'Goodness! How exciting!' she said, and she could see that Blücher was enjoying the attention, too.

Lady Caroline, appalled at the interruption, began to hurry the children out of the parlour, but bluff old General Blücher merely chuckled. He went to the door and opened it to the crowd to give them what they wanted. His hands were raised in supplication, beseeching the crowd to treat him gently.

Had he understood what his fate would be he might perhaps have instead retreated with Lady Caroline, for as soon as he opened the door the mob entered and swarmed him.

Within seconds, he had been lifted bodily into the air and carried through the doorway on willing shoulders, banging his head on the way. They took him off down the street, huzzaing louder than ever.

The guests looked shocked at this turn of events, clearly worried that they might be next. The Capel sisters could barely contain their glee. Maria thought it all the best of fun and couldn't wait to write to her grandmother about their first adventure in the little parlour in Dover. Certainly, this crossing looked like it would be more enjoyable than she had imagined.

In all they had to wait a full week at the Ship Inn before they could get a suitable crossing for them all. Ships were hard to come by, with so many people crossing to the Continent or returning to England. Even General Blücher reported that he'd been forced to sleep a night in his carriage, although Maria suspected that might have had more to do with the lateness of the hour than the lack of a room.

By the time the family finally left Dover, the celebrations had died down, diminished no doubt by pounding heads and empty purses. Finally, they stood on the deck of a sailing ship heading to Calais. The crew were too busy to pay them much notice and Maria, Georgy and Harriet huddled by the gangway, watching workmen loading their possessions while the rigging and decking creaked around them. Maria had never travelled in such a fashion before, and felt rather nauseous at the thought of the ship on the dark deep water and the buffeting waves. The smell of the sea and the ship was sharp and tasted of adventure.

'Well, I'm not sure about sea travel,' Maria said, 'but goodness! To think of the people we've met so far, and we haven't even reached Brussels yet!'

Her sisters smiled their agreement.

'Isn't it extraordinary to think,' mused Harriet, 'that we shall be one of the very first families to leave London and live abroad in over ten years.'

'I hope we shall set the trend, then,' said Maria, laughing, 'for I do not wish us to be the only ones there!'

'I do,' Georgy shot back. She leant past Harriet to say to Maria, 'for I wish to get my pick of the officers!'

Harriet sighed as the other two laughed, and the ship sailed away from the harbour, signalling the beginning of the voyage.

CHAPTER II

The Ribbon Box

'We are so gazed at whenever we stir out, it is quite disagreeable, I suppose from the difference of Dress, & the numbers — Ah voici les Belles Anglaises is heard on all sides...'

Lady Caroline Capel to the Dowager Countess of Uxbridge

Lady Caroline Paget, as she was before her marriage to John Capel, had been an exceptional beauty in her youth, and even now people commented upon her dark wide eyes and pretty oval face. A portrait of Lady Caroline by the renowned artist John Hoppner, baby Harriet on her lap, hung at the Paget family home in Wales. Whenever they visited Plas Newydd, Lady Caroline took her children to see the portrait and they would stand in front of the painting, gazing at the unlined face of their mother and laughing at what a tiny baby Harriet had been.

Lady Uxbridge remained a dominant force in her daughter's life even after her marriage, and her overbearing nature had not always been conducive to Lady Caroline's matrimonial happiness. Within a year of the wedding, and with Harriet well on the way, it was clear that John Capel had lost control over their finances. After some discreet probing, Lady Uxbridge discovered that Capel was frequenting the gambling clubs of St James's far more often than was socially necessary for a man of his standing.

There was little that Lady Uxbridge could do to support her daughter, who refused to confront her husband until the problem spiralled out of control. Before long, Lady Caroline, Capel and their children were forced to spend several months of each year with Lady Uxbridge, who paid for their upkeep and for the small army of nurses, governesses and teachers needed to support their growing family.

At their last visit Lady Uxbridge, whose great age required her to use a walking stick, joined her daughter in the gallery. Lady Caroline, gazing at the Hoppner painting while holding Adolphus in her arms, could hear her mother's stick hitting the paved floor, and wondered when she would have the chance to take in such comforting familiarities again. The old lady joined her.

'My dear Caroline,' she said, 'how many years have passed since your time in Hoppner's studio, and how your brood has grown in those years! It gives me such pleasure to see your daughters flourish as you did.'

'Thank you, Mama,' said Lady Caroline, hesitantly. She sensed her mother had more to say on the matter. Indeed Lady Uxbridge continued in a far less romantic manner.

'But, oh! How could you take them away from me? How could you leave your mother at such an age? And to live among *foreigners*, too; it really is too much. What have I to live for, if I can't see my beautiful granddaughters make good matches?'

Lady Caroline sighed, not knowing how to convince her mother of what her husband had insisted was necessary.

When Lady Caroline had first been introduced to society she had been the talk of the town and could have married anyone of her choosing. It had been a surprise when she had, at the age of eighteen, accepted the hand of the Honourable John Capel, younger son of the 4th Earl of Essex. Lord and Lady Uxbridge had thought her impulsive. They wanted her to wait for an offer from an elder son who stood to inherit land, money and even a title of his own, but Lady Caroline knew her mind and wouldn't be dissuaded. From the beginning of their attachment Capel had professed to love her with such devotion that she felt sure he would be a committed and constant husband. In some ways she had been right in her estimation of John Capel, and in other ways she had woefully underestimated how easily he could be led astray.

Without Lady Uxbridge, there was no doubt the Capel family would have fallen to the dogs. Titles and family influence were not enough to keep you from debtors' prison or from exile on the Continent. Lady Caroline was enormously grateful for the support her family had given, but also ashamed of their near-constant need for support. Now they were leaving the country, Lady Caroline would never again be able to seek a private audience with her mother to explain her latest trial and seek advice. Such matters would have to be trusted to the written word and afterwards thrown into the fire.

On their last day together at Plas Newydd, Maria and Georgy, who liked to think they were the closest to their dearest grandmama, had wept at their final parting, each kneeling by her side, their heads in her lap. The old lady, not prone to fits of emotion, had quietly stroked their heads and seemed very moved. It was with great sadness that Lady Caroline finally marshalled the children out of the library. She didn't know when she would see her mother again.

࿐

As the ship made its slow and steady progress across the channel, Maria felt increasingly excited and hopeful for what lay ahead of them. She would rather have stayed in London, but this was undoubtedly a chance to make her mark; back in England her status was still that of a child and she'd led a closeted life, but now she would finally be engaging with society as an adult.

Maria was also excited at the prospect of seeing their uncle, Lord Uxbridge. He was Lady Caroline's eldest brother, and when their grandfather had died two years previously he had become the 2nd Earl of Uxbridge. He was perhaps the most famous cavalry commanders of the time, leading the Guards and Household divisions. He was also a true bon vivant, a lover of fine clothes and the frivolities of life.

The Capel children were in awe of their uncle. In their eyes he could do no wrong, and his visits couldn't come soon enough. Lord Uxbridge, in turn, loved his army of nieces and nephews and delighted in showing them his ceremonial sword and the details of his dress uniform, with row upon row of gold frogging contrasting to the brilliant red cloth.

Yet, despite the fun the Capel children had with their uncle, there was always an underlying tension, and Maria had noticed that often her papa and uncle exchanged terse words.

She knew what this was about, although it was never openly discussed.

There had been a horrible scandal six years previously when Lord Uxbridge had eloped with Lady Charlotte Wellesley, sister-in-law to the Duke of Wellington. At the time Lord Uxbridge had been married with eight small children, but he could not be dissuaded from his passion for Lady Charlotte and wanted her to be his wife. Such a feat was as difficult as separating oil from water, as divorce was only possible through an Act of Parliament and at colossal expense, but nothing would put their uncle off his prize.

The scandal reached its peak when Lady Charlotte's brother challenged Lord Uxbridge to a duel. How both parties escaped uninjured was anyone's guess. Honour somewhat restored, it was decided that a divorce for both parties was now the only option. Lord Uxbridge was made to pay the enormous sum of £20,000 in damages to Lady Charlotte's husband, but joked to his sister that his new wife was worth every penny. Lady Caroline had not seen the funny side and didn't speak to her brother for several months.

Rightly or wrongly, there had been much blame placed at the feet of Lady Charlotte. She'd had to leave behind her children, rarely seeing them afterwards, and society never treated her the same again. Her decision was seen by most as an abomination of all that was right and true about married life. A woman had a duty to her family, and for that Lady Charlotte had been neither forgiven nor forgotten, but pushed to the margins of society, excluded from most gatherings and rarely invited to dinners or balls. She had lost the protection of London's society ladies who would tolerate a discreet affair but not a brazen rebellion such as hers.

Lady Caroline still adored her brother, but this aspect of his life wasn't open to discussion with her family. Maria had received the uncensored details from the staff in the kitchen at their grandmother's house, having bribed them with sugar violets and been sworn to secrecy beforehand. Lord Uxbridge's new wife had never once come to visit them and only the elder sisters had seen her occasionally at evening functions, before their mother had swiftly moved them away.

～⁓～

The family made slow and painful progress through France and into the Kingdom of the Netherlands. The two carriages drove over roads in dire need of repair, jolting and rocking them with increasing brutality. The view from the windows was dull and unchanging, the sky a murky grey. Each night they stopped in taverns or boarding houses, and if no accommodation was available they made do with sleeping in the carriages. Many hours on the road led to sore heads, backs and stomachs, and a number of cross words passed between them as tempers shortened.

A full three weeks later they finally arrived on the outskirts of Brussels. As they trundled through the city streets the sky seemed to lighten, and the mood of the carriages' inhabitants, by now close to mutiny, also lifted as their destination finally came into view.

The carriage came to a halt, the horses whinnying and stamping their hooves, throwing up loose gravel from the road.

As the coachman helped Maria down, she saw that on the left side of the street was a park sheltered by a thick hedge and surrounded by iron railings. On the right stood a uniform row of townhouses in pale stone. Capel led them down the street a little way, reading the numbers on the doors, and stopped. As soon as Maria saw the house, she knew the gruelling journey and the family quarrels had been worth it to live in a house as impressive as this one.

Maria pushed against the heavy wooden panels of the door, and without a creak it swung inwards to reveal an elegant hallway.

'Lord!' she exclaimed on entering. 'It's much grander than I thought it would be.'

The house had high ceilings and large sash windows facing the park. A staircase with cast-iron balusters and a mahogany handrail curved upwards to the two floors above. Maria could just make out a circular skylight at the very top, lighting the floors below.

There was a great noise behind her and several of her siblings rushed past and clattered up the stairs, shouting to each other and laughing as they went.

Harriet joined her and Maria exclaimed, 'How divine this place will be when we've properly attended to it and all our things are in their place!'

Harriet looked pleased but a little hesitant. She stared up at the tall ceilings of the front hall, ornamented with carvings and lit by a fine, if slightly dusty, glass chandelier.

'However shall we afford such a place?'

Before Maria could reply two servants came past,

staggering under the weight of one of their mother's trunks.

'Never mind that, Harriet. Everything here is said to be as cheap as dirt; surely that's why Papa chose Brussels for us, so we must make the most of it. I, for one, intend to enjoy myself to the full. I can't wait to sneak into town and see what fun we can have.'

'Oh, Maria, how can you speak so! We're not children any more!'

'No, thank heaven!'

Maria was making little headway with her insistently sensible sister. She rolled her eyes, but not so Harriet could see, instead turning away from the entrance hall. As she did, she saw Georgy careering towards them.

'My, this place is a vast improvement on our house in London,' she grinned. 'From the carriage I saw no fewer than twelve uniformed officers. Quite a sight for sore eyes, I must say.'

'Georgy, we saw plenty of soldiers in Dover,' said Harriet primly.

'But not officers, dearest sister, and those soldiers weren't planning on staying in Dover, and neither were we. These men are our neighbours; what could be more thrilling? There are sure to be lots of balls!'

To demonstrate her enthusiasm to dance, she swept Harriet off round the hall in a parody of popular dance the pas de Zéphyr. Even Harriet had to laugh at the serious expression of the gentleman suitor Georgy was now impersonating.

Still in this attitude, Georgy called across to Maria, 'My truest love, my stars and moon, meet me at the outskirts of the city at dawn, and let us run away together!'

Maria responded with equal gusto, 'Run away with you when I see you dance with another? What kind of love is this?'

'Can a man such as I not love two women at once?'

Harriet looked shocked, and Maria and Georgy laughed harder. Georgy released Harriet from her clutches.

'How strait-laced you have become, Harriet,' Georgy said, a little out of breath. 'Are you preparing yourself for a curate husband?'

Seeing Harriet's face darken, and keen to forego a row, Maria grabbed each girl by the hand.

'Come, sisters, let's explore the house.'

Harriet could not, however, be induced to join them; she went to locate her luggage and ensure it had arrived safely. Georgy and Maria disappeared down one of the two wide corridors that led off from either side of the entrance hall. What a house they discovered! Quite apart from the comfortable reception and dining rooms on the ground floor, upstairs they found rooms furnished with grand, if old-fashioned four-poster beds and comfortable armchairs. Window seats looked over the medieval ramparts and the Palace of Laeken, residence of the king. Servants threw open the windows to the clean, cool air of the summer's day, lighting the interiors they would soon call home.

Maria's back ached from sitting in the carriage for so long and she felt as if she could sleep for an age, yet at that moment she felt more awake than she had in months.

After exploring all the rooms and following a short argument with their mother about which was to be theirs, Maria and Georgy settled themselves on the window seat of a particularly fine bedroom at the back of the house. It had walls covered with delicate paper depicting bluebirds in trees with pale yellow flowers. The large double bed sat under an awning of ochre silk and would easily accommodate both sisters. There could be no thought of the two of them not sharing a room. Maria had shared a room with Georgy all her life, Harriet having long ago insisted on her own room so she could read late into the night.

The days of their childhood already seemed a long time ago, full as they had been of seemingly endless days in the nursery or on walks with their governesses. Back then, they would play fairies, nurses and often weddings, using the toys in the nursery or clothes borrowed from their mother's wardrobe. Their imaginations needed little encouragement. They took on any character under the sun, devising plays, poems and ditties to perform to their patient parents at teatime.

Under the covers at night, in the dim light from the candles burning on their side tables, Maria and Georgy would gossip about family members and tell each other's fortunes from the lines on their palms. As they grew in age their whispers took on more serious undertones, but the confidences were no less treasured.

'I saw the governess and the groom speaking in whispers last Tuesday in the stables, I swear I did.'

'I wonder what they could mean by it?'

'That's not the last of it. They went together into the stable for a full ten minutes, I counted each minute as it went by. I think they're in love. What will Mama say if they get married!'

Whatever little secrets they discussed were written down

in their very best hand on a slip of paper, rolled and sealed with wax, the necessary materials having been purloined from their papa's study. The papers would be solemnly handled, for they contained what were great secrets to these innocent girls. The notes were tucked away in the large box of ribbons that had begun its life as their mother's least favourite hatbox. Mounds of ribbons, the delight of many a young girl's childhood games during wet afternoons, were carefully wound into thick coils and laid neatly in the box. Into these coils were tucked the secrets they had written out and sealed forever.

The box was kept in a place of great secrecy. In some cases, such as when they discovered that the governess was indeed leaving them to marry the groom, Maria and Georgy were delighted with themselves for their intelligence-gathering, really believing that they'd had some part to play in the romance by secreting the note in the ribbon box. Who knew what power the box contained?

Many months had passed since Maria and Georgy had played in this way, but the importance of the ribbon box remained undiminished.

As the Capels' numerous servants brought in their luggage from the carriages, directed by Maria and helped by Georgy, they both kept a special eye out for the ribbon box. It was Maria who spotted it.

'There!' she exclaimed, and carefully retrieved the box.

The fabric that decorated the outside was a faded jade-green and white stripe, and the sides of the lid were fragile and frayed, but the contents remained nestled safely inside.

It took only a few minutes for Georgy and Maria to decide

where this most precious object from their childhood should be stored. In the corner of the room stood an impressive armoire, a mahogany piece with an inlaid design of roses and acanthus leaves. As the structure was suspended on thick wooden legs, the box slid easily underneath.

'There,' Georgy exclaimed happily, 'we have made it home already.'

There was much to do that first day, not least because there were so many children to deal with, and Lady Caroline's enormous wardrobe to transport. The servants who had joined them from England worked tirelessly to get everything organised. Their efforts were hampered by the antics of the children, who were vocal in their demands for a certain box, case or cricket bat. Only Harriet waited patiently for the boxes to be gone through methodically and gave useful instructions to ease the stresses of the day.

The younger children were running riot, unable to contain their excitement after having spent far too long in the carriages. By late afternoon, Lady Caroline begged a headache and retreated to the rooms she had reserved for herself, with an adjoining bedroom for her husband. A pleasing dressing room completed the suite. Lady Caroline Capel now sat in quietude, having shut the door on the children rampaging through the house, and sipped tea from an elegant bone china cup.

She shut her eyes and leant back on a chaise longue she had moved to catch the cooling breeze from the window. The journey had been strenuous, and despite her pleasure at seeing their new house she was filled with unease. How would the family fare in this new town with so many foreign customs and expectations? Was the town already aware of their financial situation? Was it known why their departure from London had been so quick?

At first, Lady Caroline had not understood what occupied her husband's time when he went out to socialise with his male friends. His behaviour had been normal among his peers and she had thought little of it. After about a year of marriage her mother had broken the news that Capel was spending night after night in any gambling club that would allow him entry, but by then it was too late.

Capel would come home, despairing at the vast sums he had lost, downcast and forlorn, promising never to take such risks again. He would never tell her exactly how much he had lost. Years passed and Lady Caroline wished for any other occupation that would satisfy him. Even a passion for other women would have been better than the danger he put them in, and although she hated herself for thinking it, might also have led to fewer pregnancies, which brought their own worries.

She was sure Capel loved her, which was more than could be said for many of her contemporaries' marriages. Throughout the long years of their union he had remained committed to her and their growing family. Each time Lady Caroline had been brought with child, Capel had delighted in the addition to their family, despite the growing strain on their already stretched finances. Capel even feigned indifference as to whether each arrival was a boy or girl, although Lady Caroline could tell from the sheer delight on his face when she had shown him their first son, Arthur, after five girls, that this made had him the happiest of all.

So, despite the problems in their marriage and the threats of debtors' prison that had beset them during their last few weeks in London, Lady Caroline could not think too badly of her husband. He had brought them here to Brussels to make a new life for themselves, and she was going to make the most of the opportunity. She sighed and tried to calm her swirling thoughts.

Lady Caroline opened her eyes, wondering if she had dozed off for a second or two. The light seemed somewhat different, more settled. She looked around at her beautiful surroundings. Indeed, she would be very happy and comfortable in this new home. She rose and set aside her teacup, before heading downstairs to join in the chaos of unpacking.

The day ended with an informal supper of bread, cheese and cold meats that the cook had procured from the local market, having exclaimed in delight to Lady Caroline on her return how cheap everything had been. Although Lady Caroline tried not to show it, she was extremely pleased to hear these words. In London, Lady Caroline had been mortified when their credit was refused at the shops. All promise of presents for the Christmas just past had been in peril until Lady Uxbridge had come to her daughter's rescue.

The meal began with a solemn prayer directed by Mr Capel who, despite not being particularly religious, believed prayer set the tone for the evening. The Capel children shifted in their seats; it had been a long day and they were famished. A hurried 'Amen!' was shouted as soon as it was clear their papa had finished. Plates were piled high, and the serious business of filling hungry stomachs began in earnest.

Lady Caroline looked across at her husband as they all began to eat. John Capel wasn't particularly distinguished looking, being of average height and, she supposed, average good looks, although she still saw the kindness in his face that had first appealed to her all those years ago. His clothes were plain, comfortable and well worn. He wasn't a man who cared for fripperies or expensive cloth, a small mercy considering how much money he disposed of in other areas of his life.

'My dear,' she said to Capel, who was contemplating a piece of foreign-looking cheese with interest, 'do you think many other English families are to arrive soon? I'm so looking forward to receiving them, I don't believe there's a better house to be had in the area.'

Capel regarded the cheese a little longer and replied, 'Whom do you hope to pounce on first, my love?'

'Well, I've heard that Lady Charlotte Greville is soon to be passing through on her way to the Continent.'

Capel's expression hardened and he lowered his fork to the table.

'Lady Charlotte Greville? That woman is the mistress of the Duke of Wellington, yet she's the first friend you think of to invite to this house? You surprise me, Caroline.'

Lady Caroline glared at her husband; she didn't wish to hear the word 'mistress' spoken in front of the children. Luckily they didn't seem to have noticed, focused as they were on their plates.

She held her ground and replied, 'She is first rate, to be

sure. Her relations with the duke do not diminish her position in my eyes. Do we not all revere him so?'

'We do!' piped up Maria, and her elder sisters nodded vigorously in agreement. 'I, for one, would be delighted to be his mistress!' she quipped, causing her sisters to explode into giggles. Lady Caroline did her best to stifle this outburst with one of her most practised stares; she thought it prudent to change the subject.

'I've heard that the Duchess of Richmond and all their children are also to come and join us in Brussels. The duke is to command the reserve force.'

Lady Caroline revealed this information lightly, hoping not to hurt her husband's feelings. His lack of military experience was a sore point, sure to be exacerbated by the number of military men stationed in and around Brussels. Lady Caroline's personal interest in the Richmond family was largely centred on the duchess, another key ally like Lady Charlotte Greville, although the duchess' sharp tongue and love of gossip meant she couldn't be entirely trusted and was best kept at arm's length.

Lady Caroline wondered whether they would find a house suitable for a family of their size, as they had as many children as the Capels.

Capel took his time before responding. 'You're quite correct, my dear. I had a letter from Richmond himself, just before we left to make the crossing. They hope to live here on an "economical plan", so he says.'

The children were excited to hear the Lennox children were to join them in Brussels.

'This is too exciting!' said Georgy. 'How I adored Lady Sarah when we last saw them at Brighton.'

'You barely spoke to her, Georgy, and it was I who wrote afterwards,' retorted Harriet. 'I feel sure *we* shall become the best of friends.'

'Mama, might they be able to take a house near ours?' said Maria, excitedly. 'Can they take their lessons with us? It would be grand to have the same dancing master. Do you think you can manage it?'

'I have no idea, Maria, we shall have to see.'

'That's enough, please, children.' Capel looked exhausted; he pushed his plate away. 'You are clearly all tired, and in any case, it's time for bed.'

Indeed, the party had begun to wilt. Little Algernon was asleep in his chair, his cheek resting against one hand, a half-eaten piece of bread clutched in the other. Harriet removed the bread, gathered the sweet boy in her arms and took him upstairs to the nursery. Slowly the rest of the family followed suit, having first kissed their mother and wished their papa a good night.

After the room had emptied, Capel moved down the table to join his wife, taking his glass with him.

'How many they are now,' he mused, as he poured himself and Lady Caroline a small measure of wine. 'Somehow, in this new place they all seem so much older.'

'The girls especially insist on being treated as adults now. How they interrogated me when I told them we were leaving London!'

'Indeed, I fear they'll become quite a handful here. From

what I've heard society is far less rigid here than at home and, of course, there are sure to be officers looking for mischief.'

'How will we settle them all?' Lady Caroline fretted, suddenly anxious again. 'I suppose the boys will go to a profession; the army or perhaps the clergy, and the girls...' She paused in her train of thought, admiring the small band of gold on her left finger, which had sat there unmoved for so many years.

'I hope they will all make as happy and successful a marriage as we have,' Capel suggested lightly, tracing a finger slowly over Caroline's sleeve, 'for I know all I do would be unbearable without you to guide me. Without you, our family would be rudderless.'

Despite her tiredness and the events that had unfolded between them over the years, Lady Caroline suddenly felt a burning warmth for her husband and took his hand, pressing it to her lips.

'Together, we can make a success of it. Whatever comes,' she said.

Capel's expression of warmth and love was everything she needed in that moment. They rose from the table and she led her husband up the unfamiliar staircase and along the corridor to their private rooms.

CHAPTER III
Haberdashery Dandies

'Lord Hay, son of Lord Erroll is a new recruit & a most agreeable one, he is very poor I hear, is very good-looking I know & particularly Gentleman-like.'

Lady Caroline Capel to the Dowager Countess of Uxbridge

There was much to occupy the Capels and their servants in the days following their arrival in Brussels. Finally, their many trunks and packages were unpacked, books lined the walls of the spacious library and wardrobes were filled with clothing and trinkets. The drawing room, painted a pleasing blue and with five large windows that looked out on to the park, was reorganised to accommodate the best furniture in the house.

They had brought with them a pianoforte for the girls to play, and were pleased to discover a harpsicord already in place in the music room. Rugs warmed the fine parquet floors, and sketched portraits of the children in oil and chalk hung on the walls of the entrance hall and staircase. Before long the house felt like home.

As was the custom, no one called in for several days after their arrival, allowing the family time to settle and make their house ready for guests. Lady Caroline was reluctant to let the girls loose in town before they'd made friends with some of the Belgian residents, and gave her elder daughters job after job to keep them out of trouble.

From the windows, the girls saw finely dressed men and women pausing opposite the house to peer in. The ladies wore fine hats and smart pelisses, just like those they'd seen in London. They gazed at the house, chatting excitedly to their companions, presumably discussing who might have recently moved in. The girls were keen to respond to their questioning looks, but also a little apprehensive as to what reception their English ways would receive.

It was only a matter of time before Lady Caroline's resolve weakened and she agreed to let her pleading daughters go into the town, on the condition that they were accompanied by a servant. They were left in the hands of Lady Caroline's lady's maid, Julia. In the past, and to her great satisfaction, Maria had found Julia to be easily distracted. She had once enjoyed a whole hour alone in Vauxhall Gardens when Julia had got talking to one of the boys selling ices. Maria had high hopes they might be able to give her the slip once again.

Harriet, Georgy and Maria hurriedly put on their best day clothes and headed into the town. They walked down the the avenues of the Parc Royal and past the octagonal pond in the centre. Exiting the park they found themselves on cobbled streets and down increasingly narrow lanes, past small shops and homes wedged in beside each other. Chimney smoke mingled with the enticing smells of cooked meat, bread and pastries. The locals went about their daily business, most ruddy faced but friendly enough, the ladies with shawls tied under their chins and the men with woollen scarves and leather hats.

They arrived at the main area for shopping and found the most delectable items in the windows of the shops: chemises of the palest silk, satin shoes, straw hats and bonnets all in the most modish colours of the day. They soon lost Harriet, who got distracted by a well-stocked English bookshop. Next, they came across an area devoted to haberdashery shops, each store filled with rolls of fabric, reams of beautiful ribbons and copious quantities of the famous Brussels lace they had heard about from their mother.

The exchange from their own currency made these items gloriously affordable, and so for the first time in their lives they had the ability to purchase, within reason, whatever they wanted. Maria spotted an emporium selling buttons, ribbons and trinkets to satisfy every whim, and the two sisters darted inside. Through the window they could see a concerned-looking Julia, clearly struggling to keep an eye on all three sisters. Perhaps sensing that Maria and Georgy warranted closer observation, she came to the door of the shop they were in.

Maria instinctively went to stall her.

'Julia, could you kindly go and help my sister with the books she's purchasing? I'm sure I've just spotted her struggling.'

Julia could hardly refuse such a sensible request and hurried off to help their eldest sister.

The emporium turned out to be quite the best the girls had yet visited. Swathes of fine fabric hung from hooks and wires on the ceiling, creating walkways of delicate colour. Maria's eyes were drawn to a row of exquisite fans hung across the back wall and she made her way over to them. She was now quite alone, Georgy having gone to the upper floor to see what was on offer there.

'What luxury…' she sighed, quite enchanted by the shop. Dreamily, she ran her fingers along a row of hanging ribbons. As they parted, a gentleman was revealed to be standing on the other side of the central display table, engrossed in the purchase of some gold buttons. He seemed to be a little younger than her papa, and a military man, by the looks of his dress and demeanour.

He certainly looked and dressed like an Englishman, and Maria wondered if she'd ever seen him in London. She thought perhaps not. Hidden by the rows of ribbon, she took measure of his looks. He was tall, with striking blue eyes, his hair was dark, and a long straight nose and rather thin lips completed the picture, but the overall look was not displeasing.

Dared she find some way to introduce herself? If she'd been with her mother she knew she wouldn't have. When introduced to anyone of the opposite sex she was expected to curtsey and the ensuing conversation was usually stilted and awkward. Despite this, Maria found the man interesting and didn't want to lose the opportunity to make his acquaintance. She moved a little closer.

Quite fortuitously, she felt herself brush against a box of buttons that hadn't been put back in its proper place. She leant into the table a little more and the box tumbled to the floor, buttons flying in all directions. Startled by the amount of noise they made, Maria felt embarrassed, hoping it wasn't obvious she'd done it on purpose. The gentleman heard the clatter of buttons and hastened over to help.

'Oh dear, what scramble have we here, madam?'

Maria was already kneeling on the floor, but she sat up to greet him, rather taken aback by being addressed as 'madam'.

'Well, I suppose this is a novel way to view all the buttons on offer without having to rummage through the box,' she said, hoping he wouldn't think her too silly and juvenile.

'I commend your ingenuity, but let me help you up.'

Before Maria could protest, he had taken her arm and helped pull her up. By now the shop owner had bustled over and taken over the retrieval of buttons from all four corners of the shop floor, muttering darkly. Georgy had heard the commotion and come halfway down the stairs, but on seeing Maria talking to the gentleman was now walking down the rest of the steps as slowly as possible.

'Well, what an unusual and diverting way to make your acquaintance, Miss...?'

'Capel. My name is Maria Capel. We've just moved into the city from London.'

'And I am Edward Barnes. I'm very pleased to meet you, Miss Capel. I'm stationed with the army here in Brussels.'

Georgy now joined them, several strips of ribbon draped across her arm. Barnes smiled down at her.

'Delighted, madam,' he said, when Maria introduced them, and Georgy beamed. They chatted about the date of their arrival in Brussels, the weather and the great quantity of ribbons available for sale in the shops of Brussels.

Maria saw Julia making her way over to them, looking cross. Her expression told them they needed to move on. Julia took from Georgy the quantities of ribbon she had over her arm, as she clearly had no intention of buying them, and began to return the items.

At that moment another man entered the shop. He was about Maria and Georgy's age, with a mop of golden-brown hair and wide blue eyes. He wore a dark blue military uniform with gleaming gold buttons and knee-high boots. His shirt and cravat were shockingly white, and starched right up to the neck, showing the fashion of the moment. He was without doubt a bon vivant to match even their uncle, Lord Uxbridge, and seemed to shine so brightly that he put their new friend, Edward Barnes, quite in the shade.

The young man gazed imperiously around the little shop while leaning on a walking cane. It was as though the little group had been transported right back across the Channel to the fashionable St James's area of London, where dandies and rakes roamed the streets in expensive clothes, ringing up debt, keeping mistresses and drinking to excess, all for the sake of their personal image.

'Lord Hay, well met.' Their new friend swept past the two sisters and grasped the young man by the hand and elbow. 'Quite an entrance you make, even in this humble establishment. What brings you here?'

If Edward Barnes was put out by such an entrance and the intrusion into their conversation, he carried it with good humour. For his part, Lord Hay responded with a laugh, clearly delighted to be the centre of attention.

'Thank you, General. As you know, General Maitland likes his boys to dress the part.'

'Indeed, Maitland always surprises me with the attention

he gives to such matters. I must say, I don't give a fig what my men wear as long as they turn up on time and are sober enough to perform their duties.'

'You're a general!' said Maria before she could stop herself. That certainly impressed.

Lord Hay turned to Maria and instantly she felt herself blush. His eyes were a brilliant, piercing, laughing blue; they darted through her like a dragonfly on water.

'A general, indeed,' said Lord Hay. 'But not just a general, it is General Sir Edward Barnes who is accompanying you on your shopping expedition today.'

'Oh,' stammered Maria in response, 'we're not—' But before she could finish, General Sir Edward Barnes was replying with a smile.

'It does well to do away with formality when meeting in such circumstances. The ladies and I have simply met each other by chance. It appears you share with them a love for the finer fripperies of dress, so let me introduce you to my new friends, the Misses Maria and Georgiana Capel.'

Lord Hay bowed formally, and Maria and Georgy bobbed curtseys in reply. His manner was most curious, displaying the kind of nervous energy and excitement that Maria associated with her younger brother Arthur.

'Capital, capital, how novel to meet you both in such circumstances. We are seemingly of one mind when it comes to the finer details of one's wardrobe,' he said. He looked from one sister to the other, then added, 'I do hope to see you both again soon. Brussels is always short of decent dancing partners, with so many military men about. Do you like to waltz?'

This question appeared to be directed to Maria who ventured to reply, 'I'm afraid our father doesn't approve of the waltz, he finds it too...'

Feeling unable to say that their father had banned them from dancing the waltz as he deemed it too racy, she could think of no appropriate end to the sentence. She glanced at General Barnes and saw his eyes sparkle, as though he knew exactly what Maria had been trying to articulate.

He said, 'Well, Hay, you and I shall certainly do our best to convince these girls' papa of the merits of dancing, even if the waltz is banned from their dancing cards.'

'You really must waltz, there's no dance to better it,' Lord Hay insisted. 'We shall have to persuade your father.'

'Are there many balls planned for the coming weeks?' ventured Georgy.

'Oh, a tremendous number! Just you wait and see. They're such fun. I'll make sure your dance cards are filled and introduce you to all the most irresponsible officers.'

Georgy looked thrilled at these words, but Maria saw a slight frown form on General Barnes's older and wiser face. She wondered whether either gentleman was married. It was hard to determine, as men didn't wear a ring as women did. Lord Hay, at any rate, seemed too young and carefree to possibly be in possession of a wife, but General Sir Edward Barnes was a harder card to read.

Julia rejoined them and insisted they return home. No doubt she was thinking of what Lady Caroline would say if she heard that two of her daughters were lingering in a shop speaking to two men to whom they had not been formally introduced.

Fearing a reprimand if they made a fuss, Maria and Georgy bade a hasty goodbye to their two new acquaintances and they all headed towards the door. Before they had quite made it, Lord Hay pulled Maria back by laying a hand gently yet insistently on the sleeve of her gown. General Barnes was already at the door, holding it open first for Julia and then Georgy, before turning to follow the two women on to the street.

Alone in the shop for a matter of seconds, Lord Hay turned Maria towards him, maintaining a gentle pressure on her arm.

'I do hope to see you again soon, Miss Capel,' he said, looking intently at her. There was no hesitation in his gaze; he looked at her with complete confidence that their paths would soon cross again. Maria had never met a young man in possession of such self-assurance. It was quite dazzling. She tried to hold his gaze, but instinctively glanced down. When she looked up again, she found that Lord Hay had yet to look away.

To her astonishment, he pressed into her hand a long piece of exquisite lace ribbon in the style Brussels was famous for, about the width of her wrist and rolled into a loop.

'It would be my honour to dance with you when we're next fortunate enough to meet. Perhaps you might wear this little trinket when that day comes.' Though his eyes twinkled and he smiled, a tiny flash of hesitation that she might not respond favourably to his advances crossed his features.

Maria flushed with delight and smiled back at him; a pleasurable warmth rising from the tips of her toes to her now-rosy cheeks. Before she had thought of a response they were out on the street, the ribbon curled in the palm of her hand so the others couldn't see it.

Outside, the norms of social behaviour were once more respected. The two gentlemen bowed goodbye to each of the ladies, who curtseyed their response, and the Capels headed off up the street the way they had come.

Julia glared after the two men and attempted to chastise the girls, but Maria was impervious to her grumblings and Julia quickly quietened. Maria showed Georgy the beautiful ribbon Lord Hay had given her, laughing at the look of shocked pleasure on Georgy's face. She took pains to hush her as Harriet made her way over to them, weighed down by a number of purchases. Maria quickly placed the roll of ribbon in the small drawstring purse that hung from her waist.

The younger girls told their sister about meeting the two men, one older, and well-meaning, the other handsome and lavishly dressed, but they made no mention of the ribbon. Maria didn't reveal the words that had passed privately between her and Lord Hay, as Harriet would no doubt disapprove of a connection being made in so casual a manner.

Once upstairs in their room, Maria secreted the gift in the ribbon box, along with a slip of paper describing their first adventure in Brussels and the two men she and Georgy had already befriended.

CHAPTER IV

Ladies in the Park

*'This is without exception the most
Gossipy Place I ever heard of...but
as some of us have made the rule
of only visiting those we knew in
England much Jealousy & Envy is
excited against the Ladies in the Park
as we are called, & even the Ladies
in the Park continue to squabble
amongst each other.'*

Lady Caroline Capel to the Dowager Countess of Uxbridge

A few weeks had passed since the girls' shopping expedition, and the Capel family were now fully settled in their new home. Lady Caroline was dressing for a ball that had been organised by Lady Charlotte Greville, whose connection to the Duke of Wellington had so shocked her husband at dinner on their first night. Now that Lady Charlotte was in Brussels, however, Capel had suppressed his objections, knowing that she had been a great friend and supporter of his wife in London and could do much for her in Brussels.

Lady Caroline sat on a comfortable velvet stool at her dressing table and gazed out of the window. Julia deftly pulled at her brunette locks with a short-bristled brush, twisting sections round and securing them with hairpins topped with tiny diamonds. Relishing the quiet moment when the children were distracted and she had Julia all to herself, Lady Caroline allowed her mind to wander.

It had been marvellous good luck that the Capels were one of the very first English families to arrive in Brussels. Not only had they taken one of the finest houses in the city, but they had been able to make friends with well-respected local families who had shown them great kindness and civility. In the last week alone Lady Caroline and Capel had met a number of admirable Belgian families. Yet, while the company had been stimulating and the customs of the Belgians entertaining, Lady Caroline greatly desired the companionship of her own people.

She felt a little uneasy making her way through Brussels society without the support of the army of female companions who had always given her confidence back in London. Thus, Lady Charlotte Greville's ball was to be an important evening for her. She wished fervently that her friend would settle permanently in Brussels and hoped to use this evening to persuade her of the city's many merits.

Of course, no number of Gothic buildings, spacious squares and elaborate dance halls could make Brussels equal London for society, glamour and prestige. In London, Lady Caroline was at home among the most respected and revered women in society, with the power to make or break newcomers. Lady Charlotte Greville was one such member of this elite set.

It was a cruel world where women were judged harshly on their dress, manners and accomplishments. Once a woman became an outcast, either through scandal or bad manners, she was rarely welcomed back into the fold. Her brother's second wife had met with such a fate, and Lady Caroline had not intervened on her behalf. She knew it was better to be inside this gilded cage than on the outside looking in. So she gladly welcomed Lady Charlotte and her husband to Brussels, in the hope that similar families would join them. It would be marvellous to have the town filled with English families to match the thousands of British soldiers stationed there.

To give the Bruxellois their due, they were very able dancers, and Lady Caroline had heard that several British officers were taking lessons in order to brush up on the variations of the quadrille and the waltz that were popular in Brussels. Her own daughters had been taking twice-weekly lessons since their arrival, which were loved by all except Louisa, who could never remember the steps.

But how the Bruxellois ladies flirted with the English gentlemen! Lady Caroline had been shocked and amused in equal measure, with many an officer having to push away his native dancing partner when she became too amorous. Lady Caroline would certainly be doing everything in her power to ensure that such a display was never made by one of her daughters. Tonight they would be put to the test, as Lady Charlotte's ball was to be the eldest Capel girls' first foray into the adult society of Brussels.

Lady Caroline counted her blessings that they'd managed to secure a house in such a fine location on the Rue Ducale, facing the royal park where all the fine ladies and gentlemen of Brussels went for their afternoon strolls. By arriving when they did, the Capel family had also been able to foster early friendships with the officers stationed on the outskirts of the city. Many of them had already made calls to the Capels' house. Such amiable and helpful men they were, too.

Their officer friends had smoothed the way for the family as they settled in, ensuring they had everything they needed and offering to make introductions to all manner of interesting individuals. As they sat across from her at tea, Lady Caroline couldn't help but wonder if any of these officers would do for one her girls. How neat that would be! Perhaps, if she were lucky, one of her daughters might have an agreement with one of them by the time too many English families arrived in Brussels and created too much competition.

One of the first officers to make a visit to their house was General Sir Edward Barnes, a charming man Lady Caroline hadn't known in London. She and Capel had sat across from him in the morning room, taking tea.

'General Barnes, how pleasant of you to call on us. It's so lovely to meet more Englishmen living here.'

'The pleasure is all mine, madam; my fellow officers and I are delighted to have another family join our ranks.'

Just then Harriet, Georgy and Maria had returned from their morning walk and entered the morning room.

'Ah, girls, do come and meet our new friend, General Sir Edward Barnes.'

The girls came forward to make a formal greeting, but to Lady Caroline's annoyance Maria and Georgy smiled far too warmly. Ever sensitive to the glances and giggles of her teenage daughters, she perceived a flicker of recognition pass between the three of them. Barnes smiled kindly back at them, but made no mention of having met them before.

'General, we are very pleased to make your acquaintance,' said Maria.

'Ladies, believe me, the honour is all mine.' He made a formal bow.

After Barnes had left, Capel told them that their guest had served with distinction on the Duke of Wellington's staff throughout the war in the peninsula.

Lady Caroline had certainly been impressed by his manner and charm, which seemed to be rather unassuming for someone of his experience and position. She had to admit she had thought him handsome too, but did not want to dwell too much on that thought.

General Barnes would indeed be a perfect match for one of the girls, yet Lady Caroline had to remind herself of the long journey ahead before any such arrangements could be made. The first problem to overcome would be the girls' complete and utter lack of a fortune. Only a wealthy older gentleman or one with a fortune to inherit would be satisfied with their lack of dowry, and only such a gentleman would be welcomed by the family as able to provide the kind of lifestyle the girls' birthright demanded. The lack of a dowry would put off many suitors. Beauty, wit and good breeding could only get you so far, and many ladies had been left on the shelf for less.

Another problem that was making itself increasingly apparent was her daughters' complete incorrigibility when it came to behaving themselves. Harriet could be excused from such a condemnation, as her manners and character were largely most agreeable and placid, but Georgy and Maria were proving more of a worry. Their confidence had been amusing as young girls, and they'd usually known where to draw the line, but now they were young ladies, ready in theory to be married and have families of their own. Lady Caroline worried that the heady mix of officers, parties and punch might make either of them slip from the social tightrope stretched out before them.

She was also exasperated by Maria and Georgy's impertinence and overconfidence when speaking with members of the opposite sex. Only the previous week, when another officer had come to call – the young and jaunty Lord Hay – Lady Caroline had seen him wink at Maria, and she had responded not with the frosty stare that was clearly called for, but an undignified giggle and violent flush of the cheeks.

Lord Hay's father was the Earl of Erroll, an acquaintance of theirs in London. Lord Hay was already known in London to be quite the angel to look at, but by all accounts a rake-in-training. The fact that his reputation preceded him at such a young age was not, in Lady Caroline's opinion, a good sign. His manners were quite different from those of the charming General Barnes, but Lady Caroline had to admit there was a rather thrilling buzz about the room when Lord Hay came to visit that wasn't present when General Barnes called for tea.

Aside from General Barnes and Lord Hay, quite the most unique of their visitors was the young Prince of Orange, whose father was the sovereign prince of the Kingdom of the Netherlands. In London, the prince was known to be a fool. He had, not so long ago, been chosen by the Prince Regent as a suitable match for his beloved daughter, Princess Charlotte, but after a lot of toing and froing, she had refused to marry him.

Princess Charlotte, who was all delight, poise and spirit, was reportedly appalled when stories of his drunken behaviour reached her. Rumour had it the final straw came when the prince was supposed to be meeting the princess, but was instead found to be unconscious with drink, hanging out of the back of a carriage. Princess Charlotte, having standards for public conduct that would not be lowered even for a royal heir, broke off their engagement, and Lady Caroline couldn't blame her.

The prince had returned to his home city of Brussels, where he famously rowed with his father, who hated how much the young prince loved the English and their customs. A true Anglophile, the prince was therefore destined to be a firm favourite in the households of all the English families in Brussels.

After his initial visit to the Capel house, he began to stop by with increasing regularity. They soon learnt that the prince had a great dislike of being announced in the formal manner and would go to great lengths to avoid the servants, preferring to make his own way through the house. Lady Caroline and the girls would invariably be found in some state of relaxation in one of the sitting rooms, hemming pocket handkerchiefs or battling a tricky piano piece in the music room.

'I do hope I'm not interrupting,' he would say, his head popping around the door, his accent thick but charming.

'Your Royal Highness, you startled us!' Lady Caroline would say. 'No, of course, you aren't interrupting. Harriet, call for tea, will you?'

Lady Caroline had begun to notice a familiarity between the prince and Georgy, and had to admit that the two looked very sweet together. The prince would be a catch of epic proportions, but the thought of it made Lady Caroline uneasy. Clearly the elder Prince of Orange would never approve the match. From Princess Charlotte to a penniless aristocrat; that would be quite a turn-up for the books! At best, the flirtation might lead to Georgy meeting a more suitable match, a man closer to her own class, but it was a risk. Lady Caroline planned to keep Georgy distracted in the hope a more suitable gentleman would soon catch her eye.

Lost to pondering while preparing for the ball, Lady Caroline was taken aback by the sudden arrival in her room of a brightly coloured parrot followed by a mixed assortment of her younger children, Louisa, Horatia and Algernon, all laughing heartily. The parrot flew shrieking right over Lady Caroline's head, and took refuge on top of the armoire in the corner of the room, looking distinctly ruffled.

'What in heaven's name is that bird doing in the house?' demanded Lady Caroline.

Algernon replied enthusiastically, 'Mama, do say we can keep him. He would be the best pet.'

At this, the parrot squawked. He seemed much happier now he was out of the clutches of the children.

'Answer my question, children,' said Lady Caroline, trying to employ a disapproving tone of voice.

Again, it was Algernon who was brave enough to continue under his mother's penetrating glare.

'He was outside the front gate, just sitting there, looking

quite lost, so we thought it would be nice for him to join us, and he came quite willingly. Until, that is, he saw Father, then he flew off.'

The bird squawked again, rather unhelpfully. Lady Caroline fought off a sudden desire to laugh. Capel, who had a dislike for birds, would no doubt be displeased, but there was no denying the animal was beautiful and would, it was true, make a charming pet.

'I have no time for this nonsense. Your sisters and I are going to a ball this evening. We will see to removing the bird later.'

She returned to the looking glass. In the reflection she could see the children peering at her, none of them wanting to leave the room. They loved to see Lady Caroline at her toilette, a privilege she rarely allowed, preferring to ready herself for an evening's entertainment in peace. Today she could not resist allowing them to watch her.

Lady Caroline patted her hair to ensure the hairpins would remain securely in place while she was dancing.

'What a fine job Julia has done, don't you think?' Lady Caroline said to the children. She applied some scent from a glass bottle to her wrists and décolletage, and clipped on pearl earrings. A little rouge was gently dabbed on to her lips and cheekbones. The children waited patiently for Lady Caroline to announce her toilette complete. Even the parrot took advantage of the distraction and flew down to the side of the washing basin. He kept quiet and watched, occasionally shifting his weight from foot to foot and ruffling his wings.

'*Voilà*!' She finally announced to her reflection, unable to keep a smile from her face at the sight of her children gazing avidly at her. They broke into a round of applause.

Julia, who had gone to fetch a broom with which to flush out the parrot, returned.

'Julia, perhaps we can leave the parrot for now; I'm growing rather fond of him already,' she said. Her mood had lifted immeasurably.

Julia propped the broom against the wall and fetched Lady Caroline's favourite cream fan, a shawl and a small, beaded reticule.

Lady Caroline rose and made her way from the room, escorted by her happy family, holding hands as they chattered and laughed together.

After sending the little ones down the hall to the nursery, Lady Caroline went downstairs and was greeted by a most pleasant sight. Standing in the entrance hall, checking the fit of his uniform in the looking glass, was her eldest brother, Lord Uxbridge. She ran down the last few steps and flung herself into his arms.

The siblings had always been close, having grown up together first in the Welsh countryside and latterly in the Uxbridge residence in London. Their temperaments were similar, and each was fiercely protective of the other.

'Whatever are you doing here? This certainly is a surprise.'

Lord Uxbridge planted a kiss on her cheek. 'I wanted to see my sister and her growing tribe and ensure they've not yet been swept away by the officers I hear have been visiting you.'

'Oh, Paget, how can you say that? The girls are more than ready for a suitable match.'

'Yes, and Brussels will certainly be the place for such a thing, if it can be managed.'

'What do you mean, "if"?' she replied, in mock outrage.

'Well, I say they are the most charming girls I ever laid eyes on, but with not a penny to rub between them, what's a lad to do?' He raised his shoulders, grinning mischievously.

Lady Caroline gave her brother a playful knock on the arm.

'Hush, my! They'll be coming downstairs soon and tonight is their first ball here, so don't bring them down with harsh truths.'

Before Lord Uxbridge could reply, voices were heard on the landing and the three eldest Capel daughters began to make their way down the stairs. Seeing them in their finery, Lord Uxbridge turned to his sister.

'My dear, I take my words back with penitence, I don't think you will have a wink of trouble getting these beauties down the aisle.'

Lady Caroline smiled in agreement.

CHAPTER V

Waltzing into Danger

'The P. of Orange says he intends to be very merry & to have Balls and Breakfasts without end. He has an overgrown staff already & it is likely to be increased.'

Georgy Capel to the Dowager Countess of Uxbridge

The elder Capel girls had been thrilled when their mama had said they could attend the ball, for all their visitors had been discussing it. They'd thought that Lady Charlotte's relationship with the Duke of Wellington would mean they wouldn't have been allowed, but perhaps Lady Caroline had interceded on their behalf. When they had been told their papa had agreed they could go, the news had been greeted with whoops and cheers, and immediate discussions on who would wear what, and dance with whom.

'You shall dance with the prince, Georgy, of course!'

'And you with Lord Hay, Maria!'

'Who will be dancing with General Barnes, I wonder?'

Even Maria, Georgy and Harriet, so new to the adult world of romance, knew that their hostess that evening was greatly admired by all the English gentlemen in Brussels. Being the lover and confidante of the top military leader in Europe had its benefits, and so the affaire was accepted by society as long as it was managed discreetly.

Lady Charlotte and her husband were passing through Brussels on a tour through the Continent, and were so delighted with the place had managed to secure the last fine house looking on to the park, near to the Capels.

Maria felt a little awed at the thought of seeing Lady Charlotte Greville that evening. She had once spotted her on the arm of the duke at a ball in London, and had thought that she'd never seen a woman so confident and at ease in her own skin, whereas Maria felt quite at odds with herself as she sat at her looking glass. She wore a simple evening dress that she supposed was pretty, but she knew it would look mediocre next to other dresses there. Taking a deep breath, she felt her ribs press against the corseting of her gown. How nervous she felt, and she couldn't put her finger on why.

Maria hoped she didn't look too plain. As a young and unmarried woman, her mother wouldn't allow her to wear any jewels, and noticeable make-up was equally frowned upon. Maria and Georgy had long ago managed to purloin an old pot of rouge from their mother's dressing table, but this could only be used in small quantities for fear their mother would notice the enhancement.

Outside the window she could hear sounds of people on the street, chatting, laughing and calling out to each other. On the landing her sisters barged into each other's rooms to borrow a piece of lace or trinket. Maria considered her reflection in the looking glass.

'Lord! My first proper ball; how shall I remember this

evening in years to come?' she said to her mirrored self.

She turned her head to one side so she could see her dark hair contrasting with the lace ribbon Lord Hay had given her. It was curled across her crown and behind the ringlets that framed either side of her face. Hopefully the ribbon was obvious enough to one who knew to look for it.

Whenever she had seen Lord Hay in the weeks since their initial meeting with General Barnes, Maria had become increasingly interested in him. And his clothes! At each visit Lord Hay wore the most splendid pieces, not an item out of place, satins and breeches and cravats that must have cost a small fortune, and all worn with such an air of fashionable disinterest, as though each had been casually thrown on. How plain Maria felt in contrast. Would she even be noticed among the hundreds of other young ladies at the ball?

Her swirling thoughts didn't stop there. She worried, too, that Lord Hay's fondness for her was tempered by his knowledge of the family's financial situation. She felt ashamed of the façade they kept up: the large house, fine clothes, pictures and books lining the walls of the library. Did they really deserve to attend balls such as Lady Charlotte's when they hadn't the means to keep up this lifestyle? Surely Lord Hay, a younger son, would not be interested in marrying a penniless girl like Maria. Yet when they spoke she felt such a connection. Could she dare to hope he would see past her situation? She felt another flush of frustration at her father.

Georgy entered their room, patting her newly set hair that curled upwards and was secured in place with tiny fabric roses. She shut the door hurriedly and grinned.

'Maria, I am so full of excitement for what this evening could hold, I could explode!'

'I, too. There seems to be a family of worms squirming away in my stomach.'

Georgy sighed, sitting down carefully on the bed so as not to crinkle her skirt. Looking across at her sister, she noticed Maria's hair.

'Oh, your ribbon, it looks delightful! What a calling card Lord Hay has given you.'

Maria smiled. 'He probably won't even remember, and oh, sister! What if he thinks me a fool for wearing it so plainly? Whatever could I mean by it, anyway!'

'Why shouldn't you wear it? It's a very fine piece of lace, and complements your dress perfectly. No other person will know the real story behind it. It's a secret for you to carry around with you, that only you and I know, and perhaps Lord Hay, if he's sharp enough to spot it.'

Maria liked the sound of that.

'Perhaps you're right. If nothing comes of it then no matter, I shan't bother him. In fact, there'll be so many people at the ball it's possible I won't even see him.'

She joined her sister on the bed.

'Do you think we shall see the Prince of Orange?' Georgy asked coyly.

'I hope so, for your sake!' said Maria, nudging her arm.

'Oh, Maria, stop! We've seen him but a handful of times and he's been so kind to us all. I don't know why everyone thinks he has singled me.'

'He can't keep his eyes off you, that's why. Oh, and the

fact that he visits our house more often than can possibly be explained without some romantic notion or other. Honestly, this is how it starts! Mama has noticed. So really, all that's left to do is fall properly in love and be married before Michaelmas!'

'Stop!'

'You shall be a princess!'

Maria laughed at her sister's squirming discomfort, her own anxiety about the ball temporarily at bay.

The minutes had ticked by happily and soon it was time for them to leave. After Harriet joined them, the three sisters linked arms, admiring each other's gowns. Harriet was in palest yellow, Georgy in a charming blue and Maria in cream. Looking down, they saw their mother with a tall man in a splendid Hussar's uniform. As they descended and the lit chandeliers in the hall brought the pair into focus, they recognised their beloved uncle, Lord Uxbridge. Their mother looked pleased at their entrance.

'Girls, come downstairs and don't keep your uncle waiting.'

'Sorry, Mama!' they cried, and they quickly descended the last of the stairs like ducklings swimming back to their hen.

Lady Caroline looked ravishing in a gown the colour of butter with fashionable points of white fabric hanging along the edge of the neckline. She looked every bit as glamorous as her daughters dreamt one day to be.

Their uncle possessed even more confidence and swagger than the last time he'd called. He wore a splendid uniform with gold frogging across the front and edges of his dress jacket. They embraced him gladly.

'My, you girls have turned into such beauties! Whatever are we to do with you?'

'Introduce us to some charming young men, if you would,' replied Maria, with as much enthusiasm as she dared, deliberately not catching her mother's eye.

Lord Uxbridge roared with laughter.

'Well, you are certainly filled with just the same joie de vivre as your mother was at your age.'

'I still am, brother,' Lady Caroline retorted, tapping her fan against his arm, 'tempered only by the presence of so many daughters snapping at my heels.'

'Aye, I know the feeling, my dear. So many little ones to steal the limelight from you. More on the way for me, too!'

Lady Caroline looked uncomfortable with the direction the conversation had taken. There was an awkward pause, so Maria stepped in.

'Uncle, are you escorting us to the ball? Please say yes!'

Lord Uxbridge turned to his niece, stood to attention and clicked his heels together.

'Ladies,' he cried, 'it would be a pleasure, *and* an honour.'

All embarrassment was forgotten. After their father had joined them, they left the house and began the short walk to the residence Lord and Lady Greville had rented on the opposite side of the park. Lady Caroline linked arms with her husband and led the way. Maria walked with her uncle and marvelled at his jaunty walk. As they strolled through the park, enjoying the evening light that swept the wide promenades, Maria felt a little more confident. She couldn't have hoped for a greater entry to the ball than to have their famous uncle with them to smooth the way for introductions.

Now was the time, when she had her uncle to herself, to

impress him with her grown-up wit and charm, but just at that moment she could think of nothing either witty or charming to say. Luckily, Lord Uxbridge was quite at ease and at length began the conversation himself.

'So, my little niece, I hear you have been catching the eye of quite a few of my fellow soldiers.'

Maria was not in the least surprised at his choice of topic, her uncle loved gossip, especially when it was not of his own making. She laughed. 'Why, surely you would rather talk on a more delicate subject, the weather or some such? What would my mother say if she could hear us?'

'Oh, la! We are both now far too old to be bandying about with such dull and mundane topics. The weather is the weather, but to love is the greatest subject of all to discuss with those we trust. You trust me, do you not, Muzzy?'

'Of course, Uncle.'

Maria glowed at the use of her pet name.

'You can rest assured I am to be counted upon to look out for those closest to me; that's something Charlotte is always telling me I do best.'

Maria said nothing to this mention of his wife, but her uncle didn't seem to require an answer. Instead she said, 'Well then, who is it you have heard me in connection to?'

'Well, Lord Hay I hear has become quite friendly of late.'

Maria was a little taken aback, but also pleased their names had been connected. 'You are acquainted with the gentleman, then?'

'To a degree. He's made quite a show, despite his age and lack of experience.'

Maria wasn't sure if this was a compliment or not, and Lord Uxbridge's sidelong look told her he knew more than he said. She looked quizzically back at him.

'What is it, Uncle? He seems kind-hearted to me, but we've known him but a few weeks.'

Her uncle pondered her words. 'All I will say is, be careful of that one, until you know for sure he is yours. That is my counsel,' he said.

At that moment Georgy and Harriet joined them.

'Really, Maria, you are keeping our uncle all to yourself; very greedy, I might say. Let us all share in your conversation!' Georgy said.

Without skipping a beat, Lord Uxbridge began to tell Harriet and Georgy about a new form of quadrille he had been dancing in Paris.

Maria pondered her uncle's words as they joined the crowds surging towards Lady Charlotte's house. The thudding in Maria's chest had settled, although her palms still felt hot beneath her elbow-length gloves. She was keen to break through the bottleneck caused by the hosts greeting guests in the antechamber to the main ballroom. The other attendees were merry, being quite used to such congestion.

Finally, it was their turn. Lady Charlotte greeted Lady Caroline and Capel, and then turned her attention to their uncle.

'Why, Lord Uxbridge, how delightful to see you. I'm thrilled you are able to join us for our little party.'

Maria looked around at the hundreds of people crammed into the small rooms leading from the street and wondered how such a party could ever be called *little*.

Lord Uxbridge made an elegant bow to the hostess, and hastily introduced Maria and her sisters before they were swept forward by the crowd behind them.

'Ah, yes, as beautiful as I'd heard,' Maria heard Lady Charlotte say, as their time was done and they made their way to the main ballroom.

With Lord Uxbridge beside them they made their way quickly through the crowd, his aura as bright as the jewels worn by the ladies and the medals pinned to the men's chests. Heads turned towards them as they progressed, and Maria felt proud to be at his side. She couldn't see Lord Hay and wondered whether she would ever be able to spot him through so many people.

The large room which served as a ballroom in the house was decorated with garlands and lavishly lit by hundreds of candles. The effect was quite entrancing. The babble of noise risked drowning the music from the small orchestra playing from the corner of the room. Losing their father in the throng, the Capel girls made their way with Lord Uxbridge and their mother to the refreshment table for a drink. Lady Caroline handed each sister a small measure of punch in an elegant glass, along with a warning look to be careful not to enjoy too much.

At that moment Lord Uxbridge leapt forward with a shout of recognition and pulled a distinguished-looking foreign gentleman towards them. Maria was struck by a flickering darkness in his eyes; his brow was furrowed and his expression concerned. Here was a man with a serious disposition. He and Lord Uxbridge were clearly close friends, for each slapped a hand around the other's shoulders. Lord Uxbridge turned back to the ladies.

'May I introduce you to Baron Ernst Trip, who served with me as an aide-de-camp on the Walcheren campaign. After that he fought old Boney in Portugal. A truly capital man and a great friend. We have seen much together.' Turning to Lady Caroline he said, 'Sister, you of course already know Trip from our time in London.'

Lady Caroline made an elegant curtsey, but other than that her only response was a thin smile. Maria guessed she was none too delighted at Baron Trip's re-entry into her life, and wondered what the reason could be. In turn, Lord Uxbridge's little speech was met with only a small smile of gratitude from Baron Trip. He bowed formally to them all as Lord Uxbridge made his introductions.

'Trip is a man of few words, but when they are uttered, they count,' declared Lord Uxbridge with good humour. 'Tell me, where are you stationed now, dear chap?'

The baron had a low voice that was barely distinguishable over the rumble of the crowd around them.

'I have the honour to be on the staff of the Prince of Orange.'

'Capital! You'll have a hoot with Lord March there too.'

The baron didn't seem to be paying much attention to Lord Uxbridge's words; he was looking directly at Harriet. Maria saw Harriet was holding the gentleman's gaze.

Turning quickly then to their mother, Trip said warmly, 'I hear the prince has already made himself at home in your residence, Lady Caroline. I would be honoured to visit you all soon, should that be welcome.'

Lady Caroline seemed at least partially mollified by these words, and said, 'Indeed, my lord, that would be pleasant. The prince is welcome to join us whenever he likes, and we extend the same invitation to his fellow officers.'

To this the baron made another bow. 'I look forward to the occasion,' he said. He made to move away, but then he hesitated and turned to Harriet.

'I wonder if I might have the honour of the first dance, if you're not already taken?'

As they had only just entered the ball Harriet was, of course, free to accept his invitation.

'Thank you, sir,' she said, 'that would be very pleasant.'

Maria noticed her sister was a little more flushed than usual, clearly pleased to have been singled out by Baron Trip.

'Capital! Capital!' Lord Uxbridge was delighted. 'I see my nieces will be in high demand here.' He turned to his sister. 'I see Mr Creevey over there and would have a word with him, for which I will borrow Trip for a few moments, and then release him back to Harriet.'

With that, he disappeared into the crowd with his friend.

After a few minutes, Baron Trip returned to take Harriet to the area of the room that had been set aside for dancing. She didn't look back as she was led away, seemingly enchanted by the attentions of the gentleman. The dancing started, a popular jaunty number that was familiar to them from their dancing lessons. The crowd's attention was drawn towards the dancers, just out of view from where the group stood. Maria was happy to drink in the scene, sipping her punch.

A short while later General Barnes joined them, looking

very smart in his dress uniform. After bowing to them all, he turned to Maria.

'My dear Miss Maria, may I have the pleasure of this dance?'

Maria had hoped that she might dance initially with Lord Hay, as it was generally known that the first was often taken with your particular favourite. She was rather taken aback by General Barnes's abrupt manner, and there was a pause as she struggled to reply.

'Maria will be delighted, *dear* General Barnes,' said Lady Caroline, giving her daughter a look.

'Yes, thank you, sir, I *should* be delighted.' Maria had found her voice, and just in time, conscious that she might appear ungrateful. General Barnes made a short bow. Not wanting to meet her mother's eye for fear of a reprimanding look, she took General Barnes's proffered arm and smiled at him as warmly as she could.

Before they left to take up their positions for the next dance, the Prince of Orange joined their party. He looked splendid in a British officer's uniform, a choice that would surely have annoyed his father had he been present. He really was as skinny as an otter, but Maria thought the effect of the uniform stood him in good stead, and he wore it with pride, quite the most important thing in her opinion. Georgy looked delighted and Maria saw the prince give her a twinkling look.

It was no surprise to anyone that the prince had come over with the intention of asking Georgy to dance. Georgy accepted the invitation and curtseyed her thanks. Lady Caroline met Maria's eye, as if to say, *that's how you do it, young lady*.

'Marvellous!' said General Barnes happily. 'Lady Caroline, you must be delighted to have all three daughters engaged to dance, for I see Harriet is taking another turn with Baron Trip.'

'Indeed, nothing could make me happier,' their mother said warmly.

As the girls were both led away, Maria looked back and couldn't help but feel a little sorry for her beautiful mother, left alone as her daughters went off to dance. She looked a little out of sorts, raising a glass of punch to her lips, her eyes searching the room. Where had her father disappeared to? His absences were becoming more and more noticeable since they had moved to Brussels. Maria felt sad he wasn't a more consistent companion to her mother. She wondered whether he had found any gambling establishments in the city since their arrival, but before she could dwell anymore on this worrying prospect, General Barnes had engaged her in conversation and she lost sight of her mother through the crowd.

Maria, General Barnes, Georgy and the prince watched the dance finish. Maria enjoyed the repeating patterns of red uniforms on pale coloured dresses as each pair swept expertly across the floor. General Barnes and Maria enjoyed another quick glass of punch before it was time for them to take to the floor. As the music started again, Maria felt the benefit of the dancing lessons they had been taking; everyone around them was much older than her and she reckoned they would be strong dancers. Luckily, Lady Caroline had even let them learn how to waltz, on the understanding that they were not to mention it to their papa.

General Barnes spun Maria around gamely and with great confidence. This was probably the hundredth waltz he had danced, and it showed. Did he sense that it was Maria's first? In any case, if she wasn't to dance with Lord Hay then she was very happy to have been asked by General Barnes, who was well liked by all and the most senior military friend they had made. As they turned around the floor, Maria saw that by dancing she got a better view of the room. Within a minute or two she had spotted Lord Hay. She hoped he could see her dancing with General Barnes and the thought made her smile all the more widely.

General Barnes, too, was smiling, and throwing out snippets of conversation in the usual fashion. He knew the steps well, even if he was a little heavy footed, and so occasionally missed a beat. When the dance was over he made a deep bow, in return to which Maria curtseyed as elegantly as she could, for she was mightily out of breath and didn't want to show it. Their fellow dancers crowded around them. They crossed the room together and Maria did her best to steer General Barnes to where she had seen Lord Hay, determined that she should cross paths with him.

'How do you find life in Brussels so far, Miss Maria?' General Barnes enquired as they walked, leaning close so he could hear her reply above the noise around them. Maria's plan was working; they were getting closer to where she had seen Lord Hay.

'Very well, thank you. In fact, I like it better than London. Everyone is so gay and welcoming. Although the society is smaller that seems a positive to me now, as everyone knows one another already.'

'Quite true,' he replied.

Lord Hay was only feet away and looked over to catch Maria's eye. Maria felt herself redden as he flashed a wide smile that was full of mischief. The crowd swelled again as the next set of dancers took the floor, propelling Maria and General Barnes further towards Lord Hay, and finally they were within conversational distance.

'Good evening to you both.' Lord Hay bowed.

Maria saw that Lord Hay was with another lady. The woman seemed not to be English but a Bruxellois, and she didn't greet them, but blushed and curtseyed. Maria's eye swept over her gaudy dress and unnaturally painted face. These local women were so very different from the English. Lady Caroline had called them 'loose' on two separate occasions, and although Maria was not completely sure what she had meant by the term, she guessed it had a lot to do with being 'flirts of the highest degree', another of her mother's favourite slights.

As they chatted, Maria felt some distaste for Lord Hay's dance partner, although she wasn't quite sure why. It perhaps had something do with the way her hand rested across Lord Hay's arm and chest. Yet she couldn't deny that the older generation of her own class didn't set much of an example with their behaviour. Glancing over Lord Hay's shoulder, she could see a lady her mother's age hanging off the arm of a man a good deal younger who was definitely not her husband.

General Barnes seemed also to feel the awkwardness of their meeting.

'Miss Capel,' he said, 'shall I return you to your mother? Good evening, Lord Hay, madam.'

He was courteous yet firm. Lord Hay flashed Maria one last grin and was gone. Maria was no expert, but he appeared to have drunk rather a lot already.

Barnes led her away, and before long they were back in the eyeline of the dancers and spotted Lady Caroline. As she rejoined her mother, who Maria was pleased to see was now chatting conspiratorially to their hostess, she saw that Georgy was dancing with the prince again. She was flying around the room, and seemed to Maria to shine all the brighter for being so happy in the prince's presence.

'Ah, you are back. Did you enjoy your dance, my dear?' said Lady Caroline, pulling Maria's attention away from her sister.

'Yes, Mama. General Barnes certainly is a good teacher of the waltz.'

'How delightful, but don't tell your papa, will you!'

The following hours were spent most pleasantly. Maria managed to drink five more small glasses of punch without a single reprimand from her mother, and she danced again three times; another with General Barnes, then with another acquaintance of the family, General Ferguson, and finally with the Prince of Orange. The dances were great fun but after several hours Maria found she was starting to flag. Her new shoes were pinching around her toes and she felt quite worn out from trying to keep up with all the adult conversation. Often, the chatter was peppered with army terminology she didn't comprehend and was of little interest, although she felt she ought to concentrate in case she was asked an opinion. She hoped that wouldn't happen, as she feared she would embarrass herself.

Only the mention of Napoleon's name piqued her interest. Some questioned what was to become of him on the remote island to which he had been exiled. Would he ever be able to return? Maria had been brought up to fear Napoleon, but many revered him. His short, portly frame had been the source of many a caricature and cruel joke in London, but the mention of his name was often also accompanied by hushed voices of admiration, for his bravery and valour were legendary. Indeed, it was known to all that in Brussels there was still a lot of open support for Bonaparte.

As conversation swirled around her she began to feel increasingly out of her depth, not least as the edges of speech grew hazy with sleepiness and drink. Just as Maria was beginning to wish that her mother would stop dancing with Lord Uxbridge and allow them all to make their way across the park to their beds, Lord Hay appeared at her side. Maria choked slightly on her punch.

'Miss Maria, I see you have finally shaken off General Barnes.'

'Lord Hay! Well, I...' Maria found she was stammering again. Why were her responses always so undignified?

Lord Hay seemed not to notice or mind. 'Might I have the pleasure of this last dance? I have been hunting you down with an eye to seeing you in action. I hope you've been practising your steps!'

Maria felt a bolt of excitement and anxiety and was inordinately thankful that her mother wasn't there to hear her blusters. Lord Hay strode with her across the room, holding her hand slightly raised from his own, as though presenting a prize. They certainly seemed to turn heads as Maria was led, yet again, to the dancing area.

It was another waltz. Without hesitation Lord Hay pulled her towards him, his hand taking her waist. Maria felt the hairs on the backs of her arms rise. As they began to turn about the room, Maria had a chance to examine Lord Hay more closely. He wore the standard dress kit of an ensign in the Foot Guards, but the cut of the cloth was only a little short of extraordinary. It was so figure-hugging as to be almost indecent, and he had a broadness across the chest and shoulders that set off his slim hips perfectly. Confidence rose from him like a perfume.

Maria's sore feet were quite forgotten as they spun together again and again across the floor. Maria felt she was floating with each rise and fall, so assured was Lord Hay in his handling of each phase of the dance. Her senses were heightened and she was keenly aware of the feel of his hand at her waist, the rustle of her satin dress, the sparkling warmth and chemistry fizzing between them. Maria was unable to hide her delight. What would her father say if he could see her waltzing with such a man as Lord Hay? Then the music swelled again and she had to concentrate on the steps so she wouldn't stumble and ruin the moment.

Maria didn't want the dance to end, or for her feet to return to the mundanity of walking, but of course it was soon over and she and Lord Hay were both out of breath, laughing and grinning at each other. Lord Hay made her a deep bow and Maria's curtsey was equally elaborate. When her eyes lifted, they met Lord Hay's with a new kind of intensity. Together, they made their way away across the hall, away from the chatting dancers.

'Miss Capel, how well you dance. Let's not make it our last together.'

'I would very much like that, Lord Hay.'

At this he frowned slightly. 'What say you to abandoning this formal way of talking? I hate all this lord, lady and miss nonsense. Do you have any objection if I call you by your Christian name?'

Maria didn't know what to say. She had never called anyone except her siblings by their Christian names. Even her uncle she called Lord Uxbridge now he had inherited her grandfather's title. This was definitely something that her mother wouldn't approve of. Before she could fashion a suitable response they had come close enough to Lady Caroline to meet her eye, so Maria simply smiled, and hoped that would satisfy Lord Hay for now.

It was time for them to make their way home. Lord Hay and Maria exited the ball as a pair, behind Lady Caroline and the others. At the entrance, their papa reappeared, looking flushed and a little disordered. Maria was distracted enough not to notice the glare Lady Caroline was giving him.

At the entrance to the park, Lord Hay made to return to his lodgings.

'Thank you all for a most charming evening,' he said, mostly to Maria. 'It's going to be great fun having the Capel family in town, I'm sure.'

He bowed and strode off through the knots of people heading homeward in various states of inebriation and exhaustion.

By now, dawn was keen to join them so the family

hastened across the park to their house. Heavy-headed from the wine and dancing, they were relieved to reach home and have the door shut behind them. After kissing their exhausted father and frosty mother good night, the girls removed their shoes and climbed the stairs. By now, light was chalking the sky, a hazy glow heralding daybreak. Georgy and Maria bade Harriet goodnight on the landing, then fell into their bed fully clothed, the room spinning, heads and feet throbbing.

Maria couldn't believe the fun they'd had and was already thinking ahead to the next ball they might attend. No wonder their mother and father frequented balls so regularly. How often had Maria been taking her breakfast when her mother had finally returned from a ball? Now she knew why! Her body ached but sleep wasn't forthcoming. She rose from the bed, pulling sleepy Georgy up with her. They removed their dresses, helping each other rather haphazardly with the buttons and stays, and got into their night things.

Georgy collapsed back into the bed and fell asleep almost immediately. Maria resisted a little longer. She sat at the dressing table and carefully removed the lace ribbon from her hair. Barefoot, she padded over to the large wardrobe and returned the lace to the ribbon box, before quietly pushing it back into its hiding place.

Lord Hay hadn't mentioned the ribbon as she'd hoped he would, despite the exaggerated turns of her head she'd made during their waltz together. Perhaps she'd been childish to take the gift to heart, for it seemed Lord Hay had forgotten all about it, but she wouldn't let such a detail spoil her perfect evening. Rejoining Georgy, she fell into a happy slumber.

CHAPTER VI

A Meeting

'I do not know whether you are acquainted with the Young Prince, I am sure you wd. like him, if it was only for his Good nature to us. He comes in without even being introduced by a Servant, at all hours, just like a tame Cat.'

Maria Capel to the Dowager Countess of Uxbridge

Following Lady Charlotte's ball, the Capel girls began to settle into the rhythm of their new lives. Pleased with their behaviour, their mother agreed that the eldest Capel girls were ready to be let completely out into society, and so like early summer flowers finally open to the sun, the fullest and most exciting phase of their lives started.

Soon after the Lennoxes arrived in Brussels, Maria, Georgy and Harriet paid them a visit. The Duke of Richmond had managed to secure a house large enough for his whole family, but it was in an unfashionable part of town, in the industrial area, a carriage ride away from the area the Capels called home. The elder Lennox girls, Ladies Mary, Sarah and Georgiana, were thrilled to see their friends again.

'Do tell me,' asked Lady Georgiana as they took tea

together, 'have you made any interesting connections since you've been here?' They could tell by her tone that she meant those of a romantic nature.

'Yes, I've heard you've caught the eye of the Prince of Orange, Georgy,' said Lady Mary.

Georgy looked embarrassed, but pleased.

'Indeed she has,' Maria answered for her. She steeled herself to ask, 'Tell me, have you made the acquaintance of Lord Hay yet? We first met him in a rather unusual way, at a haberdashery shop of all places.'

'Yes, we've had the pleasure,' said Lady Sarah. 'He visited us a few days ago with General Maitland. I must say I thought General Maitland to be a fine gentleman indeed...'

'Sarah, don't you think he's a little old for you?' Lady Georgiana said.

'Not in the slightest,' Lady Sarah replied, her chin set.

'Lord Hay is undeniably handsome, but he certainly made his mark in London before coming here,' said Lady Mary, clearly wanting to change the subject.

Maria was intrigued. 'In what way?'

'Oh, you know what these men are like – or rather, should I say boys? Let's just say he was behaving in all the ways your mother and mine wouldn't approve of.'

Maria didn't feel she could press for more information, and in any case the conversation was already moving on. Her interest in Lord Hay, far from abating, grew in intensity with everything she found out about his reputation.

They saw a lot of the Lennox girls and their parents as they were often invited to the same dinners, receptions and picnic trips. Balls were less frequent, making them all the more special. The day after they attended a dinner or ball, the Capel sisters would rise late. After slow mornings, afternoons were filled with visits to friends or receiving guests in the drawing room, walks and occasional dress fittings. A short quiet time was enjoyed before they readied themselves for each evening's activities, for it was in at night that Brussels truly came alive.

It was rare to spend an evening at home, although Lady Caroline did insist on occasion that the girls went to bed straight after supper.

'I won't have you looking careworn, you must look your best at all times,' she declared. 'You simply can't stay out all hours, please. Nothing ruins good looks more quickly.'

Maria didn't really believe this. Seeing her mother in the family way so many times had led her to think that it was bringing babies into the world that damaged a woman's health more than regular late nights. After each birth Lady Caroline had to battle harder to regain her shape, and each time Maria saw the lines around her eyes and mouth deepen, and her hair lose its shine. Lady Caroline was undoubtedly still beautiful, but she was no longer the youthful woman in the Hoppner portrait at Plas Newydd.

Neither Maria nor her sisters had much idea of the process by which babies were created, except that a man and woman had, of course, to be married before such arrangements were made. Weighing up whether marriage was worth the sacrifice when considering the number of children you might end up having was a popular topic of debate among the Capel girls, with their younger sisters Louisa and Horatia vehemently opposed to the idea of husbands.

'All men save Papa and Uncle Uxbridge are *beasts*,' Louisa had declared during their last discussion on the topic.

Maria was reflecting on this subject during one early autumn walk with Harriet and Georgy through the park outside their home. The sun was warm and pleasant, the park virtually empty. They turned from the far west avenue on to the main promenade.

Although of course Maria did want to marry one day, she knew that as soon as she did she would be separated from her sisters. There would be the responsibilities of marital life, the demands of her husband and most likely distance to contend with, too. Until one of them married they were free to spend their days as they pleased, living in each other's pockets. That was the way it had always been, and particularly on such fine and contented afternoons as these she was reluctant to let go of the life with her sisters that she'd always enjoyed.

Yet marriage did seem to be an unavoidable conclusion for them all. No other option seemed open if she wanted to make a home of her own. Whether their mother would allow them to marry solely for love was questionable. Despite their financial situation, their mother still had exacting standards as to the sort of man they should be considering. The want of money was a concern of the highest order, but Maria still felt the pressure to make a 'good' match.

She felt sure her sisters would make better matches than herself in the end. Harriet now had a number of men who made a beeline for her when she entered the room at a dance or dinner. Georgy had a fine figure that caused Maria great envy, afflicted as she felt she was with a body that went straight up and down and warranted very little positive commentary.

Maria had been surprised to find that Georgy was reluctant to talk about the attraction she and the Prince of Orange evidently shared for each other.

'Gee, do tell me what you and the prince were whispering about yesterday evening.'

'Well, you know, we really weren't speaking for long. Just a few moments before Mama hauled me off to dance with someone else. Just the normal things, really.'

'Oh, come, I wasn't born yesterday. You two are as thick as thieves.'

'How jealous you sound, Muzzy!'

'I'm not jealous, I'm thrilled. But I do want to be let in on your whisperings!'

Georgy would not be swayed. Perhaps she didn't want to jinx the match.

Maria loved all her sisters and was especially close to Georgy, but despite her protestations she did feel a little jealous of the attentions paid to Georgy by the prince. She and Lord Hay had, since her first ball, danced together several times, and each time Maria had experienced the same level of thrill and excitement as that night at Lady Charlotte's. No other man she had met in Brussels stole into her thoughts so often.

At the end of each dance she and Lord Hay would grin their pleasure at each other. At night, Maria's dreams were a confused tangle of lips and bodies, and in the morning she felt embarrassed. She didn't discuss these dreams with her sisters, as close as they were. If she was dreaming of such things, did this mean she was ready to marry, and that Lord Hay was the one she wanted to be her husband? She undoubtedly desired him. From the increasing amount of time they were spending together, and from the way he looked at her and held her, surely he felt the same way?

Yet, at that first ball he hadn't noticed that she wore the ribbon he'd given her, nor had he mentioned it again, and so it had remained tucked away in the ribbon box. Lord Hay was also changeable. Sometimes he went for weeks without visiting, and then he'd visit several days in a row. Maria had on several occasions seen him dancing with other women. This was, of course, the natural way of things, yet the way he looked at these women suggested to Maria that his affections might not be reserved solely for her.

The sisters were walking genially, passing conversation in the relaxed way only those who really know each other well could. Harriet was pensive and Georgy was humming a gentle tune to herself while twirling in her hands a leaf she had found on the path. As they turned the corner they were met with quite a scene. There before them was the Prince of Orange, who was stumbling along the path supported by none other than Lord Hay. They were both dressed in evening clothes that looked like they'd seen better days, despite it still being only the middle of the afternoon.

Maria was at first delighted and then dismayed as she took in the scene. Both men were staggering badly, Lord Hay weighed down through his efforts to support his taller friend, who was close to unconsciousness and bearing down on Lord Hay with his full weight. As the sisters drew closer, Lord Hay became aware of their presence. His eyes were bloodshot, his face pallid. Maria's first thought was that both had been poisoned or injured in some way, but then she realised they were both absurdly, embarrassingly drunk.

Lord Hay, realising the awkwardness of the situation, attempted to straighten the prince into a more upright position.

'Ladies, good morning,' he said, slurring his words rather spectacularly. 'I, er, do apologise for our condition. The prince, as you can see, has been taken, um, rather ill.'

Despite his hesitant and halting words there was a glint in his eye. He clearly found the situation rather amusing. So, indeed, did Maria, who was struggling not to laugh.

'Well, sir, it seems you have both made quite the night of it,' she replied.

Harriet said under her breath with a glance at her sisters, 'Perhaps a little too much.'

Maria looked over to Georgy to see if she too found the situation amusing, but this was not the case at all. Georgy looked disgusted at the state of the prince. It was undeniable that the prince looked far less desirable than when he was gallantly sweeping her around the ballroom floor. His face was bloated, greenish, and he was quite without speech, managing only a few incoherent mumbles.

Maria could see that Georgy was looking at the prince's cheek, her eyes narrowing. Maria looked too and saw that there was an unmistakable red lipstick kiss sitting there. Now she no longer wanted to laugh. A very awkward moment followed when no one spoke. How Maria wished their mama, who knew how to handle any social situation, was with them.

Then the prince made a most unbecoming noise in his throat, suggesting he was about to lose last night's supper, at which point Harriet took control of the situation, not wishing any of them to see the prince so indisposed.

'Come, Georgy, Muzzy, let's be getting home,' she said, taking each by the arm.

Lord Hay met Maria's eye. 'Muzzy?' he said, smiling sleepily at her.

Maria was dragged away by her sisters before she could reply. They left the two men to stagger off down the path. When Maria looked back she saw that Lord Hay had sat the prince down under a large tree and propped him up against the trunk, then collapsed next to him, creating a cloud of dust. They both settled down in a heap.

'Disgraceful!' declared Georgy. 'I'm only glad that Mama wasn't there to see such behaviour.'

Harriet agreed, adding, 'Did you see their clothes? They clearly hadn't been to bed and were sneaking back through the park to their billets.'

'Well, I thought it was very amusing,' said Maria. 'They're young, so why shouldn't they have some fun? Their responsibilities with the army don't seem very arduous.'

'It's hardly gentlemanlike behaviour, Muz. I'm sure General Barnes would never behave in such a way,' said Harriet.

'No doubt about that!' laughed Maria.

They had reached the front steps of their house, so naturally the incident could be discussed no longer. Their little adventure must not be brought to the attention of Lady Caroline. When they returned to their room, Maria suggested to Georgy that she might want to slip a piece of paper about their adventure into the ribbon box, but Georgy wasn't in favour of the idea; she clearly wanted to forget the episode as quickly as possible.

Maria, however, found it quite impossible to stop thinking about Lord Hay, how he now knew her pet name, and the look he had given her as they had parted. All these memories she planned to write down when next alone, to be secreted in the ribbon box.

That afternoon, despite the girls' secrecy, Lady Caroline did find out about the drunken adventures of the Prince of Orange and Lord Hay. She was trying to enjoy a rare moment of peace and quiet in the drawing room, alone except for the parrot, who was keeping her company while cleaning his feathers. Lady Caroline found the presence of the bird rather calming and was glad she'd allowed it to stay in the house. At any rate, he entertained the children and was a great talking point for guests, perhaps lending the Capels an air of the exotic they didn't completely deserve.

Lady Caroline was starting to feel rather restless and so was delighted when the arrival of General Barnes was announced by a servant. He had walked through the park to visit the family and was chuckling to himself as the servant left them to make tea.

'Dear Barnes, what has amused you so?' Lady Caroline asked, holding her hand out for the general to kiss. He took the seat nearest her.

The parrot began to stir from the perch they had fashioned for him near the window. It was clear the parrot had not taken to General Barnes. He had refused to step on to his arm when he would do so easily for others and was now staring fixedly at him.

Lady Caroline ignored the parrot and waited for General Barnes's response.

'I have just discovered that young scoundrel, Lord Hay, fast asleep under one of the large trees on the slopes by the pavilion; dead drunk, of course. And who should be with him but the Prince of Orange, heir to the realm and in quite the same state, no less! They both appeared perfectly at peace with the world, curled up next to each other and snoring away.'

Lady Caroline affected to be scandalised by such behaviour, although in truth stories of such drunken escapades were the norm for anyone who'd grown up in London during the time of the Prince Regent's excesses.

For the sake of propriety, she declared in false outrage, 'That prince! His behaviour is quite as bad here as it was in London, when Princess Charlotte threw him over. He is no better behaved than our regent!'

'Quite, and it hardly reflects well on the army to have two of its brightest sparks lying dead drunk in a park, but there you have it.'

'Did you leave them lying there?' she asked, as she settled herself more comfortably on the sofa next to General Barnes.

'God, no, I gave them both a good kick and sent them on their way.'

Lady Caroline laughed, and it seemed the most natural thing in the world to touch the general's arm as she did so. How easily he joined in her mirth. Their eyes met and Lady Caroline felt a jolt of happiness, her earlier boredom at an afternoon ill-spent forgotten. General Barnes was such a tonic, and how well she felt when he looked at her like that, as though he didn't want to be anywhere else in the world.

The parrot suddenly took flight from his perch and launched himself across the room, flying so close to General Barnes that he ducked to avoid being scalped by the bird's claws. Both the parrot and Lady Caroline shrieked, the latter jumping up in alarm. Just then, Maria, Georgy, Harriet and their younger sister, Louisa, entered the room to join their mother, finding them in a state of disarray. The spell between Lady Caroline and General Barnes was well and truly broken.

The new arrivals curtseyed to General Barnes and settled themselves in chairs around the room as Lady Caroline tried to calm herself, straightening her dress and shooing the parrot out of the room in punishment. General Barnes spoke warmly to the girls and it was as though nothing out of the ordinary had happened. Lady Caroline felt a little confused and flustered. Perhaps the flight of the parrot and the arrival of her daughters had been fortuitous after all.

CHAPTER VII

By Moonlight

'On the Prince Regent's birthday
we had a Magnificent Parade
& Feu de Joi which extended all
round the Park. Lord Wellington,
who attended it, was reed with
enthusiasm. In the Evening Lord
Clancarty gave a very Good
Ball to 500 People.'

Maria Capel to the Dowager Countess of Uxbridge

The heat of the summer was now upon them. The Capels sheltered from the sun's blaze, windows thrown open to a non-existent breeze. They couldn't understand how the Bruxellois coped with the heat, as none of them ever opened the windows of their houses.

In their house on the Rue Ducale the parrot seemed to be the only member of the family who didn't mind the weather. He spent much of his time in Capel's study, taking up residence among the books and papers that filled the room. He was really quite chatty, although what he said was usually unintelligible. He was most likely to start babbling when Capel was trying to doze off the excesses of the previous evening in his favourite chair, which did not endear him to the creature.

The parrot also had a habit of walking the passages of the

upstairs floors at night. One such evening Maria was woken by what she presumed to be the parrot hopping and flapping past their room. After listening for a few more minutes, however, she realised that the noise was not coming from the corridor but from their adjoining dressing room. The floorboards were creaking, and there were rustlings and whispered voices. Her heart seemed to miss a beat. This was not a member of their household. What on earth was going on? Dare she go and look?

She decided she did dare. A path to the dressing room door was lit by shafts of moonlight shining through the gaps in the curtains. She lowered her bare feet to the floor and quickly pulled on her dressing gown. Taking a deep breath for courage, she crept across the room and, before she could convince herself not to, flung open the door.

To her horror two strange men stood there, their arms filled with clothes, books and even the lamps that usually lit the room. The room was instead lit by the lanterns the two men had set on the floor, which was strewn with the girls' possessions: hats, dresses and trinkets alike. The two men had lined and grubby faces, were dressed in dark clothes and looked shocked at the interruption. They immediately made a break for the window, which had a wooden ladder up against it on the outside.

'Stop! Stop, thieves!' Maria was so shocked that she was surprised any words came out at all. The men of course paid no heed and were down the ladder in a matter of seconds.

'Mama, Papa!' Maria's shrieks brought Georgy careering into the room.

'What on earth is going on, Muz?'

'Georgy, we've been robbed, go and get Papa!'

Maria dashed to the window and looked out, but could see nothing in the darkness. Her heart was thudding painfully in her chest and she took a deep, shuddering breath of cool air.

'Well,' she said into the blackness all around her, 'I can now see why the locals keep their windows shut.'

When she turned back to the room she saw her mother and father looking appalled.

'Strangers, in my house? It will not be borne!' their papa shouted.

Lady Caroline was already in tears. 'And to think, they were so close to our girls; it doesn't bear thinking of!'

Maria had been thinking along the same lines. Anything could have happened to them if the burglars had ventured into just one more room.

'I shall certainly be reporting this matter, girls,' said their father, 'and we'll do our best to get your things back.'

Maria didn't hold out much hope for that. Slowly the shock subsided, helped by a cup of sugared tea brought by the cook. They began to take stock of what had been taken. Lady Caroline procured pen and paper and began to note the items of jewellery that had been stolen, to give to the jewellers and goldsmiths in town in the hopes the pieces could be recovered. By now all the children were up and the older ones helped Maria and Georgy begin to make some sense of the mess. Of course, Harriet was the most help.

'Perhaps you'd like to come and sleep in my room for a while,' she suggested, and both Maria and Georgy agreed that would be comforting. 'I'll have the maid make up a spare bed.

I think we're a little big for all three to share now.'

'I suppose this will soon be remembered as a great story,' said Maria, 'but right at this moment it feels rather awful. It's not as though much here is of serious value, but most of the pieces of jewellery were gifts from Grandmama or our uncle. I suppose I shall never see them again. And much of our clothing is gone, too, or spoiled.'

Georgy sniffed. She had been close to tears for some time.

'Cheer up,' said Louisa, trying to lighten the atmosphere. 'It's only two days until the Prince of Wales' birthday celebrations, you're sure to have so much fun!'

At this, tears began to fall freely down Georgy's face.

'But now I have nothing to wear!' she wailed.

Maria gave Louisa a look.

༻❀༺

Whether they had suitable clothes to wear or not, the Prince of Wales' birthday celebrations, organised for the twelfth of August, were soon upon them. The regent was in London but parallel events were being held in Brussels in his honour. On the morning of the birthday the girls were up early to ready themselves for the day. Each had a wash, a basic affair with a tub, buckets of water and an overworked servant to help matters along. After dressing, they went down to breakfast.

After a hurried meal, Harriet, Georgy and Maria headed into the library to find the Prince of Orange languishing on one of the sofas, trying to make the parrot say 'Your Highness'. The bird babbled back unintelligibly. Unlike General Barnes, the parrot seemed to be able to tolerate the prince, but he wouldn't go near him or speak directly to him, as he would with the Capels themselves.

The prince sighed in exasperation and rose to greet each girl in turn.

'This bird does not appear to be swayed by my efforts to befriend him.'

'I'm afraid he doesn't take too kindly to our visitors, particularly the male ones, but he is growing mighty fond of us, and he particularly likes Maria,' said Georgy.

'Even Mama, who professes to hate all animals, seems rather taken with him,' said Harriet. She sat nearest the window and Georgy and Maria took their seats around the prince. They were used, by now, to finding the prince taking his ease in their house.

'The thing is,' he'd told them on an earlier occasion, when they had been shocked to find him already in the drawing room, 'I have a hatred of court life. My father's way of things is far too rigid.' So he let himself into people's houses and simply wandered about wherever he liked, waiting for someone to stumble across him. Hence his nickname, the Tame Cat.

They had by now brushed over any awkwardness arising from meeting the prince and Lord Hay drunk in the park. Georgy seemed to have fully forgiven her beau – really, it was impossible to be cross at the gentleman for too long as he was such good fun, and since that day he'd been markedly caring and affectionate towards her. Neither had mentioned the incident, but the prince's behaviour made it clear he knew, or had been reminded of, what had happened.

Maria guessed that Lord Hay would have filled in any

blanks in the prince's memory. Now all was forgiven and it was Georgy who sat closest to the prince, their bodies turned towards each other, and it was to Georgy that the prince directed much of the ensuing conversation.

'And how are you ladies since the awful burglary? I hope it hasn't shaken you too much?'

'Not too badly, thank you. Harriet was kind enough to allow us to lodge with her for a few days, but now we're back in our own bedroom.'

'Yes, because you snore, Georgy!' Harriet said.

Georgy threw a cushion at her good-humouredly.

'You were very brave, Maria, to go and confront them,' said the prince.

'Oh, not really, the parrot would have had more of an effect, I'm sure,' said Maria. 'As it was, I did little aside from gawp and shriek!'

'Imagine how much more they'd have taken though, Muz, had you not been there!' said Georgy.

The prince seemed to be on the verge of saying something. He took a deep breath.

'Yes, I hear you lost rather a number of items that meant a great deal to you. Miss Georgiana, I hear that your favourite embroidered fan was one such item taken?'

'Yes, indeed.' She sighed sadly.

'Well, might I present you with another, in the hope that it might be of some use at this evening's celebrations?'

With a flourish, he pulled from behind the sofa a small box that he had concealed there. It contained an exquisite fan made of amber, about the size of two ladies' palms. Georgy brought it out of its box, blushing furiously, and held it up to the light. As she opened the fan it cast prisms of orange across the floors and walls. Georgy grinned shyly, hesitating to meet the prince's eye too soon, yet still the gentleman looked thrilled at her reaction.

Harriet and Maria were able to express their delight more openly.

'Your Highness, what a delightful present,' said Maria.

'It is truly beautiful. Georgy, you lucky thing.' Harriet looked as delighted as Maria felt.

'You really are too good to our sister, sir, for you know how very much she regretted the theft of our things,' said Maria.

Georgy still seemed to be struggling for the right words, but at length she said, 'My lord, I am so grateful for this beautiful gift. I shall forever treasure it.'

'It is no more beautiful than she who holds it.'

Maria looked at the pair as she and Harriet made their excuses and melted away into a corner of the room, allowing Georgy and the prince some privacy. Settling on a window seat with Harriet, Maria saw the pair laughing together as he practised using the fan on himself, falling back in an act of fainting against the sofa. They sat a fraction closer to each other than their mother would have approved of.

Looking out of the window, Maria prodded Harriet and pointed out on to the street. Who should be walking past their house just at that moment but the great Duke of Wellington! Quite forgetting the pleasing scene behind them, the two girls pressed themselves against the glass for a better look. They had known the duke was back in Brussels but this was the first chance they'd had of seeing him, and what a vantage point!

The duke was accompanied by a man the girls knew by sight as his quartermaster, General Sir William De Lancey. Luckily for the girls, the duke and Sir William were met at that moment by General Maitland of the Foot Guards, and the group stopped to talk just opposite the Capels' house. The duke and General Maitland shook hands vigorously. Maitland looked delighted to meet the duke, who was tall and slim with a distinctive hooked nose. Even from this distance the duke's infinite confidence in himself and the world around him was palpable.

The duke's replies to Maitland, muted through the pane of the glass, were short and concise, his countenance serious. Maria's face was now so close to the glass that her breath was creating a mist and obscuring her view. In irritation, she rubbed the pane with the sleeve of her dress, not thinking that the movement might be seen. The three men turned and saw Maria and Harriet gawping through the glass. Gasping in embarrassment, they fled from the window, collapsing on to the floor below in fits of laughter.

The prince and Georgy, disturbed from their tête-à-tête, realised what they'd been up to and joined in the laughter. After lifting their heads to peer through the window and confirming that the three men had continued on their journey, Maria and Harriet, red-faced, returned to the sofas and happily entered into a hearty gossip about the man everyone was discussing – the Duke of Wellington.

The duke seemed to Maria to be a mysterious individual, although the basic story of his life was well known. He was the third son of a minor aristocratic family who lived then in Ireland, and as a child no one had thought he would amount to much. Yet on joining the army he'd proved himself a very capable soldier, a strategic organiser and a great leader of men. While serving in India he rose quickly through the ranks and returned after twelve years with a knighthood and a fortune in Indian loot. He had gone on to fight Napoleon tirelessly for six years on the Continent.

The French had never beaten the duke in battle. Maria had heard the two commanders had never even met on the battlefield and now she supposed they never would. The victorious soldier, the greatest military leader of his age, had been granted a dukedom by his grateful nation. So, having been born humble Arthur Wesley, he was now the 1st Duke of Wellington, and a field marshal, too. As he already had a wife and two small sons, his family dynasty was secure.

Wellington always had around him a group of loyal military men, usually from noble families, who'd fought with him during the war in the peninsula. These men were his aide-de-camps and other junior officers from the Guards regiments. Although the duke was a disciplinarian when it came to matters of business and war, he was known to be close to these men, who he called his 'family'. The rank and file under the duke followed him loyally, but he was also feared for he insisted on complete discipline. Any troublemakers were punished severely.

The girls were thrilled to have spotted the duke as he was known only to be in Brussels for a short time, passing through the city on his way to take up the position of British ambassador in Paris. His presence in the town had been the cause of much excitement, and whispers of whatever event or theatre production he was attending would invariably lead to swarms of people making their way there to see if they could spot him.

He could often be found in the company of Lady Charlotte Greville, who was looking even more smug than usual. His attendance at the celebrations for the Prince Regent's birthday that evening would no doubt add an extra frisson to the occasion, and certainly made the Capel sisters look forward to the event even more than usual.

That afternoon, a special parade to mark the Prince Regent's birthday was to take place and would be passing directly in front of the Capel house. The family crowded on to the pavement to see it, the little children nestled into the skirts of the elder ones, hands held securely. Other families soon joined them, lining the streets around the square as people of all walks of life joined together to watch the spectacle. Soon row upon row of militia marched past to delighted cries and cheers. The soldiers wore their best and most brilliant uniforms, and the brass bands played with great enthusiasm.

As soon as the Duke of Wellington could be seen through the crowd, walking alongside his 'family' of aide-de-camps, the crowd roared and surged forward. The officers around him held back the most enthusiastic of the throng, and the duke was able to pass by the Capels unmolested. He nodded to them as he went by. Next to him walked the Prince of Orange, who waved cheerily and most un-militarily, giving Georgy a wide smile. Maria saw their mother giving her sister a disapproving look, but Georgy was delighted.

Lord Hay was at the back of the group, looking poised and dignified. Maria thought he wasn't going to look at them, although he must know he was passing their house. At the very last minute his head turned and he smiled slightly in their direction. Maria felt gratified.

As the last regiment marched away, the crowd began to disperse. Capel ushered his excited children back into the house, where they were to prepare for the evening's entertainments. The ball was to be hosted by the ambassador Lord Clancarty, whose duty it was to organise an event of suitable magnitude to celebrate the Prince Regent's birthday. The ball was to be held in the Hôtel de Ville, a rather grander establishment than the home of Lord and Lady Greville, which was a short carriage ride away from the Parc Royal.

The Capel family arrived there soon after nine o'clock that evening. Almost immediately, Maria spotted Lord Hay through the crowd. He was standing near the Duke of Wellington, who saw them and made his way over.

'Good evening, Capel,' the duke greeted their father. He indicated Maria and her sisters. 'It's a fine thing to see your daughters out with you.'

'Why, thank you, my lord. They are certainly pleased to be joining the fray, I can assure you.'

The duke smiled.

Their papa pressed his advantage. 'We would be honoured if you would like to visit us one afternoon. You will usually find Uxbridge in attendance.'

'I would like to, but we leave tomorrow.'

'Then, as this is your last evening in Brussels, I wish you a joyful one. The regent's birthday is as good an occasion as ever I saw one.'

It was a polite exchange, but short, and the duke moved on to greet another acquaintance. As he went, he nodded to each of the Capel girls, who curtseyed in return. Maria felt the familiar thudding of nerves in her chest at being in the duke's presence, and was secretly pleased when they were out of his orbit. She would certainly have had little to say to him had he turned his attentions to her.

Within an hour the Capel girls had been swept to different parts of the room. Georgy, under the watchful eye of their mother, was dancing with the Prince of Orange, and Harriet was talking to Baron Trip in a far corner. Maria fetched herself another glass of punch, making the most of the opportunity while her mother's attentions were distracted. She thanked the attendant for the glass and sipped it happily while absorbing the scene.

What a thrill to see hundreds of couples whizzing past across the dancing floor again. She felt a little dazed, probably the result of not having had time for supper and of drinking more punch than she was used to. She looked up to see General Barnes making a beeline for her, but before he reached her there was a firm hand on her elbow, and she looked to her right to find Lord Hay pulling her away.

'May I have this dance, Miss Muzzy?'

Had she heard him correctly, had he just used her pet name? Smiling, Maria placed her glass down on a table and went with him. Had she looked back, she would have seen that General Barnes seemed rather put out.

Maria and Lord Hay took their place with the other dancing partners and were soon joined by General Barnes, who had taken Lady Sarah Lennox to the floor instead of Maria. She smiled at them both as they passed, but General Barnes didn't look very pleased to see Lord Hay and Maria dancing together yet again.

The dance was of course a waltz. Lord Hay put his hand on her waist and Maria felt the familiar prickles of excitement running down her back. It seemed madness that no matter how often they were in each other's company, they were so rarely able to exchange words privately. Despite being in a room full of couples this was their best chance, so Maria began to speak.

'You dance so well, Lord Hay.'

'You know you can call me James, if you prefer,' Lord Hay replied instantly.

Before she could give it a second thought, she said, 'Of course, and you may call me...well, Maria, should you wish.'

'I rather prefer Muzzy,' he replied, smiling mischievously at her.

'Oh! That's just a silly name my family call me.' Maria blushed harder than ever.

'It reminds me of that rather funny incident in the park, for which I am glad to see you have forgiven me.'

'Of course. It was rather amusing, wasn't it?'

'From what I remember of it, indeed. In any case I think Muzzy is a most delightful name. In fact, I have a new grey mare who arrived this very morning, and she is almost as sublime as you. May I have the honour of naming her after you, may I call her Miss Muzzy?'

Maria grinned with delight at his words before she could think of a suitably ladylike response. She had certainly never been called *sublime* before. Lord Hay's hand gently squeezed hers. Maria felt a little giddy as they swirled past the other dancing partners. To her shock and utter delight, as they turned past the far wall of the ballroom Lord Hay leant towards her and gently kissed her bare shoulder, just above the neckline of her dress. Maria's only response could be to meet Lord Hay's eye, and not look away. She had forgotten to breathe some moments before.

The waltz ended and they sprung apart to politely clap the band. As soon as the applause was over, however, Lord Hay grabbed Maria by the arm.

'Follow me, Miss Muzzy!' he whispered.

Off he dashed, pulling her towards a door that led away from the ballroom. Maria looked back to see if any of her family were likely to see her leave. She spotted her mother deeply engrossed in conversation with Lady Charlotte Greville and the Duke of Wellington, and knew she was safe. Lord Hay had already disappeared, so she turned and slipped out of the room, closing the door behind her.

Maria let her eyes acclimatise to the darkness. Through the wall she could hear the muffled steps of hundreds of soles, the swish of dresses, laughter and chatter. A little hesitantly she walked down the corridor before her. One side had windows and the other bookcases interspersed with oil paintings in dirty gold frames. Lord Hay was waiting for her behind one of the bookcases, and jumped out at her as she came past. She shrieked and quickly tried to stifle the sound.

'Lord Hay, you can't do that!' she scolded him, her hand to her bosom.

'Please, I asked you to call me James.'

They began to walk down the corridor together. It was a brilliantly moonlit night, the windows on their right throwing shafts of silver for them to walk through.

'What if someone should hear us, or see us?'

'Other than the servants, no one will come down here unless they're up to no good,' he replied confidently. 'And so what if they do come? Are we not walking and talking, as friends?'

Maria didn't reply, for he was right; they were only walking and talking. Yet, despite her ignorance about such things, she doubted very much if they were just friends any more. Lord Hay had again taken her by the waist with one hand, and they walked so closely together that barely an inch kept them apart.

They were also walking further and further away from the ballroom. They were completely, inexplicably alone. What were they were doing, and what would her mother say if she discovered them alone in this way?

They stopped to gaze out of a window with an excellent view of the city below them, lit by the moon and the glow from the many bonfires built to celebrate the regent's birthday. The town looked thrilling, alive with people thronging the streets. The devil-may-care attitude of those in the ballroom seemed to be reflected in the world outside, too.

Maria and Lord Hay looked down on groups of young men and women staggering through the streets, laughing and leaning on each other for support. One had a bottle of some sort that he swigged from before passing it to a lady in their company. To Maria's shock and delight the woman took the bottle and enjoyed a hearty slug. She laughed, leaning out of the open window to see better. A welcome breeze cooled her face.

'You see, pleasure really is the order of the day here in Brussels,' Lord Hay said. He was also watching the woman.

'This really is an extraordinarily place,' murmured Maria. 'I'm growing so fond of it.'

'I'm sure you find it quite shocking, and this really is only a fraction of what the city has to offer.'

'I'm sure that's true, Lord Hay,' replied Maria a little tartly, 'but don't imagine that this is the first I've seen of such things.'

'Do call me James,' he said, and moved a fraction closer. He too was leaning against the open window, but now their bodies turned towards each other. Maria hesitated, yet there seemed no way out of the situation now, and it felt so easy being this close to him.

Finally, she said, 'Yes, James.'

Lord Hay smiled mischievously, as though he had just won a wager when the odds had been against him.

'What more would you like to see of such matters, I wonder?'

Before Maria could answer he had reached out and touched the tips of her fingers with his own; soon their hands were curled together. Neither said a word. Maria could barely breathe. Of course, she knew that being alone with Lord Hay was very wrong, but it felt so thrilling, and so right, and she didn't want the moment to end.

'You really are quite divine, Miss Muzzy,' he said, pulling

her a fraction closer to him, the air between them thick with intent. Was this to be the setting for her first real kiss? Just as she thought it, the kiss happened, their lips meeting easily and eagerly, and it seemed to be the most natural and delicious thing in the world. Maria felt a rush of something like hot water boiling through her body. Lord Hay drew her close to him, pressing her up against the gold buttons of his dress uniform, his mouth searching for a response that Maria was unsure how to give.

Maria felt a sudden flutter of concern – what was next, after one had been kissed? She had no experience of such matters and nor did her sisters. It seemed, however, that Lord Hay was no novice when it came to kissing. After a few more moments he gently released her from the embrace, but kept his hand pressed into the small of her back, her body still flush with his. The moment and the kiss had been perfect, and they smiled sheepishly at each other.

Then the spell was broken by the sound of laughter coming from the far end of the corridor nearest the ballroom. They broke apart, excitement turning to fear and the hot liquid in Maria's body cooling as quickly as it had heated. Who was about to disturb them? Had her absence from the ballroom been noted?

Before she could think of what to do or say, Georgy and the Prince of Orange burst upon them. They were holding hands and Georgy was flushed with pleasure. She laughed at the look of shock evidently plastered on Maria's face, and the prince was equally jovial. Lord Hay, too, looked amused.

It was Georgy who spoke first. 'How thrilling to have burst

in on you in this way; you both look as though you've been caught doing something you shouldn't!'

Far from disapproving, Georgy looked delighted.

'Sorry, old boy,' said the prince to Lord Hay, 'but Mother Hen is on the warpath and we thought it wise to come and round you up rather than leave her to send out a search party.'

'Very sensible,' said Lord Hay, springing into action. 'I'm sure, in any case, there's a bottle of claret in the smoking room we ought to be seeing to.'

The two men quickly escorted Maria and Georgy down the corridor to the ballroom. The gentlemen made two short bows to them, and before he departed, the prince grabbed Georgy's hand and kissed it. Lord Hay was already walking down the corridor towards the promised bottle of claret.

Maria and Georgy slipped through the door and back into the ballroom. Only a few seconds later they were spotted by Lady Caroline, who was standing with Harriet, both craning their necks as they searched the crowd for the missing sisters. They strode over, looking cross but relieved.

'There you are! Where have you been, Maria? I didn't see you in either of the last two dances.'

'I needed a breath of fresh air, Mama.'

'Well, kindly take it escorted next time! But never mind that now, I spoke to General Barnes a while ago and he would like to dance the next with you. Let's go and find him.'

Maria had no choice but to locate General Barnes and dance with him, which was by no means unpleasant, but not a patch on her experience with Lord Hay.

'Why, Miss Maria, you seem quite buoyed up this evening,'

General Barnes said when they finished their turn.

'Well, it's a lovely evening to celebrate, don't you think?'

'What are we celebrating, might I ask?'

'Why, the Prince Regent's birthday, of course!' But in Maria's mind she was celebrating something far more exciting.

Some time later, Lady Caroline noticed the lateness of the hour, or the earliness of the next day depending on how you looked at it.

'Goodness!' she exclaimed, 'I think it's time we were all in bed. Although where your father has got to, I have no idea.'

Their papa had yet again disappeared, and although they went from room to room, they couldn't find him. They had all noticed their father's disappearances were becoming increasingly common, and Maria felt sure he was gambling again, although where he was finding the other players she didn't know. The thought dulled the happy glow that her adventure with Lord Hay had given her. What if their papa lost so much money they were forced to leave Brussels like they had London? Maria would hate to uproot their lives again when she'd become so taken with the city, and particularly with a certain gentleman who lived in it.

Maria could tell her mother was upset by their papa's disappearance and was doing her best to hide it.

'It looks like we shall be escorting ourselves to bed, girls,' she announced in a hearty manner that fooled no one. 'Off we go, please.'

In the carriage, they laughed and gossiped about the evening as best they could, although Maria suspected that she wasn't the only one keeping parts of the evening to herself, for

Harriet seemed much quieter than usual. When asked what the matter was, she said that her new shoes were pinching, but Maria wondered whether it had anything to do with Baron Trip, with whom Harriet had been talking and dancing for most of the evening. She seemed a little dazed, gazing off into the distance and not joining in the sisters' chatter.

Georgy and Maria couldn't discuss the subjects closest to their hearts until they were back upstairs and getting into their night things. Maria checked Lady Caroline had turned in for the night before confiding in her sister what had happened with Lord Hay in the corridor.

'What do you make of it?' Maria said anxiously, when all had been revealed.

'Why, he seems more than a little in love with you already!' Georgy squealed. 'How romantic to kiss by moonlight.'

'It was more a case of being kissed, to be honest. I didn't really know what to do once we started.'

'What was it like?'

'Quite strange, but not at all unpleasant. He held me so close it felt indecent, but very nice.'

Maria could feel herself blushing again.

'I was glad of your arrival, to be honest. I was quite without my wits. What could I have been thinking!'

'Oh la! Muz, I think you were feeling rather than thinking!'

'Well,' Maria said, suddenly wishing to change the subject, 'what do you make of your evening with the prince?'

'He's so charming, I feel quite bewitched by him. But Mama and Papa disapprove so.'

'He's a prince! How could they possibly disapprove?'

'You know full well he'd never be allowed to marry a commoner such as me.'

'We're not really commoners, and you should be allowed to marry whomever you choose.'

'Oh, Maria, you know it doesn't work like that. The prince will have to marry a princess from another royal house.'

'Well, Princess Charlotte wouldn't have him, so I don't see why you can't!'

The two sisters continued to talk late into the night. The candle by their bedside burned for hours, wax dripping unnoticed on to the nightstand. All their hopes and desires for what could happen in the coming months were freely shared, ideas and exclamations dancing around the room, flickering in the candlelight. Maria voiced her concerns about the strange behaviour of their father and Georgy tried to reassure her.

'You know most fathers have a flutter at the tables, Muz. I doubt it's for large sums. Try not to worry.'

Their adventures kept them awake until the sun began to creep in through the curtains, when they finally fell into a deep impenetrable slumber, tangled among the covers, the candle still burning.

CHAPTER VIII
A Proposal

'General (now Sir Edward) Barnes who is really one of the most amiable & best creatures I ever met with & doubly devoted to every individual of the Family from Capel to Adolphus — He is very rich and liberal minded...& to Crown all there is nothing handsome that Lord Wellington does not say of him in Military point of view.'

Lady Caroline Capel to the Dowager Countess of Uxbridge

The day after the Prince Regent's birthday ball Maria and Georgy rose late, but even so they found few of their family downstairs. They entered the breakfast room and helped themselves to tea. Only their father, hidden behind a newspaper, and their brother Arthur, over from England for the school holidays, were present. Maria lacked the energy to stifle a huge yawn. Harriet had perhaps already left the breakfast table as she was usually an early riser, and as a rule their mother took breakfast in bed, this being a luxury afforded to all married women.

'Good morning, Papa,' ventured Maria to the newspaper

facing her. The paper ruffled and a corner was peeled back to reveal her papa, eyes darkened with lack of sleep.

'Good morning, my dear. How was your evening?'

'Delightful, thank you.' Maria was hesitant to add more in case she incriminated herself by looking too pleased, or indeed guilty. Georgy caught her eye and grinned. Maria didn't dare ask where her father had got to, knowing she would be considered impertinent.

The girls settled down to a breakfast of ham, eggs and toast. Maria was ravenous. As she was eating, a letter arrived for her and was handed over by a footman. She thought at first it was a missive from their grandmother, but the hand was unfamiliar. Who on earth had written to her? The handwriting appeared to be male. She broke the seal and unfolded the letter. The note was short. Resting an elbow on the table, she read:

Dear Miss Capel,
I so enjoyed dancing with you last night. I hope to have the pleasure of calling upon you again today, at home.
Your true & obedient servant,

Where the signature ought to have been was only a spot of ink, as though the author had placed nib to page to sign a name and then had a change of heart. How very thrilling! Maria stared down at the page, her sore head quite forgotten.

'Who is your letter from, Muzzy?' her sister asked. She

reached out her hand and Maria passed it over, for no such letter delivered at the breakfast table could possibly be kept to oneself for long. Georgy read the letter in seconds.

'Goodness! How incredibly romantic.' She met Maria's eye for a second before exclaiming innocently and loudly, 'Whoever could have sent it?'

'What's this, now?'

Capel's interest had been piqued by Georgy's words, and the newspaper was lowered to the table. Georgy read the contents of the note out to him as Maria's face glowed. Capel's face lit up as she read.

'Well, I never!' he exclaimed. 'Well done, Maria. Whoever he is, I hope he's more conversational in life than on paper, for that is the briefest love letter I've ever seen, to be sure.'

The letter was returned to Maria, who folded it back up with care. Looking down at the curled letters of the address, she felt rather put out by her father's words. Lord Hay could hardly have professed his hopes and dreams in such a note when he knew it would be read by everyone at the breakfast table. This must also be the reason he had addressed her as Miss Maria Capel when surely he must have wanted to call her Maria, or even Miss Muzzy.

'Who is the lucky fellow?' Capel asked, 'I do hope you've chosen wisely or your mother will be most vexed. I shall reserve judgment until the fellow is revealed.'

Maria smiled and felt a reluctant rush of warmth towards her father. Despite his frequent absence from their lives and the trouble he had brought them, he showed he cared when it really counted. Maria was not, however, tempted to reveal the name of her suitor. She wasn't entirely sure that her parents would approve of Lord Hay as a potential husband. As a younger son he was, like her, virtually penniless, and his reputation for drinking and revelry would hardly appeal to any prospective parents-in-law. Maria felt a little uneasy as she pondered the letter. It would be secreted in the ribbon box when she next went upstairs.

Harriet entered the breakfast room. She had been on a morning walk, escorted by a maid, and was still wearing her hat. She looked elated.

'And you, dear Harriet, what did you make of last night?' said Capel to his eldest. 'My spies tell me they saw you and Baron Trip together for most of it.'

Maria guessed that spy must be their mother.

Harriet responded, as one might expect, with blushes and mumbles at these words, her previous happiness tempered.

'Why, yes, Papa,' she managed to utter, 'I think him a most admirable gentleman.'

'No doubt. He seems an intelligent man, although I hear some strange things about his views.'

'What views, Papa?' It was Georgy who spoke, not Harriet, who was busy handing her outdoor things to one of the servants. She sat down beside them, looking uncomfortable.

'On matters of religion and the like. Not things I want to hear of his discussing with you, Harriet.' He looked uncharacteristically stern.

'No, Papa,' Harriet said.

'I'm glad to hear that, and I would like my words taken seriously. I don't want him to lead you astray. Aside from that,

I take it you like spending time with him?'

'Very much so, Papa.' Her response was clearly a little too passionate for Capel's liking, and his brow furrowed still further.

'A little less enthusiasm please, Harriet,' he sighed. 'He is but one man of perhaps many suitors, and we don't yet know the extent of his attachment to you.'

Harriet opened her mouth to respond but clearly thought better of it, and shut it again. After a moment, she said, 'Yes, Papa, you are right, of course.'

'A lady must guard her heart and mind until she is certain a man is worthy of it.'

Maria was surprised at her papa giving such sage words of advice. It was curious that Harriet looked far more agitated by their father's words she would have expected. Men had been interested in Harriet in the past but she had treated each suitor with polite indifference until they eventually lost heart and pursued another. Baron Trip really seemed to have made an impression on Harriet.

Maria was keen to hear more about Harriet's growing attachment to this mysterious gentleman, and wished she'd invited her to the late-night analysis she and Georgy had enjoyed after the ball. Perhaps she'd had a similar encounter to Maria's and was keeping the secret to herself? Maria wondered how best she could prise the information out of her.

After they'd finished their breakfasts the sisters retired to the morning room, Maria examining her dress critically in readiness to receive Lord Hay. Then she and Georgy pounced on Harriet for more information. Their sister was surprisingly eager for a chance to talk about her beau, again something that struck Maria as quite out of character.

'His full name is Jonkheer Otto Ernst Gelder Trip van Zoudtlandt,' she said in a rush, 'but his friends call him Ernst. He's been with the Dutch army since he was just thirteen.'

Maria wondered at Harriet remembering such a long name by heart, thinking that the baron must have taught it to her, and noted too that Harriet already knew his preferred christian name. She decided not to comment on either point. 'Goodness, so young!' she said instead.

'Yes, and he's even served under the Duke of Wellington. That's how he knows Uncle Uxbridge.'

Georgy looked impressed. 'I never imagined a military man being the one for you, Harriet.'

'Well, he's not like other officers. He's much more sensitive and serious than his contemporaries.'

As Harriet talked on and on about Baron Trip, about their conversations, about their dancing and how she felt she was falling for him, Maria and Georgy exchanged looks of barely concealed amusement. Their sister sounded as though she was completely in love already, having spent barely more than a few hours in his company.

It was very unlike Harriet, who was usually so measured and reasonable. Maria was pleased she was finally letting her guard down and allowing a man to woo her, but worried that her feelings for this man were becoming intense too quickly.

Georgy seemed to agree. 'Harriet, my love, I'm thrilled for you; he sounds completely divine. However, as you've spent so little time with him, can you really say you know him well enough to love him? You've only danced with him on a few occasions, no?'

Harriet looked a little sheepish. 'I have in truth seen him numerous times since we first met at Lady Charlotte's ball, at nearly all the smaller balls we have attended.' Harriet carried on quickly, as she could see that Maria and Georgy were about to interject in surprise. 'Oh, I don't mean we have talked or danced. I've seen him across the room, you see, and...' She trailed off, her eyes lowered, blushing furiously.

Maria wanted clarification. 'So, he didn't speak to you again until yesterday's ball?'

'Not as such, no, but last night things were different. For some reason we were free from whatever had been holding us back and we danced and danced and talked and talked and oh! it was such magic. I don't feel I could ever love another now I've experienced the feeling.'

The passion in Harriet's eyes was almost alarming, and something about the frantic way she was talking made Maria feel uneasy. Yet she couldn't regard Harriet too harshly for having fallen so hard for Baron Trip, for she recognised the way she felt about Lord Hay in many of her sister's sentiments. Their evening, too, had been magical, had it not?

Who was she to judge what connection Harriet had made with the baron, and where it could take her? She decided that she would do everything in her power to see the match right. She only hoped he deserved her sister's love.

'I'm so pleased for you, dearest Harriet, and I hope he'll make you very happy indeed,' Maria said, taking her sister's hand.

Harriet seemed a little taken aback by Maria's heartfelt manner, but smiled and blushed happily.

⌒⌒⌒

While the girls dissected the character, conversation and comportment of Harriet's precious Baron Trip, Lady Caroline was upstairs resting. She had yet to change out of her night things as she was feeling rather under the weather. Stopping by her looking glass, Lady Caroline noticed that her face looked a little fuller than usual, and pressing again her dress, she felt that her bosoms were swollen.

She barely wanted to admit it to herself, but she was by now well used to the early signs of pregnancy. The symptoms were unmistakable. Lady Caroline sighed and blinked back tears. How could she go through this ordeal again, and with Adolphus not even having reached his first birthday?

She couldn't resent her husband for this unexpected turn of events, even though her heart and mind told her it was folly to have another child when they could barely afford to feed and clothe those they already had. Their union had taken a positive turn since their arrival in Brussels, and Lady Caroline had welcomed Capel into her bed on more occasions of late, sensing that he was trying to make amends for his neglect of her during their last months in London.

Lady Caroline had relished these nights together, savouring having her husband to herself when he was so often absent in person or in mind. Now she supposed there was no point in regret, for a baby was coming, and they had better prepare for it as best they could.

She wondered when the best time would be to tell her husband. She supposed she should first be seen by a doctor, just to be certain all was well. She didn't want to worry Capel unnecessarily. Despite his many late nights and absences, he'd seemed happier recently and she didn't want to spoil his mood.

Lady Caroline wondered if the club Capel had recently joined had anything to do with his more positive disposition. The Literary Club had been set up for English gentlemen living in Brussels as an establishment where members could take tea and attend dinners with friends and acquaintances. Capel reported it had a well-stocked library and all the latest newspapers from England.

Since he had joined he'd seemed much happier to be living in Brussels, and also brought home a large amount of usually very accurate gossip. Lady Caroline had used these snippets to great effect with her daily companions, the other 'Ladies of the Park', so she really couldn't complain about the increasing amount of time he was spending at the club.

Battling a rising feeling of nausea, Lady Caroline slowly got dressed and went downstairs. As she entered the morning room Julia appeared with a cup of fresh ginger tea. Lady Caroline smiled gratefully as she took the cup. Although they hadn't discussed it, Julia had guessed her mistress's condition. Lady Caroline felt lucky to have such a loyal and constant lady's maid as Julia, who always knew how to help. She'd been with Lady Caroline since Harriet was conceived, and had never left her side through that birth and each one that had followed it.

Lady Caroline walked over to the window seat, near to where her husband was writing his letters, and enjoyed her tea in peace. Several yawns punctuated the easy silence. Even the parrot seemed happy to sit quietly and preen, and the morning passed amicably enough, with the children coming in and out of the sitting room at intervals, chatting warmly to each other.

Louisa was practising at the piano in an adjacent room, and her progress was pleasing to the ear. Harriet was writing in her diary with great animation, regularly looking out of the window as though hoping to see someone. Georgy was sketching and occasionally stealing glances at Maria, who was seated on one of the silk sofas, a book clasped in her lap, unread, her eyes unfocused, her back unusually straight.

Presently one of the footmen came into the room and announced that General Barnes had come to call. Lady Caroline saw a flicker of disappointment flash across Maria's face. *Whatever is afoot?*

'Do show him in,' said Capel, setting down his pen.

'How lovely.' Lady Caroline smiled. 'We can catch up on all the events of last night.' For some reason this made Georgy giggle.

General Barnes strode into the room. He held his hat in his hands and looked both animated and a little agitated.

'Good morning to you all, and I hope I find you in good health.'

Capel replied, 'Very good, Barnes, very good. I missed you at the tables yesterday, what kept you?'

Lady Caroline failed to suppress a frown on hearing Capel's words – so he had been gambling last night! She looked at him, but her husband didn't meet her eye, perhaps realising he had spoken too freely.

'I was too busy dancing with your delightful daughters. Besides, I've fallen foul of your skills a little too often of late.'

Capel mumbled a non-committal reply to this and there was a pause as the ladies in the room all glanced at each other, not wanting to join in a conversation about something of which they heartily disapproved. General Barnes seemed to realise he had hit on a sensitive subject. He fiddled with the brim of his hat and looked more awkward than ever.

'Anyhow, I wonder whether it would be possible to seek an audience with the young Miss Maria?' he said quickly and to their great surprise.

The silence became even more pronounced. The parrot ruffled his feathers and squawked, causing a slight distraction. Lady Caroline looked from their visitor to Maria, rather bewildered.

'Maria, my dear General Barnes?' Then a little of his intention became clear and she hurried on, 'Why, I'm sure Muzzy would be delighted to speak to you.'

Maria was taken aback by this turn of events. Minutes before, she had been daydreaming about Lord Hay's visit and now General Barnes was here, he and her father had spoken about the dreaded gambling tables, and now the general wanted a private audience with her. What on earth was going on? Surely such a conversation could not mean what she felt it might? She could think of nothing to say and merely gaped.

'Children, John, let's retire to the library and leave these two in peace,' said Lady Caroline. She stood up and swept

Harriet, Louisa and Georgy along with her. 'Come along, please, girls.'

As they made their way from the room the girls all looked back at Maria, their eyes wide with shock and excitement. Maria was rooted to the spot, staring, beseeching them to stay, but within seconds the door had closed.

Maria felt as though she had once again stumbled upon strangers in her dressing room. She really didn't know what to say. Neither, it appeared, did General Barnes. Again, he twirled his hat as silence settled around them once more. Finally, he spoke.

'So, Miss Maria, if I may. I had a lovely evening last night.'

'Yes, it was good fun, was it not?' At least she'd managed to say something!

'Yes, indeed. I very much enjoyed our dance.'

There was another pause.

'Why yes, as did I, of course, General Barnes.'

'I'm sure you have realised the reason for my call this morning. After you received my letter.'

So the letter had actually been written by General Barnes, that was a surprise.

'You will think me strange for not signing it, but I have to admit I lost my nerve at the last minute.'

Maria had never seen the general look so out of sorts. Here was a man used to commanding thousands of men, but alone with her now he was shy and awkward.

'I, well, um...' Maria really did not know what to say. This was all so sudden and unexpected. Maria was feeling more and more uncomfortable.

'You must realise what affection I have developed for you since meeting you in the haberdashers all those weeks ago.'

It was as Maria had suspected but she hadn't wanted to believe it. Was General Barnes really about to propose? He took a deep breath and continued.

'You would do me the greatest honour were you to consider being my wife. Nothing would bring me greater happiness. I hope you have grown to think fondly of me and would consider us a good match.'

So there it was. No bended knee or profession of love. Nothing to quicken the breath or cause her skin to tingle. Just a practical proposition. Seconds ticked by and still Maria said nothing. She was sure she must be gaping at him; really, she must say something!

'General Barnes, I – I'm...'

It was no easier to get the words out, and now Maria could feel the tears coming instead.

❧

Lady Caroline cursed herself, for if she had left the door ajar they could have listened from the corridor. As it was, they were forced to wait in the library, striving in vain to hear any sounds from the morning room. She paced about, dizzy with excitement. How quickly her sedate morning had turned upside down. Her sickness was quite forgotten.

Her dearest Maria, engaged to the wonderful General Barnes! What a great catch he was. Indeed, if she'd been in Maria's place, she would be delighted to receive such a proposal. General Barnes was steady and sensible, able to provide for and protect a young lady such as Maria. She couldn't think of a more fortuitous match.

It was true that Maria seemed to prefer men of a more adventurous nature and perhaps would find General Barnes a little dull, but she was sure her daughter would soon come to realise how superior a husband he would make to the younger officers they knew. That Lord Hay, for example, would never do. Not only did his lack of fortune rule him out, but his character was far too brash and troublesome.

Lady Caroline had been concerned over the last few weeks that Maria and Lord Hay were growing too close, so the timing of this proposal couldn't be more fortuitous. What a wonderful way to have General Barnes in their lives forever. Indeed, if she were entirely honest with herself, beneath her excitement lay a flutter of jealousy.

While Lady Caroline paced the library, Harriet, Georgy and Louisa stood in the doorway watching the door to the morning room. Capel, seated in his favourite chair by the window, seemed amused by their behaviour. Several minutes passed.

'This is so thrilling,' said Georgy.

'Do you really think he will propose? To be truthful, I didn't think their attachment was that strong,' said Harriet.

Lady Caroline hushed them. 'General Barnes would be a marvellous catch for Maria,' she said firmly.

Suddenly the door of the morning room flew open, and they all jumped back. Out came Maria, her face slick with tears. Without a word she turned and ran up the main stairs. All pretence of sangfroid abandoned, Lady Caroline and her children fell over each other to reach General Barnes, who looked like he wanted to go after Maria. He looked upset and embarrassed.

'Well, I... Well, really,' he blustered.

There was an awkward pause in which they all turned to Lady Caroline to see how to handle the situation. She offered her hands to General Barnes.

'Oh, General Barnes, I'm so terribly sorry. What has that headstrong girl gone and done?!'

When Barnes, looking more upset by the second, didn't reply, Capel also took him by the arm and steered him back into the morning room.

'Let's have a drink,' he said, despite it not yet being noon. 'Hair of the dog, eh?'

Before Lady Caroline joined the two men, she turned to her daughters. 'Harriet, Georgy, go upstairs at once and see what is to be done about this mess.' The two sisters ran off up the stairs, glad to be leaving the awkwardness behind. Louisa trailed after them, hoping, as ever, to be included in the older girls' conversations, but as she reached Maria and Georgy's bedroom the door was closed with a snap.

Upstairs, Maria was as angry as she was upset. The tears had taken her by surprise. Now she was lying on the bed, shaking with sobs, her hands balled into fists. Why, General Barnes had ruined everything! Harriet and Georgy entered the room and threw themselves on to the covers beside her.

Georgy didn't say anything but simply pulled Maria on to her shoulder and stroked her hair. Slowly Maria felt her anger soften. She let the tears fall on to Georgy's dress.

Harriet was propped up on one elbow, evidently steeling herself to speak, and Maria didn't need to see the frown on her sister's face to know she wouldn't approve of the way the conversation in the morning room had played out. No one spoke for a while, but eventually it was Harriet who broke the silence.

'Maria, whatever can you mean by this?' she said. 'General Barnes is a dear creature to us all, and a fine match for you.'

Maria said nothing. Even Georgy, usually on Maria's side, said, 'Can you really not bring yourself to marry him?'

'I cannot,' Maria said glumly, her voice muffled within Georgy's embrace.

'General Barnes is the kind of match we all hope and pray for,' said Harriet. 'You should be delighted that he proposed so quickly. No other chance may come your way.'

Harriet's words could have been those of her mother, father or even her uncle. She spoke sense, but Maria didn't want to hear it. She shrugged free from Georgy and sat upright. She turned to her eldest sister, anger flaring up again.

'You would wish me to marry someone I could never love? You could truly ask such a thing of me?'

Her look must have been fierce, for Harriet looked sheepish. She didn't reply, and it was Georgy who spoke next.

'We thought you were fond of each other. Is it not so?'

'I am indeed fond of him, but I like to think a little more than *fondness* is necessary to sustain a happy marriage. And how could it ever be so, when even if I did feel more than friendship towards General Barnes, it is Lord Hay whom I wish to marry?'

The tears were falling freely again. Her sisters said nothing, for here was the truth, and the harsh reality was that nothing in Lord Hay's actions during the past few months had come even close to a proposal. This was surely another cause of the tears rolling down Maria's face.

'Oh, what a mess. What's to be done?' Maria pressed her palms against her eyes and cheeks, halting her tears in their tracks and leaving her face wet.

Georgy had her arm around her again. 'Dear Muzzy, please don't cry. Whatever happened can surely be put right, in time.'

Maria sniffed. A handkerchief embroidered with blue forget-me-nots appeared beneath her downcast eyes, a peace offering from Harriet. She took it and dried her tears.

'It was just such a shock, I suppose. Although I knew he thought kindly towards me it never occurred to me that he'd propose. It all just seems so rash.'

'So he actually asked you to marry him? He had not even spoken to Papa yet; he knew nothing of it!'

'Yes, he proposed. I suppose he planned to speak to Papa afterwards.'

'Did he get down on one knee?' asked Georgy, ever the romantic.

'No, not a jot of it, it was as though he was inviting me to a dinner party.'

'How odd,' said Georgy. 'I thought men had to get down on one knee for it to count. I'm sure Papa did so for Mother, I don't think she would have taken him otherwise.'

'The whole thing was so entirely unromantic.'

'What did you say in reply?' Georgy clearly wanted more detail.

'Virtually nothing, I'm afraid. I began to feel more angry than anything else.'

Georgy was indignant. 'Why were you angry? It's a compliment to be asked for your hand in marriage!'

'I was angry at him for asking, and for risking the friendships he has with our family for nothing.'

'He obviously doesn't think it nothing,' said Harriet. 'Didn't he give you some hint as to why he thought you were interested?'

'He sent the letter that arrived this morning. The one I thought was from Lord Hay. I barely even remember dancing with him at the ball.'

The reality of what she had done pressed down heavily on them all. Maria felt wretched, yet knew that she'd made the right decision. Despite her initial interest in him, when she'd orchestrated their meeting in the haberdashery shop, she'd never since felt romantically inclined towards him and hadn't any notion he felt that way towards her. How blind she must have been! She had certainly never imagined marrying General Barnes, despite the obvious benefits of the match.

She knew her sisters thought she should have accepted General Barnes, or at the very least thought about the offer for a time. It would have been the mature and polite way to react. Maria had potentially damaged one of the most important friendships they had made in Brussels. There was no telling how their mother would react when she heard what had happened. Often a good match for one daughter led to even better matches for younger sisters. In this way, Maria's decision had been both selfish and rash.

Harriet couldn't resist one last attempt at making her sister see sense.

'Can nothing we say persuade you, Maria? You might never receive the offer of such a match again. To be settled with a man such as General Barnes is something we all wish for.'

Maria would not be swayed. She turned to them and spoke calmly yet firmly.

'May I be alone, please? I need to think.'

Georgy and Harriet slid off the bed and left the room, Harriet looked disgruntled, Georgy a little sheepish. Maria knew they would be recalled downstairs immediately to relay to their mother what she had said.

Maria didn't want to argue with her sisters but she knew, however hard it was for them and the rest of the family, that she had done the right thing. Her only great power in life was that she could choose who to marry, and she wouldn't throw herself away on someone she could never bring herself to love. It was possible she wouldn't be asked again, but Maria was willing to take the risk. As she lay back down on the covers and stared up at the ceiling, she wondered how many hurdles she would have to overcome before the gamble paid off.

PART II

~~~~~

JANUARY 1815

CHAPTER IX

Club Tricks

*'It don't seem the least like
Christmas here; I have never felt
so out of England as now.'*

Lady Caroline to the Dowager Countess of Uxbridge

'Capel, wake up, man! It's your trick next, I believe.'
'Yes, come along, old fellow, it's not like you to be caught napping at the table!'

Capel had indeed been caught in a reverie. He quickly looked down at his hand and placed a card randomly on the table.

'Forgive me, gentlemen, I have rather a lot on my mind this evening.'

They were sitting as a four, two pairs of partners opposite each other, in the genteel surroundings of the Literary Club. Capel couldn't recall the name of his gaming partner. The hour was very late. Glancing at the clock on the mantel, he realised several hours had passed in a blur.

He really ought to be getting home, but he and his partner had won the last game and only had to get another to achieve the best of three. They were so close, having three points to the other side's two and needing only five to claim victory. Sober, Capel would have known the next stage could take hours, but as it was, he took another large mouthful of port and tried to concentrate as best he could.

Capel had been distracted all evening, but he didn't confide in his fellow players the causes. Firstly, he suspected his wife was with child again. She hadn't said as much, but there were signs. How they would cope he didn't like to think. They could barely afford their lives in Brussels as it was, cheap as things were, and that was without yet another mouth to feed. He loved his large family, and adored each of his children, but as he got older he wondered how he would find the energy to manage an even larger brood.

Really, though, what was bothering him more was that he was lying to his wife about what he really got up to at the Literary Club. It was not just the gentleman's membership club it claimed to be. It did have an excellent selection of newspapers and periodicals, as well as a lending library and a well-stocked bar. It was also true that one could always find a friend, old or new, with whom to share the latest news and a well-earned drink. This was how the club presented itself to the outside world.

But the club was in fact a gambling establishment where one could play faro, loo, piquet, Basset or, Capel's favourite, whist. Since their arrival in Brussels, Capel had visited with increasing frequency. His wife had no idea of what really drew him to return to the club time and time again. Often, he would go with every intention of simply relaxing with friends and reading a newspaper or two, but as the hours passed the gambling tables became increasingly appealing. He would try to put up a fight but eventually be convinced to take a seat at one of them.

'Just the one game, then,' he would insist.

Whist could be as simple or as devilish as the players liked to make it, but as the hours passed, the cruelly addictive nature of the game always grew. Capel, who had by then usually drank several glasses of claret, would find his resolve to be home by midnight quite forgotten. All his attention would be focused on bringing home victory for him and the partner sitting opposite.

'Another point for us!' Capel was jubilant.

'Aye, but there's still time,' the man to his left grumbled.

The clock struck midnight and Capel and his companions completely missed the onset of the new year, so engrossed were they in their game. Hours later, as he walked home through the bitter wind and rain, Capel saw the streets filled with people drinking and revelling. He realised he had missed bringing in the new year with his family.

Shame, repressed by the game and the port, rose in his chest again. He had lost a great deal of money that evening, more than he would ever admit to his wife. Hopefully Lady Caroline would by now be in bed and he would be able to avoid an interrogation.

Capel knew he'd struck gold when he married his wife and been blessed with so many children, but felt that was where his luck had run out. The rest of his life had been a disappointment to himself, to Lady Caroline and to their respective families. The two small jobs his family had procured for him brought in little income and were never enough of a distraction from the delights of the gambling tables. Before long, the suffocating grip of addiction had taken hold.

He was embarrassed to admit, even to himself, the number of times they'd had to lean on his mother-in-law for money. He knew, too, that the money would have been sufficient to sustain their family had Capel been able to stop gambling. His actions had turned them from a wealthy family into one that had to flee England and take refuge in a foreign country to escape his creditors.

When Lady Caroline had finally been made aware of the depth of his debt, back in London, she had cried and raged.

'Twenty thousand, Capel, twenty! How could you have been so stupid, so thickheaded? How will we ever, in a thousand lifetimes, be able to pay back such an amount?'

Capel had no answer to this and had hung his head in shame.

'I swear, if I could leave you, I would.' Instead, she had thrown her tea set at him, which had hurt rather a lot.

Yet despite the many rows, Lady Caroline hadn't abandoned him. Her threats had been empty, her anger placated by his repeated reassurances that he'd finally learnt the error of his ways.

He had reached the house and hoped his late arrival wouldn't be noticed by the family, or indeed the parrot that had taken to stalking the corridors at night like a feathery guard dog. He would, of course, sleep in his own room so as not to disturb his wife. If he woke her, he was sure to receive a cold and bitter reprimand, which he no doubt deserved.

As he settled into the chilly bed, a throbbing head keeping him from sleep, his mind wandered to his children. They had probably had a riotous evening bringing in the new year, not that he could at that moment remember where they'd intended to be for the countdown. Nothing had brought Capel more pleasure in life than seeing the children grow up. His sons, especially the eldest, Arthur, caused him the greatest joy, yet he couldn't deny that there was equal pleasure in watching his daughters flourish too. They had grown into attractive and accomplished girls, full of spirit but with an ease of manner that perfectly reflected the way his wife had brought them up.

He had been greatly disappointed when Maria refused to marry General Barnes. That would have been a fine match indeed, and would have greatly promoted the reputation of their family, reassuring other potential suitors that his daughters were desired as respectable matches despite their financial handicaps.

He had tried to reason with her.

'Maria, are you sure you're prepared to throw away your best chance of an independent life?'

But in the end he couldn't bring himself to force her to marry Barnes, despite knowing that many of his peers would have done so, and with good reason. Clearly Maria saw this attachment as nothing more than a friendship, and didn't love General Barnes in the slightest.

He'd been impressed by how quickly Barnes had recovered from Maria's rejection. Any other man he knew, himself included, would have kept clear of the Capel residence for quite some time, yet Barnes was evidently made of sterner stuff. It reflected well on him that after an absence of only two days he visited without warning one afternoon, and walked in on them all in the drawing room.

In front of them all he said to Maria, 'Dear Maria, let

us be friends. I do hope we can be, with no awkwardness or uncertainty.'

Maria, to her credit, seemed pleased at this and readily agreed. The afternoon progressed as it might have done if no such event as the proposal and subsequent rejection had occurred, which to Capel seemed quite remarkable.

The first morning of the year 1815 saw Capel woken by Lady Caroline shaking his arm. His eyes jerked open painfully, his head suddenly throbbing from the wine and cigar smoke. Lady Caroline was still in her nightgown. She didn't look quite as cross as Capel expected.

'Well, husband of mine. Can I to enquire as to where you brought in the new year?'

Capel rubbed his face with his hands and sat up quickly, feeling his stomach lurch.

'My love, really, what can I say? I met some friends at the Literary Club and, well, one thing led to another and before I knew it the clock struck twelve!'

'The children were terribly disappointed, but I shan't dwell on it. Julia has brought tea; come and join me.'

Capel could scarcely believe he had got off so lightly. He hastened out of his bed and splashed his face with water before joining his wife in the double bed they often shared in the room next door. Lady Caroline poured them both tea. The hour was not as late as Capel had thought. The house was cold and dark so they climbed back under the covers.

His wife looked at him thoughtfully as she sipped from her cup. 'I have something I need to tell you.'

'I wonder if I can guess!' Capel responded, and looked

pointedly at his wife's stomach. Lady Caroline blushed, and he knew his suspicions were correct.

'Yes, it's true, we're going to have another child. I hope you can be glad. I know it isn't what we planned.'

'My dear, every child you bring me makes me happier than anything in the world.' He leant across and kissed her.

'It appears the Lord wishes on us a dynasty, despite no fortune for them!'

'A few good marriages will set us straight, my dear, just you wait and see.'

'General Barnes would have been a good first step.'

'No doubt. I still regret Maria's decision, but she certainly seems happy with it. I do hope she hasn't done any lasting damage to his friendship with our family.'

'It doesn't appear so. He seems as good a friend now as ever. We were with him yesterday evening and had a very jolly time. I can't believe I'm saying this, but he seems to have become more attached to Harriet than he ever was to Maria. I saw them walking together in the garden the other day, and could tell by his stance he likes her very much.'

'Goodness, that would be a sensation, if he were to move from one to the other.'

'Perhaps he just wanted to cheer her up; she is so melancholic these days, isn't she? And do you know what Lady Charlotte said to me last week? She said, "Which of your daughters is General Barnes to marry? Or is he to marry *them all*?" I ask you!'

Capel couldn't help but laugh. What a situation they had on their hands. Three daughters ready to be married, surrounded by military men of varying characters, some playing straight and others keeping them on their toes.

He didn't mention it, but at times he wasn't entirely sure whether their officer friends came to see his daughters or his wife. Lady Caroline certainly still had admirers. Barnes, for one, seemed a little too attentive given how short a time he had been in their lives.

Yet his wife had never given him cause to worry, and Capel wasn't by nature a jealous man. In any case it was essential that a steady stream of eligible men came to their house, particularly if one could draw Harriet out of her low mood.

Lady Caroline was clearly in a more positive frame of mind.

'In years to come, I fully expect we'll look back on this time as the most exciting and fruitful of our lives.'

Capel leant over and kissed her again.

Harriet had always been the most restrained and sensible of the older girls, less prone to flirtation and more interested in serious discussion and analysis of the pressing matters of the day. Since the autumn, however, weighty concerns had been playing on her mind.

One moment she would be happy and gay, the next fragile, and always, it seemed, on the brink of tears. She became increasingly susceptible to headaches and began to shut herself in her room for hours on end, refusing to go to the parties she had previously enjoyed. As for those events she could be persuaded to attend, she would lose interest if Baron Trip wasn't there and ask to go home, causing arguments with her sisters who wanted to stay and fulfil the promises made out in their dance cards.

The down days had gained in frequency in the run-up to Christmas, the day of which she spent in her room, claiming another headache. Lady Caroline complained of the girl's secretiveness, that she was never to be found when called for, and that she wouldn't talk or dance with any of the officers who asked her. If only Harriet would see General Barnes as a suitable antidote to her troubles.

Georgy, on the other hand, was the life and soul of every party she attended. Her connection to the Prince of Orange had continued apace, causing many a comment from Capel's friends at the Literary Club. Rumours of their romance had even reached London, as they received a letter on the subject from Lady Caroline's mother.

Capel liked the young man but knew the match could never be. The prince was heir to the Kingdom of the Netherlands, for goodness sake. As flattering as his attentions to the family were, there was no way he would be allowed to marry anyone as lowly in status as Georgy.

The prince had recently asked Georgy to take part in a quadrille for a ball he was organising, a great honour indeed, but such was the ever-increasing intimacy between the pair that Capel had decided to invent some reason to excuse her. A few days before Lady Caroline had discovered them in the library kissing, and that had been the final straw. Capel had written to the prince to say that Georgy had hurt her foot getting out of a carriage and so couldn't take part in the dance.

Capel knew it was for the best, for nothing good could come of Georgy throwing away her attentions on a royal heir. It would only end in tears. In fact it already had, as Georgy's predictable reaction was hours of crying into Maria's lap, and she had refused to speak to her parents for several days.

∽∾∽

A few days into the new year, Capel was descending the main staircase of their house and saw Julia entering the front hall with a letter in her hand. She jumped when she saw him, and tried to conceal the letter behind her back. Her guilty expression immediately piqued Capel's interest.

'Ah, Julia, pray, is that a letter for me?'

'No, sir. It's... it's for one of the girls.'

'Well, give it to me and I shall hand it over. Who is it from?'

Julia had blushed a deep scarlet.

'Sir, I... The gentleman is an acquaintance of one of the ladies, and he wished me to give this letter to her.'

'Why was the letter not delivered in the usual way?' Now Capel really was suspicious. 'Give it to me, please.'

Julia seemed very reluctant to do so; she looked over her shoulder down the corridor to see if there was any family member she could call upon for support. Turning back to Capel's now furious stare, and with no other option open to her, she handed the letter to him.

'If there are any more letters, they come straight to me. Do you understand?'

'Yes, sir. I'm sorry, sir.'

His disquiet rising, he dismissed Julia, who scurried off towards the kitchen. Capel took the letter into the morning room, mercifully empty of both children and parrot. Ripping it open, he read the following.

Dearest Harriet,

Your letters entreat me to pity you, & to understand your actions. But you must understand me, dear heart, that what you ask, nay demand of me is not possible. What we have shared has been miraculous, but must not continue. This is the last time I shall contact you, and I have taken the liberty of returning your last letter. Please burn this, and forgive me.

Yours sincerely,

T.

Capel read the letter twice, and his fury rose with each reading until the paper shook in his hands. With the letter was enclosed one from Harriet.

I am writing this, Ernst, from the couch in the room where you once promised to be mine forever. I sometimes think it is cowardly to drag on such an existence as mine — then the remains of early prejudice tell me that it would be critical to terminate it …

The remaining pages were all written in a similar vein. His eyes fell on another section.

... Your dressing table drawer was open & I looked in hopes of finding a comb or brush which had touched that dear Picturesque brown head — but only found two old combs of mine own, one which fell out one night on the Ramparts, the other I left in your room myself on that never to be forgotten night!

Slowly Capel made sense of what he was reading. Harriet and Baron Trip had clearly been seeing each other in secret, out on the streets of Brussels and even in each other's bedrooms. What a scandal this would be where it uncovered! The letter from Harriet was dated November the previous year. It was inconceivable that such a connection had been going on underneath their noses for so long.

It is a strange sensation when shock makes you both cold and hot at the same time. Capel's fingers felt chilled on the pages as he read and re-read what his daughter had written, but his heart was racing red-hot. He never would have believed these words could be written by his normally level-headed daughter, but the handwriting was unmistakable.

How could Harriet have been so stupid as to risk everything for this man who had now thrown her aside? It was not to be tolerated. His honour would not stand for it.

Capel finally saw a way in which he could protect his family and compensate for his past failures. He would challenge Trip to a duel. It was the only honourable course of action. If he couldn't fight in the army, if he couldn't keep away from the gaming tables, at the very least he could do this to preserve the honour of his daughter and by extension, his family.

He strode into his library and, sitting down at his desk, began to write a letter. He would not see his daughter's reputation in tatters. Live or die, the matter must be laid to rest once and for all. He had turned a blind eye for too long.

CHAPTER X

Fighting for Honour

'My dear Capel has had an Affair with Baron Tripp (Harriet the Unfortunate cause)...'

Lady Caroline Capel to the Dowager Countess of Uxbridge

Perhaps Capel should have felt embarrassed that he didn't own his own duelling pistols and needed to borrow the Duke of Richmond's rather excellent and well-used pair, but he didn't. While he was at the duke's house he asked Richmond to be his 'second'. He sensed that the duke would jump at the chance to be involved in any dangerous activity that reminded him of his youth, the duke having fought two, rather rash duels himself many years before.

'If it concerned one of my daughters, I would do the same,' the duke had reassured Capel, as he expertly cleaned one of his flintlock pistols and checked the sight. 'These damn foreigners must be put in their place.'

'I must admit, Duke, to feeling a little out of my depth.'

'You'd be a fool not to be scared. If there wasn't a ban on officers of different ranks duelling each other, I would be doing it myself on your behalf.'

Capel didn't think the duke was joking.

A few days previously, as custom dictated, Capel had

written to Trip and called him out for his behaviour towards Harriet. Trip had written back in what Capel considered to be an unacceptably terse manner, refuting his claims of dishonour and misbehaviour, and denying he had ever been alone with Harriet.

Capel had seen the letters; he knew this to be a lie. Trip wrote that he would never speak to Harriet again and wouldn't approach her, but in Capel's mind the damage was done. The only honourable course of action left was the one he'd already resolved upon: to challenge Trip to a duel.

Trip agreed to his terms, and as the challenged party picked the type of weapon they would use. It was no surprise that he chose pistols, as duelling with swords had gone out of fashion some years before. As the challenger, Capel then proposed a location for the duel to take place, a 'field of honour', outside of the city limits so that arrest would be avoided. They were each to have a 'second' to negotiate before the duel took place in case a peaceful resolution could be reached.

When he woke early on the appointed morning, Capel felt sick with a mix of nerves and excitement. This was the most reckless thing he had ever done. That his wife and children were sound asleep in their beds added to his disquiet. What would they do on waking and discovering where he had got to? What if he was killed?

Ruefully, he supposed they would be financially better off if he died, and at least the disgrace he had brought on the family would be at an end. Yet he couldn't truly think they would wish that fate on him. Not when the family loved and cared so deeply for each other, despite the differences between them.

Soon, he and the duke were making their way out of the city in the duke's carriage. Before long they arrived at a barren and deserted field. The hour was early enough that the sky hadn't yet decided whether to be dark or light. A mist hugged the ground around them. Richmond gripped Capel's shoulder and grimaced.

'I see the brute is late; little wonder, I suppose.'

Capel had no words with which to answer, as his every nerve was strained to breaking point. He had never duelled anyone before, let alone a military man who would no doubt be a much better marksman. His head throbbed with adrenalin. He tried to remind himself of why he had resolved to do this.

'*For the honour of my family*,' he muttered under his breath, again and again. He didn't want to become a murderer, but he was no coward either. He had to settle this score with Trip and do right by his family.

In the distance, he saw another carriage slowly making its way towards them. The horses pulled up nearby and out stepped Baron Trip. He wore a dark cloak and looked grim. As he got closer Capel saw dark shadows around his bloodshot eyes, and his mouth was a thin line.

The Duke of Richmond and Trip's second stood to one side and spoke quietly for a few moments, then the duke looked over to Capel and shook his head. It was down to Capel to begin the proceedings.

'Well, Trip, I see you have answered my summons.'

'As you wish it, sir.'

'And you wish, do you, to proceed, rather than commit to a

full apology for the wrongs that you have done to my family?'

'I see no wrong, so cannot on my honour retract my actions.'

It was no good, the next steps were clear to everyone present.

'If that is the state of things,' Capel said, 'then let us begin and be done with it.' He hoped he sounded braver than he felt. Trip nodded curtly. Capel suddenly wondered if this was his first duel, too. His opponent suddenly seemed incredibly young.

The duke handed him the pistol. Capel and Trip turned and walked in opposite directions for ten paces, then turned back to face the other. The air was thick with anticipation. As Capel was the challenger, he was to shoot first, then Trip would have his chance. Given that Trip was the one in the wrong, he should by right and tradition either not fire at all, or fire at the ground, that being the gentlemanly way to end a dispute.

Capel waited for the signal from the doctor, which came quickly: 'Gentlemen, fire!' It was now or never. His heart was beating with such force it was surely making himself more of a target. What happened next took only a few seconds but they were the longest seconds of Capel's life.

Before he could hesitate he wrenched the pistol up and fired. Through his panic he saw Trip had also raised his weapon. His whole body seized up in horror as he waited for the bullet to hit home. Trip had fired straight at him.

～～

'So you see, my dear, we *both* fired, but as you can see,' Capel opened his arms wide, 'I survived.'

Some hours had passed and he was telling his wife the tale

in the safety of their drawing room. Lady Caroline's eyes were like saucers.

'Not quite at the same time, you see; I fired first, aiming to the right, for of course I didn't want to actually hit him. I must say the relief I felt on seeing he was still standing was immediate, for you know I'm no killer! But Trip fired also, and as you can see, he grazed my coat. I've had rather a lucky escape, I think.'

Lady Caroline could see that the right shoulder of Capel's coat had a large burn mark on it and the fabric was torn. So that's what the strange scent in the air was: gunpowder!

'By God, I can't see how we both came out of that alive,' said Capel, 'but somehow we managed it.'

Lady Caroline was so shocked she was almost lost for words.

'And you told me to visit Lady Charlotte this morning, knowing that you would be fighting a duel! John, how could you deceive me so?'

'I'm sorry, but I couldn't risk your trying to stop me. I had to summon the courage to go through with it and if I'd told you I might not have been able to.'

Lady Caroline opened her mouth to reproach Capel further, but decided against it. She couldn't truly be angry with him for keeping the information from her – and now here he was, alive to tell the rather thrilling tale, and truth be told she had never found him more attractive.

Capel continued with his tale, explaining how after the duel had ended, he and Trip had shaken hands and Trip had even managed a thin smile. Then they had bade each other a good morning and headed back to their respective carriages.

What a morning it had been! As Capel told Lady Caroline the whole story he seemed to sit up a little straighter, and by its conclusion his wife was in tears.

'And truly, Baron Trip has been romancing our Harriet?' she asked. 'You don't mean Georgy or Maria? It just seems so unlikely! She's usually the sensible one.'

'Yes, I know, but it's true, without a doubt. A great deal of underhand goings-on have taken place behind our backs, and Trip has behaved most dishonourably to Harriet.'

'I don't know whether to be furious with her or seek to console her.'

'I spoke to her before I came to you and she confessed all, with great purity of heart and many tears. I believe this will ease the anguish she has felt these last few months. Trip's behaviour has been most outrageous. They even spent time alone together in his room. That letter I intercepted incriminated him without a shadow of a doubt. Now he's called off all contact, leaving Harriet as heartbroken as we see her now.'

Lady Caroline struggled to believe what she was hearing. Her daughter, alone in a room with that awful man! She would never have believed any of her daughters would do such a thing, and certainly not Harriet. She shook her head in disbelief.

'I suppose at least we know now what's been ailing our daughter all these months,' she finally stammered.

'Yes, indeed, my dear. It's a damned serious business.'

'I cannot believe Trip,' she said, dabbing under her eyes with a handkerchief. 'I cannot believe he would shoot you when he is so clearly in the wrong. What if he'd killed you? What would have become of us then?'

'Even Richmond, and Trip's own second, were shocked at his having fired. The man really must have no soul, as he himself claims.'

'Does he really claim such a thing?'

'Yes, indeed, Paget has confirmed it. The man's an atheist, and doesn't keep his unnatural views to himself. I dread to think what horrid thoughts he has impressed upon our Harriet.'

'At least now the dreadful business is at an end, and we can say for sure that Trip will never be welcomed into our home again.'

'Indeed; anyone who tries to kill me had better think twice before trying to marry one of our daughters!'

Lady Caroline drew closer to her husband on the sofa, linking her arm with his and breathing in the scent of gunpowder and pride on his skin.

There was a soft knock on the door, which opened to reveal the wretched face of their eldest daughter, her face quite distorted with tears. She hesitated, unsure of her reception, her whole body convulsing with barely contained sobs of agony.

'My dear child,' her father said, opening his arms, 'come, let us comfort you!'

Harriet screwed her eyes up against the pain and came blindly towards them, her hands over her face. They made a space between them on the sofa and enveloped her in their arms.

Oh, to be young again, and to feel love's sting so sharply, Lady Caroline thought, as she and her daughter gave over to crying. Despite her shock and disappointment, she couldn't bring herself to harangue her daughter when she was in such a state. Harriet was a broken doll, and the pieces of her that were left sat between them. As Lady Caroline wept, she realised she'd already forgiven her and wanted only for her to be healed and whole again. The trio stayed wrapped in each other's arms for a long time, until Lady Caroline was able to get Harriet upstairs and back into bed. She couldn't be coaxed downstairs again for days.

CHAPTER XI

A Hero and a Villain

'Ourselves, Richmonds, Grevilles, Lady Sutton & Daughters are the only English of our Acquaintance who have weathered it out & we are amply repaid, for the Town is perfectly tranquil & for the present there can be no danger of Molestation... Lord Wellington is expected every hour — His name is a Host in itself.'

Lady Caroline Capel to the Dowager Countess of Uxbridge

Later that week Lady Caroline was at her writing desk penning a long missive to her mother. She wished more than ever before that the old lady was here to help them through their present troubles. Even more than needing support and guidance for herself, Lady Caroline wanted to reassure Lady Uxbridge of the true state of things before any gossip reached her. As the ink flowed across the page, she could barely believe the words she was writing.

Capel had, thank God, been able to keep Harriet's name out of the Trip business, which was a great accomplishment given Brussels' predilection for gossip. All anyone knew was that the quarrel between Capel and Trip had got to the point where shots had been exchanged, and honour had been restored on both sides. Only the two parties engaged in the duel knew the exact reason it had been called, and although whispers had been circulating that one of Lady Caroline's daughters was the cause of the trouble, few knew which it was.

As February's cold winds and rain slowly lessened, the mornings grew lighter and birds were once more confessing the joys of the morning to their friends. Harriet pined for Baron Trip, and the family supported her the best they could while they tried to focus on the many positives of their lives in Brussels. They all agreed they had come to love the city. Lady Caroline's belly started to grow, but she continued to escort her daughters to the many events that filled their diaries.

A few friends, including General Barnes, encouraged her to take it more easy. She began to sit out most of the dancing and would sometimes go home early, while the girls were busily occupied with their partners. They would instead be escorted home by a bleary-eyed Capel, often grumpy and monosyllabic while his daughters excitedly analysed the night's event.

Not all the Capel girls were to be found on the dance floors of Brussels, as winter turned to spring. Louisa was still just a little too young, at fifteen. Although she desperately wanted to join her older sisters, she stayed at home with Harriet, who wasn't yet well enough to attend parties again. Harriet was no closer to forgetting Baron Trip, and her health had suffered much from the shock of his rejection and his shooting at Capel during the duel.

Trip would, of course, never be allowed to set foot in the

Capel residence again. Such finality, far from helping Harriet come to terms with the situation, pushed her to the brink of despair. No amount of comfort or reassurance calmed her for long.

Trip had been sent to Paris and had kept his word not to contact Harriet again, but she couldn't resist writing him a number of increasingly desperate letters. Receiving no reply she fell further into misery, and confided in Georgy and Maria what she had done.

'I know it's madness, but I so wanted to hear from him again.'

'Oh, Harriet, how could you have done so when Papa strictly forbade any contact? If he finds out you wrote to him, he'll be so angry,' said Georgy.

Harriet hung her head in shame. 'He hasn't responded anyway,' she said, despondently.

Maria and Georgy glanced at each other, and Maria said what they were both thinking.

'Well, I for one am glad he hasn't responded.' Harriet looked up and seeing her expression Maria hurried on. 'I'm sorry, but it's true. I don't think more contact will help you heal. Once you send a letter, the power of your silence is lost in waiting for a reply, leading only to more heartache.'

Maria was surprised at her words, they sounded like those from a much older woman; but however much she knew them to be true, she also suspected that her words were falling on deaf ears. She was sure Harriet would try to contact Baron Trip in the future, and only hoped that he'd keep his word and not reply. She prayed he wouldn't return to Brussels.

Nothing her sisters did could raise Harriet's spirits for more than a few hours. They tried taking her for walks in the park outside the house. They brought her interesting flowers, feathers and leaves as they sat by the statues that surrounded the pond. They took her in the carriage around the Forêt de Soignes, and to visit their Lennox sister friends.

The Lennoxes called on them also, sometimes in the company of their handsome eldest brother Lord March or their younger brother Lord William Pitt Lennox. Both would pay Harriet every kindness and compliment, trying to bring her out of her shell, but it barely made an impact.

She was always polite and considerate, but Maria would often catch her looking into the distance, her face impassive and eyes glazed over. It wasn't hard to imagine what distracted her; all she wanted was Trip.

'I worry he'll do himself harm,' she whispered to Georgy and Maria one night. They had begun to squeeze into one bed to keep Harriet company. 'His mind works so differently from ours.'

Maria replied into the dark, 'No man can be worth the pain you're feeling, Harriet. Love us, love your family, but don't waste your love on him a moment longer.'

Maria believed passionately in what she said, but she was also impatient for her sister to recover. She wanted her old sister back and to forget this horrid business but feared Harriet had been taken somewhere she couldn't follow. Harriet didn't answer her. Into the silence Maria quietly prayed that Harriet would find peace in her heart and leave her troubles behind, but her prayer was full of doubt.

Maria had learnt a lot from Harriet's troubles. She had seen the benefit of not letting her heart go until she was completely sure of a man's devotion. In the confusion surrounding Harriet and Baron Trip, she'd decided to enjoy herself as much as she could without committing herself.

෴

With hundreds of British aristocratic families in residence, Brussels – not London or Paris – was now the centre of high society. As the weather improved, the girls went for more walks and drives, either around the town or through the parks. It was easy to greet people they knew, and invitations flowed in from all quarters for dinners, banquets, balls and theatre trips. Despite her concerns about Harriet, Maria had never been happier or felt more herself.

They were invited to attend a review of the cavalry under the command of their uncle, Lord Uxbridge. They would go on horseback, except Lady Caroline, who would ride in a carriage. Excitedly, they planned what to wear, sourcing silk neckties, bodices in light tweed and full skirts down to the ankle.

All the girls rode well, although Georgy was less confident than the others. Maria felt none of her sister's nerves. She adored horses and looked forward to the review with great enthusiasm, only regretting that Lord Hay wouldn't be there to see her in her new riding habit. She wondered how he was getting on with his new mare, Miss Muzzy, and wished the occasion would come when they could ride out together.

Reviews were an important part of military life. Entire regiments, in this case some seven thousand men, would gather to parade in formation in front of their commanding officers. The rank and file would prepare for days beforehand, as their uniforms and regalia had to be perfect. Anything less would reflect badly on the officers' handle on the men. A review was the army flexing its muscles; thousands of men standing to attention, a display of strength and skill. It was certainly an honour to be invited to one, especially as a guest of the commanding officer.

The day of the review was the first that year in which Maria woke to a real sense of spring in the air. A soft glow could be seen through the gaps in the curtains. The sun was up and shining brightly by the time the sisters had dressed and gone into breakfast. Harriet had begged another headache and was to stay at home.

To Maria there was nothing more liberating than riding through beautiful countryside on a crisp sunny morning. The horses were content, snorting into the cold air. Maria and Georgy were riding side-saddle, and Maria felt dressed for the part in her smart new habit.

The review was to take place on a large plain, a short ride south of the city. On arrival, Maria was stunned into silence at the scene before her. She had been told about reviews but wasn't prepared for the scale of the spectacle. She had never before seen so many soldiers standing in formation. As far as the eye could see, ranks of soldiers covered the plain, with pathways between them like streets through cities. Yet this city was unlike any Maria had seen before, for it was rustling and shimmering in the sun, sunlight glinting off the polished metal on both soldier and steed.

Maria was glad her uncle had taken the trouble many years ago to teach them which regiment wore what uniform. She quickly spotted the Dragoons, their crested helmets of black horsehair contrasting to their scarlet coats and white breeches; then the Hussars, their fur caps topped with white and red plumes.

The horses were well fed and fit, their tails docked. The English were renowned for keeping their horses well and ensuring they always got enough food and rest, and the effects were clear for Maria to see.

They rode over to the group surrounding their uncle, who looked distinguished and proud astride a stunning grey charger that was pawing the ground excitedly, keen to depart. Lord Uxbridge greeted them warmly.

'I hope you're impressed by my men; they look pretty sharp to me,' he said to Maria and Georgy.

His eye roved critically over the thousands of men who stood to formation in front of him, so still they looked like toy soldiers. The odd perspective made Maria feel a little dizzy.

'If you're ready,' Lord Uxbridge said, 'then we shall be off.'

Lord Uxbridge was accompanied by a large number of his staff who rode alongside him, leaving Maria and Georgy to follow a short distance behind. There were a few other civilians in the convoy, who they greeted with a polite nod.

One gentleman in particular caught Maria's eye. He was taller than the others and sat astride his horse with the calm confidence of someone who'd spent many years in the saddle. Before she could properly scrutinise him, the whole party moved off.

Maria glanced across to Georgy. She looked nervous and was holding the reins a little higher than was necessary, causing her horse to toss his head. Their horses were beginning to fall behind. Maria signalled to her to lower her hands, and luckily the ground was kind to them as they rode across to view the first line of troops.

Maria looked keenly at each soldier as they passed, trusting her horse to keep its footing and follow the others. Each face looked so like the one before, and soon they were a blur. Her eyes returned to the group ahead of her and she found herself seeing if she could get a better look at the man she had spotted earlier. She wondered if she could orchestrate a conversation with him.

'Shall we ride further up, Gee?' she said to her sister.

Georgy, always one to see through a seemingly innocent suggestion, immediately looked suspicious.

'Why, I wonder? Should you by any chance want to join that group of amiable gentlemen?' she said slyly.

Maria grinned. Her sister knew her too well.

'Well, not to do so would be a wasted opportunity, would it not?'

They began to trot up the path towards the group which was now some way ahead of them. Georgy looked uncomfortable, her hands were too high again. Her horse suddenly spooked, barging into Maria, causing a moment of panic as both horses fought for position on the narrow path.

Georgy called out in alarm and Maria's horse bolted away at such speed that she instantly became dislodged; before she knew it, she was flying through the air. She landed with a most inelegant *thunk* on the hard earth and her head hit the ground; the horse careered off down the path.

Maria sprawled on her front, all the air knocked out of her. Gasping and coughing, she lifted her head and saw Lord Uxbridge and the others turning their horses around to see the cause of the commotion. *How mortifying!*

She tried to get up from the damp and dirty ground, but her head felt as though it had been split open and she groaned involuntarily. A face appeared above hers, and to her embarrassment she saw it belonged to the gentleman who had caught her eye earlier.

'May I assist you? Are you able to rise?'

His accent was elegant and lilting, but he was certainly not a native English speaker. To Maria's inexpert ear he sounded French. The man held out a hand, but then lifted Maria up by the elbow and waist, steadying her on her feet and looking kindly down at her.

'Are you hurt?'

'No, I think not. Only shocked and embarrassed.'

'It could happen to anyone. I'll assist you to remount. But first, would you permit me to check your injuries? It seems as though you have hit your head rather badly.'

He carefully turned Maria's head from one side to the other.

'Are you in pain?'

'No, just a little sore.' She winced as he gently pressed her temple where she had hit the ground.

Out of the corner of her eye Maria could see Georgy and the others waiting nearby, watching her in her torment. The horse had been recovered and was snorting in frustration at being held by an irritated-looking Lord Uxbridge. Maria was sure her face was as scarlet as the sun.

'Goodness, this is rather mortifying.'

'Don't worry, I'll have you back on your horse in a few more moments. Are you sure you're all right?'

'I feel better by the second, thank you.'

His examination was complete and he declared her fit to rejoin the review. Before he retrieved her horse, he brushed down the side of her skirt which was covered in dirt and pointed out the fallen leaves that had stuck in her hair. Between the two of them they removed them as quickly as possible, smiling at the awkwardness of the task.

Maria couldn't help but notice the man's quiet, cool confidence. He looked a little older than her, and his dark hair was much too long for someone in the military. He must be a civilian guest of her uncle's. His dark eyes met Maria's, and he smiled again.

'Thank you for your kindness, sir,' she said, as he helped her back into the saddle.

'Think nothing of it.'

Lady Caroline had descended from her carriage to attend to her daughter. One of the stirrup leathers had broken, causing more fuss as it was secured to a rung at the front of the saddle. Lady Caroline did this, using the opportunity to give Maria a look that told her she would be receiving a serious talking-to when they got home.

Maria had been warned on numerous occasions that she was too confident when out riding. *Here is the proof of it*, her mother's look told her, and thousands of British soldiers, as well as their officers, had been witness to it.

Maria didn't want to see any more of her mother's disapproval. She saw the man who had helped her was now also back on his own horse. She hadn't even asked his name. He smiled at her and tipped his hat and Maria only had time to mouth 'thank you' before he rode off to rejoin his friends.

Georgy caught her eye, clearly trying not to laugh, and they moved off together. Maria felt very awkward riding with only one stirrup.

'Trust you to turn such a situation to your advantage, Muz,' Georgy said.

'Oh la! What can you mean? In any case, it was your horse who caused the ruckus, not mine!'

Georgy simply smiled knowingly at Maria, who couldn't help but grin back.

The rest of the review passed without further drama. After they had ridden the length of the line, they all stopped to watch the cavalry pass them. Maria's incident was quite surpassed by the sight of the regiment cantering in formation. The thundering of hooves and flashes of uniform quite took Maria's breath away. *This must be what being in a battle is like,* she thought.

The noise was incredible; she would have liked to put her hands over her ears but didn't want to take them from the reins given her recent fall. She looked down the line to see her uncle's reaction. Lord Uxbridge sat upright in his saddle, gazing straight ahead. This was an important and proud moment for him, as he surveyed all the troops under his command. Maria was thrilled to share in this achievement.

When they next drew up alongside each other her uncle said, 'Well, Muz, spare pity for my men who've been training for months to put on their show, only to have you steal their limelight!'

Maria felt awkward, but Lord Uxbridge didn't look cross anymore, so she asked who it was who had helped her up and on to her horse again.

'Oh, I don't know his name, he's not a military man, but a friend of the Marquis d'Assche. We are currently stationed at the Marquis's house and he's staying there also. I've heard he has a lot of very useful contacts at The Hague. I'm sure he'll enjoy regaling his friends at dinner about dusting down your habit!'

Now Maria really was embarrassed, but before she could think of a suitable retort, someone called to Lord Uxbridge and, without another word, he kicked his horse into a sharp trot and left her side.

It had been a day of highs and lows and Maria suddenly felt glad they were heading home, although she wasn't looking forward to the rebuke from her mother that undoubtedly was in store.

∾∾

A few weeks after the review, the elder Capel sisters were in the drawing room with their mother, Lord Hay and the Prince of Orange when the door burst open and General Barnes marched in, tailed by one of the servants who had been denied the chance to introduce him. They all looked up.

'Have you heard the news?'

'What news would that be, General Barnes?' said Lady Caroline. As always, General Barnes had her full and undivided attention.

'Clearly, then, you have not. By God, I can barely believe it. Bonaparte has escaped from Elba and landed in France. The army has rejoined him and the king has fled!'

The whole room gasped, men included. The Prince of Orange grabbed Georgy's hand instinctively. Lord Hay leapt to his feet.

'Then we will fight,' he exclaimed. 'Let's take our men back to Old Boney and show him what we're made of!'

Maria turned to General Barnes. 'Is it really true, General? It seems so extraordinary that he should have been able to escape the island and make his way to France unmolested.'

General Barnes replied, 'Indeed, there is no mistake. He has already reached Paris and King Louis has fled to Ghent.'

'When you think of the horrors Napoleon has brought on his country,' said the Prince of Orange, 'it beggars belief that his men should go back to him so readily.'

'They are certainly loyal to the core,' General Barnes agreed.

Maria looked at her sisters. They looked as shocked as she felt. The long-fought-for peace with France had seemed so permanent, and now in a flash they were back on shaky ground.

'Are we in danger?' Harriet asked. 'Brussels is less than two hundred miles from Paris, after all.'

'No danger whatsoever, dearest Harriet,' General Barnes

said. He sat next to her on the sofa and took her by the hand. 'It's true, however, that the English in Paris are leaving in droves, and many will seek sanctuary here. They have already begun to arrive; soon the town will be quite overrun by the English.'

'Even more so than currently, you mean,' said Georgy. She glanced over at Harriet with a worried expression; would this mean Baron Trip would be returning?

Lady Caroline's eyes were wide. 'What will happen to the army?' she asked General Barnes. 'Will they go to meet him?'

'I should hope so,' said Lord Hay with gusto, before General Barnes could answer. 'Let us go with our full strength, I say, and finish the scoundrel off for good. I look forward to the opportunity to send him packing.'

General Barnes frowned at the young man's enthusiasm. When he spoke, his voice carried a warning tone.

'War is bloody, Hay. I should not wish it so readily.'

Lord Hay was undeterred. 'It is honour, not war, that I long for, General. I am pleased Bonaparte has chosen to test us once more. I, at any rate, am ready.' Turning to the ladies he said, 'Please excuse me, I must get back to my quarters and see what's needed of me.'

He bowed, and before the Capels could rise to curtsey their goodbyes, he'd left the room. The Prince of Orange also bade them a hasty goodbye, bowing twice to Georgy before following his friend into the hall. General Barnes shook his head.

'You think them rash?' enquired Maria before she could stop herself.

'The attitude isn't uncommon among the young and untried of our armies,' he said grimly. 'They long to show their worth. I remember the feeling myself. But now I long for peace, and greatly regret that Napoleon is forcing us once again into action.'

Maria too had felt discomfited by Lord Hay's passion for battle. Over six years, tens of thousands of young men had died in battles that had already become household names: Talavera, Badajoz, Salamanca, Vitoria. At Vitoria alone at least five thousand of the Duke of Wellington's men had been killed or wounded. France had been their sworn enemy, the bitter resentment from each side insurmountable.

No one knew the exact number of deaths before Napoleon abdicated, but it was known that nearly a thousand officers had been killed and over thirty times that number of the men under their command. By the time the French had been defeated and the Capels had arrived in Brussels, there were seventy thousand British soldiers on the Continent. They had a formidable fighting reputation. But the truth was that a year later only a small percentage of that force was still there, and the danger was immense.

So many of the men wouldn't return home. Countless families would be torn apart. The children left behind wouldn't have graves to visit.

With an effort Maria pulled herself back to the room.

'But you will fight with the others?' she asked General Barnes.

'Of course. I will do my duty, but I do so, I hope, with more humility than those who have yet to see the horrors of war.'

'Will there really be a war? Could we not let Napoleon keep France, if he promises not to expand his empire?'

'No doubt that's what he will say, but all his actions have shown he won't stop until he controls the whole world. He won't rest until the whole of Europe is at his heel once more. We can't allow him to keep even *an inch* of French soil.'

'What will happen if Napoleon invades Brussels?'

'I wouldn't like to say. Looting would be the very least of it, I'm afraid. But don't fear, we'll get you away from danger with plenty of time to spare, if an invasion is on the cards. I'll make sure of it.'

General Barnes let his words sink in. He meant every word of his promise. Maria looked at him and saw his eyes were filled with sadness, and worry, too. Everything began to feel very real.

Then Harriet said, in a small voice, 'The officers have all been recalled from Paris by now, haven't they?'

Her words were met by silence of a different kind, as everyone knew why she was asking.

General Barnes replied kindly, 'Yes, Harriet, they'll be well on their way by now. All the Allied armies are congregating here in Brussels, so we can work together to overthrow Napoleon.'

Harriet looked wretched.

A few more seconds passed before General Barnes said, with an obvious effort to be more cheerful, 'Now, see here, all is not lost, for the Duke of Wellington himself is returning from the Congress of Vienna to take command of the army. With him at our helm, we surely can't fail.'

'How can that be, when the Prince of Orange has command of the armies here?' asked Georgy, looking a little put out.

'Well, he should hand them over if he knows what's good for him,' General Barnes replied harshly and without hesitation. 'This is not a matter of who outranks who due to birth or situation. We need the best man for the job, and that man is Wellington.'

Georgy didn't try to argue with him.

General Barnes was right, of course. No one could command the armies of Europe like the Duke of Wellington. No one was as experienced or held the same level of trust and respect from officers and soldiers alike.

As the news of Napoleon's escape spread through Brussels like wildfire, the question on everyone's lips was, *when would the duke return*? The thought of his presence in Brussels gave people hope, but it would take time for him to travel back to the city and the people were impatient. They wanted to see for themselves that the hero they believed could save them from Bonaparte had arrived.

With each passing day, more and more English families left Brussels, despite repeated assurances from the military that the city would remain safe. It became common to see families lugging their posessions through the streets as they left the city. The Capels, together with a number of other families, decided to stay. Here they had a front row seat as the Allied army galvanised against Napoleon, and it was sure to be a thrilling time for them all.

By now, spring had established herself in the city with a colourful, fragrant flourish. The Capel girls enjoyed the blossom trees in the park, where they walked at least once a day. It was still an excellent place to meet one's friends, and each day brought another piece of news about Napoleon or the Duke of Wellington. It was hard to believe all they heard, as the information changed so frequently.

As the days turned into a week, rumours about the duke's arrival finally seemed to become fact. Excitement over his return from Vienna reached fever pitch. The morning of Wellington's arrival saw the Capel sisters rise early and dress in their most sensible clothes, as they knew the crowds would be immense and their best things might get ruined.

They skipped breakfast and joined the crowds filling the streets. The atmosphere was charged. The sisters fought to stick together as they made their way to the Grand Place, the vast square at the heart of the city, flanked by the town hall and guilds. The buildings were painted with accents of gold than shone in the morning light. Nearby, a band was playing.

The crowd swelled, with people laughing and calling to each other. French, Dutch and English mixed with many other tongues Maria didn't recognise. People had brought flags, and children seated on their fathers' shoulders acted as lookouts.

Then a shout rang out: 'Over there, I see him!'

The crowded roared their appreciation. Maria, jumping up and down, saw a group of men on horseback enter the square at the corner nearest them. The horses slowly made their way forward, shaking their heads but otherwise coping admirably with the crowds. Wellington was easily recognisable at the front of the group.

'They're coming our way – what luck!' Maria exclaimed.

The duke wore a plain dark coat, fawn-coloured breeches and a black cocked hat. Maria had heard about his horse, the famous chestnut called Copenhagen. He was known to have carried the duke through the worst battles and still come out fighting.

The duke didn't smile or wave to the crowd but nonetheless seemed pleased by the jubilation, occasionally tilting his head in recognition of the many loud huzzas. Eventually, he rode past the Capel girls. He met Maria's eye and touched his hat. She grinned up at him, thrilled at the recognition. Then he spoke, loudly, so as to be heard over the crowd.

'Tell your father to come to dinner, tomorrow at eight.'

None of them had time to respond before the group of men passed, the crowd closing in behind them. How thrilling; a personal invitation to dinner from the duke himself! What rotten luck he had not invited them all!

CHAPTER XII
Dining with the Duke

'The Duke of Wellington gives a
Grand Fête Champêtre next week.
Mama says she is determined not
to stir from this place unless for
something very brilliant. We have
not made the same determination
& therefore mean to make Papa
Chaperone us to a Ball at the
Duchess of Richmond in a day
or two.'

Maria Capel to the Dowager Countess of Uxbridge

Capel fidgeted on the doorstep to the duke's house, his heart beating uncomfortably fast, waiting for his knock to be answered. 'Damn, they're taking their time,' he grumbled to himself. Did he even want to go through with this dinner? He could almost feel the eyes of his wife and daughters boring into the back of his head. They had watched him leave the house and travel across the park to the house directly opposite their own. He knew they would be eagerly awaiting his return.

Of course it was an honour to be asked to dine with the duke at such an important time, but what he wouldn't give to be ensconced in his library instead, perhaps with a large glass of wine, or, even better, to be seated at one of the tables at the Literary Club. He heard footsteps on the other side of the door and stood a little straighter.

'Yes, sir, may I help you?' The footman's face was impassive.

'I am here to dine with the duke. My name is Capel.'

'Very good, sir.'

The footman ushered him into the hall, and he was asked to wait, his coat and hat having been taken off him. Now Capel really did feel sick. What if there had been some mistake and the duke hadn't said to the girls that he was to come this evening, but the next evening, or at a different time? What if they had misheard him in the crowd? He waited in the hall for what felt like an age.

'Capel, how good to see you.'

Just like that, the Duke of Wellington was before him. He seemed taller than when Capel had last seen him in London. Up close, his refined features and hooked nose were bronzed and his eyes sparkled.

'I saw your girls as we came through the square. How well they looked.'

'Thank you. I must say, they become more of a handful by the day.'

'Aye, I can imagine. I am glad for my part I have only boys, although they come with their own challenges. Come and join the others.'

Capel let out his first full breath since his entry into the house. As he and the duke left the entrance hall to join the rest of the guests, he tried to relax. This would certainly be a night to remember.

'So, Capel, now we've set the world to rights, tell us, what excitement has there been in Brussels during our absence?'

They were seated around the dinner table, enjoying glasses of claret after a simple yet delicious meal. The question came from Capel's right, where sat the quartermaster, General Sir William De Lancey. To his left was the Duke of Brunswick, emptying a bottle into his glass with relish.

'More balls than I can contend with, I'm afraid. My wife and daughters are delighted, but I must say I'm finding the rigmarole rather exhausting.'

The duke chuckled, and it was General Barnes, seated opposite him, who responded.

'Your family has certainly been working hard to keep the spirits of the army from flagging.'

Capel was not sure he appreciated this remark and could not think of a suitable reply.

'I hear you and Trip got into rather a scrape some months back,' said the duke lightly.

Capel paused before responding. 'Indeed. Luckily, that's all behind us now.'

He was proud of his part in the duel, but even so, he thought it best to steer past the subject.

'Duke, in your opinion, does Brussels remain a safe place for my wife and girls?' he asked Wellington.

The duke looked round the table and back down at his glass before responding.

'Entirely, Capel. You can trust that Brussels is as safe from the French as any city on the Continent. We'll know when danger is near.'

But the duke was not yet finished on the subject of Capel's duel. 'I wonder whether I shall ever be forced into a duel,' he said, pensively.

'Surely not!' chuckled de Lancey. He drained his glass and nodded to the footman for a refill. Capel saw that his own glass was also empty and hoped the footman would fill it too.

'I don't think it would be quite the thing for the great duke to be caught duelling on Wimbledon Common,' De Lancey added.

'I wouldn't be so sure, De Lancey.' The duke looked wistful. 'There are so many surprises in life. Wouldn't you say so, Lord Fontanelle?'

This question was directed to another guest at the table. Capel had been introduced to the man when he arrived but hadn't caught his full name.

'I would, your grace,' the gentleman said. 'I'm always surprised by the extent to which passion can turn God-fearing people into killers. And not just individuals, but whole groups of people. Bloodlust blossoming in the streets, manias rising and falling with the seasons, until people come to themselves again.'

Lord Fontanelle's remarks brought a different tone to the conversation, and the men all nodded and murmured in agreement. Capel was quite struck by the gentleman and his words. He was of foreign extraction, perhaps Swiss, but with an accent so subtle and gentlemanlike it was hard to place. Like Capel, he was plainly not a military man, yet despite the presence of some of the most senior military leaders in Europe he seemed entirely at his ease.

'I presume you speak of Paris?' enquired General Barnes. 'Were you there during the Revolution?'

'Some of my family was, yes, and the stories I heard from them convinced me I knew enough of war to last a lifetime. I could see in their eyes they had been changed forever by what they witnessed. And they were the lucky ones. They escaped.'

'Tyrants come in many forms.' Now it was Capel's turn for wise words. He spoke them aloud without conscious thought, and felt a little embarrassed. How much wine had he drunk? It was probably time for him to head back to Caroline, but first he wanted to know more about the gentleman sitting across from him.

'What brings you to Brussels?' he asked Lord Fontanelle.

'I'm a guest of the Marquis d'Assche. His house is not far from here. It's an honour to be in Brussels to see the Allied armies gather their strength against Bonaparte.'

'It's good to be among friends, and to feel our strength growing,' the duke agreed. He seemed to be in a reflective mood. 'Yet it's also good to enjoy the many benefits of society that are on offer here in Brussels.'

'Is there anyone in particular you are thinking of, your grace?' said De Lancey with a smile.

The duke didn't reply to De Lancey, but said to Lord Fontanelle, 'I would trouble you for a word after the others have left.'

Indeed, the hour was late, the guests were bleary-eyed and beginning to slump in their seats. Lord Fontanelle asked Capel whether they ought to head home across the park together.

'The Marquis' house is very near yours, I think. I shall just speak to the duke and meet you outside.'

Capel didn't think to ask how Lord Fontanelle knew where he lived, and gladly accepted the offer. Slowly, the men made their way out of the dining room, down the darkened corridors to the entrance hall and out on to the road.

Capel went to thank the duke, who was clapping General Barnes on the back as he bade him goodnight. The duke took Capel's hand and, before he could be thanked for the fine food and wine, spoke quietly and quickly.

'I didn't wish to say so in front of the others, but there may well be cause for you and your family to go to Antwerp. The situation with Napoleon is fragile. Be prepared and await word from myself or Barnes, or indeed our new friend Lord Fontanelle.'

Capel was taken aback. Earlier the duke had seemed so sure that there was no danger.

'You're certain?' he asked.

'If Napoleon's men get into the city there'll be blood on the streets within hours. I've seen what his men are capable of. Looting will be the least of it. I've seen women stabbed, shot, worse. I'll ensure that word is sent to you.'

The duke was not a man to exaggerate, and anyway Capel knew his words to be true. Everyone knew of the horrors Wellington had witnessed in Portugal and Spain.

'Thank you, your grace. I'm grateful to you,' he said. He gripped the duke's hand and the two men smiled grimly at each other.

Capel only had to wait a few minutes for Lord Fontanelle, and together they walked into the darkened park. Capel's mood was gloomy, but he decided not to pass on to Lord

Fontanelle what the duke had said. If Wellington wanted the young man to know, he would have told him.

Despite the late hour, Capel and Lord Fontanelle saw couples walking through the park together, keeping close, and several bushes rustled unnaturally. A particularly obvious noise caused them both to laugh.

'Brussels really is an extraordinary place,' said Capel. 'You would never get away with such behaviour in London. Well, perhaps in Vauxhall Gardens,' he added as an afterthought.

'It's the thought of war,' Lord Fontanelle replied, 'it makes them feel like anything is possible.'

'Perhaps it is, maybe this is how life ought to be, and I'm sure my daughters would agree with you!'

'Possibly it'd be best not utter such thoughts in front of them!'

'I think that would be wise.'

'I should like to meet your family one day, if you should wish it.'

'That would be delightful; you are just the sort of chap my eldest daughters should be meeting. So many of the army men they currently consort with are the loosest of fellows beneath their fine uniforms.'

'Well, I can't promise to be an angel in that regard.' He indicated the fine cut of his coat.

Capel smiled. 'But you are no bon vivant, sir?'

'Not in the strict sense of the term, no; I appear to have grown too sensible for that.'

'Well, I, for one, am glad there is at least one decent man roaming the streets of Brussels.'

They came to the edge of the park and bade each other farewell. Lord Fontanelle shook Capel's hand warmly and headed off down a side street. Capel went in the other direction and let himself into his house. Right up until those last remarks by the duke, he really didn't know when he'd enjoyed an evening more.

To dine with the Duke of Wellington was an honour he would always remember, and what a charming man Lord Fontanelle had been. He hoped to meet him again but couldn't see that their paths were likely to cross a second time unless he was a member of the Literary Club, and he didn't seem the type. In fact, why he'd been at the Duke of Wellington's table was a mystery.

'How was your evening, my love?'

Capel had tried to be quiet as he crept into Lady Caroline's bedroom, but she had woken and was stirring sleepily. He quietly undressed and got into bed beside her. By the time he'd settled under the covers she'd already gone back to sleep, but he answered her anyway.

'Rather fascinating, not to mention insightful,' he said. 'A night I will never forget.'

As he lay in the darkness, he decided that he would heed the duke's warning and make plans to move his family to Antwerp. He would tell no one, but he would prepare. He couldn't risk them being trapped in Brussels, should Napoleon's army win. Some might think him unpatriotic, but he knew of the horrors the French had committed, and it would kill him to see any such thing happen to his wife or children. He had protected them once and was ready to do so again.

CHAPTER XIII

Heat Rising

'I should suppose the Commencement of Hostilities (If they ever do begin) cannot be far distant — But Nobody can guess Lord Wellington's intentions, & I daresay Nobody will know he is going till he is actually gone.'

Lady Caroline Capel to the Dowager Countess of Uxbridge

The pace of life in Brussels took on an even greater urgency now the Duke of Wellington and his military staff had returned. The Capels received fewer calls from their favourite officers, but when General Barnes, Lord Hay or the Prince of Orange did make it to tea, they came with gifts of gossip and titbits of information that more than made up for their absences.

On their walks around town it was now commonplace to see officers riding to deliver messages, run errands or attend to important business. They spoke to their companions in low voices, with a sense of pride and certainty in their position in the midst of all this hustle and bustle, having been drilled for years in the parts they must play when war was coming.

Maria, on the other hand, was quite at sea. As an unmarried woman with few family members in the military, she felt lost in this new world of war and was growing increasingly anxious as to the part she was to play in it all. Yet, it was undoubtedly thrilling to be living in the heart of Brussels, at the centre of it all, and she was confident there was no immediate danger to their staying in the city.

It was understood by those in the know, and Maria had it on good authority from Lord William Pitt Lennox, that Napoleon was planning to stay in Paris and build up his strength, giving the British and Allied forces in Brussels time to do the same. Maria had heard that Wellington had several spies deep in Napoleon's inner circle, who sent out information when they could.

Yes, they would be safe in Brussels, surrounded by allied armies from across Europe. The Prince of Orange had thankfully relinquished his control of the combined forces, leaving the Duke of Wellington in sole charge of orchestrating armies across five nations. Then there were the Hanoverian troops, linked to the British through King George III, and troops had also been sent over from Austria and Hungary.

The Prussians were to play a crucial part in the proceedings. They were led by General Blücher, who the Capels had met and been so entranced by all those months before in Dover. The Duke of Brunswick was also in town already, having attended the same dinner party as Capel, at Wellington's headquarters. Like Blücher, Brunswick was besieged by well-wishers and admirers wherever he went.

Even though an invading army was heading their way, parties and dinner dances continued apace; indeed, barely a week went by without a grand ball. Lady Caroline insisted the girls attended every one they could. They became so tired they started using face powder to hide the dark circles under their eyes. Maria thought at first that their mother wanted them to find suitable matches before the officers went to war, but then realised that Lady Caroline wished only to keep them busy as her own disquiet about the situation grew.

It had been a year since their arrival in Brussels, and as the weather brightened, each day seemed a little warmer than the last. They turned from winter's heavy satins, sarsenet and wools to cooler taffetas and lighter linens. Georgy took out the fan the Prince of Orange had given her the previous year, holding it up to the spring light in the drawing room. The prince had been so busy recently that they had barely seen him, and Georgy looked a little plaintive as she turned the fan over in her hands.

When Maria went and sat by her, Georgy brightened.

'Don't worry about me, Muzzy,' she said. 'I don't pine for the prince in the way Harriet does for Trip. I enjoy his company, but I know nothing can come of it in the end.'

'It seems none of us are destined for a smooth run to the altar.'

'Oh, there was never a chance of that for the prince and me. So far, you are the only one to have got anywhere near marriage!'

'Yes, and I ran for the hills!'

They both laughed. Everything that had happened to them

so far had been swept away by the news of Napoleon's escape. All that mattered now was to enjoy these heady days and nights as they passed in a blur, snatching moments of reflection in the peaceful moments before they fell asleep. With war on the horizon anything seemed possible, even probable, and what had passed was already a distant memory. The thought of being Lady Barnes seemed more improbable than Napoleon walking into their sitting room at that moment and joining in their conversation!

Just then Harriet entered, tears streaming down her cheeks. Through gasping breaths she told them she had seen Baron Trip out on the street when she had been running errands with Julia and a few of their younger siblings. Algernon was hugging the folds of her skirt, trying to comfort her.

'What did he say? What did he do?' asked Maria.

Baron Trip had stood there, stared at her and then walked away. Harriet was quite inconsolable. She lay her head on Maria's lap, her face in her hands, and gave herself over to sobs that shook her whole body. Looking down at her eldest sister, Maria felt her heart harden even more against men like Baron Trip.

Would it have been so difficult for him to speak cordially to her sister, or even just to have nodded a polite greeting? How lucky Maria had been to keep her friendship with General Barnes after the disastrous proposal so many months before. He had been the ultimate gentleman, she now realised. Baron Trip was a scoundrel, and more than ever she was glad that her father had called him out and fired a shot at him.

After coaxing Harriet upstairs, they gave her a few drops of laudanum to quiet her. Their father was likely to be home soon, and they didn't want him to see Harriet in such a state or he would no doubt force them to reveal what had shaken her so badly. Harriet took the drops greedily, knowing they would afford her a few hours of peace. She crawled into bed fully clothed and pulled the covers up to her chin, despite the heat of the day.

'Sleep now, my love. When you wake, you will be stronger,' Maria said, although this was more of a wish than a certainty.

On the other side of the house, Lady Caroline was writing another long letter to her mother, beginning with the words:

You will be interested to hear that the Duke of Wellington has hardly improved the morality of our society, as he has given many parties and makes a point of asking all the ladies of loose character...

The Duke's actions were quite against the strictures of the 'Ladies of the Park', despite Lady Charlotte Greville being, in some eyes, of 'loose character'.

Another such individual whom Lady Caroline was also now seeing rather more of was the admittedly ravishing Lady Frances Wedderburn-Webster, who it was said had once fought off the advances of Lord Byron. The fact that she was married and currently heavily pregnant didn't seem to have put off the Duke of Wellington.

Only that week Lady Caroline had heard a scandalous rumour that the duke and Lady Frances had been seen disappearing into some bushes in one of the parks. Adding insult to injury, Lady Frances' mother had turned up in a carriage, having got wind of what the duke and her daughter were up to. She searched the park for them but luckily didn't disturb the lovers.

Lady Charlotte Greville was still also vying for the duke's affections, but now had to share him with Lady Frances. Even though Lady Caroline counted Lady Charlotte as one of her closest allies and friends in Brussels, they rarely discussed the nature of her relationship with the duke.

A small part of Lady Caroline was jealous of the attention and special place in the social hierarchy afforded to women such as Lady Charlotte. In fairness, her friend was very discreet about her dalliance with the duke, which was particularly impressive considering how many stories of the his liaisons peppered the spring days of that year.

Rumours spread from house to house like an absurd game of Chinese whispers, until it was hard to separate fact, fabrication and pure fantasy. Such was the power of these rumours they now had their own name, a 'Bruxelles story'.

One such story that reached Lady Caroline's ear gave her great cause for disquiet. She had been visiting the Duchess of Richmond with Lady Charlotte, who had informed her that Lord Waterpark had left the Literary Club one evening with debt to the tune of £15,000. A truly shocking sum, they'd all agreed, before moving on to another subject.

At the time, Lady Caroline fought to hide how this

information alarmed her. The Literary Club was a gambling establishment! How easily Lady Caroline had believed Capel when he'd told her it was a dining establishment with a fine library. She'd been so eager to accept that her husband had seen the errors of his ways.

It wasn't customary for couples to share a bedroom every night, so Lady Caroline didn't always know what time her husband took to his bed. He usually spent a few nights each week with her, and on other nights he kept to his own rooms. When he shared her bed, he came to her at a regular time and seemed content and happy. Now Lady Caroline wondered what he had been doing on the nights he slept next door. Was he frequenting the Literary Club, and letting his gambling habit take hold once again?

Lady Caroline tried to bring her focus back to the letter she was writing to her mother, for she needed to phrase the next part with care. If Capel had lost more money, if his gambling demons had not been beaten, then the family was in danger not only from Napoleon's forces but from a threat inside their own home.

Brussels had been a blessed relief from the money troubles that had plagued them in London. Everything was so cheap, and the girls had been delighted with the clothes and trinkets they could buy. The rent on their house was reasonable, at only £100 per annum. With another child on the way, every penny counted. Now it seemed that Capel was once more throwing their successes away to satisfy his lust for cards.

Lady Caroline felt a kick from the baby and paused, her dip pen raised a few inches from the notepaper. She rubbed her stomach. Desperation swelled in her, and her hand shook slightly over the page. She didn't want to make a scene with Capel, despite her frustration and anger at his many inadequacies.

Their relationship had been put under so much strain by his creditors in London, and they'd enjoyed such a renaissance since living in Brussels. The baby growing inside her was a result of that, and she didn't want to jeopardise the progress they'd made and the happy family home they had established in the city.

Capel the gambling addict, who came home sweating and weeping from a night of near ruin, run to ground by men who claimed to be his friends, was not the man with whom she had fallen in love. He wasn't the husband who had held her at night as she'd wept about Maria's refusal to marry General Barnes, or Harriet's depression. Lady Caroline didn't have the energy to continually reprimand Capel for his betrayal of their family. She wouldn't sacrifice their happy family home for that.

Stretching her aching back, she looked out of the window and across the ramparts. The evening was still and peaceful. She would ask for help from the one person she could always rely on: her mother. Going back to the letter, she refreshed the ink on her nib and poured out her needs as best she could.

Mother, I'm afraid we may be in need once again. I can't be sure Capel has returned to the Green Table, but I have my suspicions. Would you consider sending me funds in case they are needed? I would keep them secret from Capel, I promise.

When she had finished, she sealed the letter with wax and went downstairs. Her mother had helped them many times before, but Lady Caroline worried that this might be one time too many. She was also saddened that she had, for the first time, written without the knowledge or consent of her husband.

With war about to break out again she had no idea how long it would take her letter to reach Lady Uxbridge. She passed the letter to Julia with firm instructions to keep its existence a secret, and joined Georgy and Maria in the drawing room. They explained they had taken Harriet up to bed, and why.

'I don't know what to suggest for that poor girl,' Lady Caroline sighed.

'There's nothing we can do, Mama, except love her and pray one day she is healed.'

Lady Caroline nodded, looking pensive.

'I entreat you girls,' she warned her daughters, 'to heed my words. Many women throw their lives away on men who don't deserve their trust. Guard your hearts jealously, and even when you're married, don't trust your husband completely, or indeed any member of your family except the women. When times get hard, they're the only people you can fully rely on.'

Her sternness shocked Maria and Georgy. They both looked solemn and nodded their agreement to these sad, wise words.

⚬⚬⚬

Over the following weeks, Maria found it easy to take her mother's words to heart. One only had to glance at Harriet to be reminded of what happened when you let your heart rule your head. Yet her initial attraction to Lord Hay had hardly diminished since their first meeting and she blushed when thinking about their stolen kiss at the Prince Regent's birthday ball, all those months before.

Lord Hay had been absent on military matters for some time and Maria missed him acutely. When she heard that he was back in Brussels she expected to receive a call from him, or a letter, but neither were forthcoming. As the days passed and she still didn't hear anything she began to worry.

Finally, she saw him, at a ball held to the east of the city. He looked as smart and confident as ever. Her heart began to beat wildly. She gave Georgy a look and her sister caught Maria's meaning immediately. They made their way over to the area of the room where Lord Hay stood speaking to the Duke of Brunswick.

It wasn't long before it was impossible for Lord Hay to ignore their presence and he came over to speak to them. The duke asked Georgy to dance. She seemed reluctant to accept, which Maria found surprising as her sister knew how desperate she was to speak to Lord Hay. Georgy was led away, but looked back over her shoulder, seemingly unhappy about leaving Maria and Lord Hay being alone together.

They both spoke at the same time.

'Hello, how nice to see you.'

'Good evening, Miss Capel.'

They both smiled. Maria was surprised he was addressing her so formally.

'Oh dear,' she said. 'How are you, it's been some time since we have seen you?'

'Yes, it has been a busy time and I've been out of the city training the men. It feels like we are finally preparing for battle.'

'Well, we've missed your visits. Louisa is quite bereft.'

'Ah, I shall have to make it up to her,' he said, but he seemed distracted and not his usual flirtatious self. He wasn't meeting her eye for more than a few seconds.

'Is everything all right? If I may say, you don't seem your usual jovial self.'

'Yes, everything is well, I just rather thought you might have...well...' But Lord Hay didn't finish his reply. He was looking to his left and saw that General Barnes was advancing towards them. 'Never mind, clearly I was in the wrong. Let's not mention it again.'

'Whatever are you talking about, Lord Hay?' said Maria, but General Barnes was upon them before she could push him for an answer.

Hay turned to Barnes and greeted him heartily, leaving Maria utterly confused. *What was Lord Hay talking about?* She was bewildered.

The rest of the evening passed in the usual blur of dancing, drinks and dinner. Maria tried to speak to Lord Hay again but gave up when it became clear he was avoiding her. She didn't want him to see her desperation, for desperate was how she felt.

On the way home she recounted to Georgy what Lord Hay had said. 'Can you think of any reason for his behaving in such a way?' she asked. Georgy said she could not, but Maria noticed she too didn't quite meet her eye.

Summer didn't wait for the family to ready itself, but burst upon them one day. They happily abandoned their pelisses and shawls and replaced them with fine linens and parasols. As they packed away their spring clothes one afternoon, Maria and Georgy were reminded of the robbery the previous summer. This year, they would be keeping their windows firmly secured against intruders.

In the first week of June, they tried to acclimatise to the warm weather, wearing thin muslin dresses and cooling themselves with fans. They rarely ventured outside during the hottest hours of the day, but in the late afternoon they continued to make calls to friends, or even better, receive visits themselves.

One day, Lord March and Lord William Pitt Lennox called. Maria was sitting with Georgy, Louisa and Horatia. Harriet was upstairs with another headache. Their mother was also present, looking a little careworn but still beautiful, in a pale yellow dress that had been let out several times to accommodate her growing stomach. Adolphus and Amelia were playing at her feet.

Adolphus, still too small to know much about what was going on around him, was happy to amuse himself with a coloured rattle, but Amelia, who had just reached her third birthday, was in raptures at the visit from Lord March, and sat gazing at him with her mouth slightly open. Lord March, clearly charmed by the attention, took Amelia up on his knee and she sat there happily as he told them about a ball that his mother, the Duchess of Richmond, was planning. It sounded like a grand affair.

'Do you think it's right to have a ball at the moment, Lord March? Could the army not soon be in disarray if a move from Brussels becomes necessary?' Lady Caroline enquired.

'I wouldn't worry, for Mama asked the Duke of Wellington directly, and he said it was perfectly safe to hold a ball. He was quite certain it would be undisturbed. Indeed, Lord Wellington is to throw one himself the following week, to celebrate the anniversary of the Battle of Vitoria.'

'Well, in that case, I wish your mother the very best with her preparations.'

What Lady Caroline really wanted to know was whether she and her daughters were on the guest list, but she was too polite to ask. Luckily Lord March had perfect manners and understood the situation exactly. He shifted Amelia to one knee and produced a stack of cards from the satchel he had brought with him.

'My mother wanted me to pass on your invitations and very much hopes you can attend.'

There was one for each of them. The beautiful cream card was so thick it stood up on its own. In the top left-hand corner their names were handwritten in a most elegant script.

'How lovely! Your mother always does these things so tastefully. Of course we would love to come.'

'It looks set to be a wonderful evening, and made even more so with the presence of you and your daughters,' said Lord March cordially.

'It should be a decent evening, Mama is borrowing the band from the army and the plate from the British Embassy,' said Lord William modestly.

Lady Caroline nodded. 'Yes, it's convenient to have friends in the army to smooth such things over. Our dear General Barnes—'

Before she could finish, Maria interjected, not wishing to hear her mother talking about General Barnes yet again, something that had become increasingly common of late.

'I should think your house well situated for a ball. How many are you inviting?'

It was Lord William Pitt Lennox who answered. 'Oh, about two hundred, Mama says. Not all military types, but a good spread. That should liven things up somewhat.'

'Won't most of the men be in uniform?' asked Georgy.

'Yes, I should think a large proportion. Rather inescapable here, eh?'

Maria thought how true that was. She was seriously considering whether she could ever be induced to marry someone serving in the army. The life seemed so inconstant, so full of fear and anxiety. To think your husband might be called away at any moment to live for many years in a foreign country, with little or no leave to visit his family. Surely that couldn't be conducive to a happy marriage?

'I should think that those not in uniform must feel rather inadequate next to those in it,' continued Georgy. 'After all, there is nothing more appealing than a man in uniform.'

'Georgy, honestly!' said Lady Caroline.

But Lord March and Lord William laughed.

'We agree,' said Lord William, 'hence our choice of career! The ladies respond very well, I can assure you.'

Seeing the look on her mother's face, Maria enquired

after Lord William's recent riding accident. He had taken a bad fall during an amateur horse race and lain unconscious for several hours, much to the horror of his family and the vexation of his commanding officer. Lord William's injuries meant his name had been put on the sick list, so he was unable to participate in active service.

'A damned nuisance, to be sure, but hopefully I shall be back at it in time to dance with Boney's men.'

General Barnes was introduced just as the two Lennox men were making to leave. When the flurry of greetings and farewells had subsided, General Barnes turned to Lady Caroline.

'I should like to take some air. Lady Caroline, would you care to join me?'

Maria felt rather vexed by General Barnes's request. Had he not just received a healthy dose of clean air on his journey over? But Lady Caroline looked delighted at the suggestion and rose from her seat to join him.

'Capital,' said the general. He turned to the girls. 'Ladies, I shall see you anon.' He and Lady Caroline exited the room, arm in arm.

'What utter cheek not to invite us as well!' Maria exclaimed, turning to Georgy. 'Do you not think so?'

Georgy was laughing. 'Honestly, Maria, you can't reject General Barnes and then care that he should wish to see Mama alone.'

'Can I not? It doesn't seem proper to me.'

'They're friends, that's all,' Georgy replied airily.

'Well, I don't care for it one bit, and I'm sure Papa wouldn't, either.'

Georgy settled back to her reading, leaving Maria feeling quite out of sorts for the rest of the afternoon.

CHAPTER XIV

Secrets

'The Duchess of Richmond gave a sort of Farewell Ball on the 15th — at which all the Military in and about Bruxelles were present...'

Lady Caroline Capel to the Dowager Countess of Uxbridge

There was a tension in the air that seemed to grow with each dawn. It was as though a force of nature was winding around them, around Brussels itself, spiralling ever tighter. Behind this force was the knowledge that war with Napoleon was now inevitable and would be upon them in a matter of weeks. What exact form the storm would take, no one knew. Wellington was certainly playing his cards close to his chest.

Something about the Duchess of Richmond's ball made it seem special from the off, and yet it started like all the others. By the early evening of the 15 June, Maria and her elder sisters were washed and in the upstairs bedrooms, discussing how they would like their hair styled. Harriet had agreed to join them that evening, which made Maria and Georgy very happy.

They sipped tea and chatted; it was a peaceful time, yet there was a flutter of excitement in the air. The little ones at their feet wanted to hear more about the men they knew – who wore what uniform and who they most wanted to dance with. The girls slipped their feet into satin shoes and were helped into simple yet luxurious pale muslin gowns by Julia, who was looking more frantic by the hour as the demands on her time grew increasingly unreasonable. She would no doubt be glad to see the back of them so she could relax in the kitchen with the cook and enjoy her evening off.

Maria was applying some powder in the little bathroom adjoining the room she shared with Georgy. She was in a pensive mood. She felt more and more that Georgy was keeping something from her, but she couldn't put her finger on what it might be.

Her sister was usually an open book but had recently become vague and non-committal, and most strangely of all she never seemed to want to discuss Lord Hay with her. Whatever could be going on? Maria had begun to think perhaps Georgy had set her own sights on him, but when she was clearly still besotted with the prince this didn't make sense either.

Maria went back into the bedroom and sat on the bed. She watched Georgy having her hair fixed by Julia, who was by now an expert in the pretty curled styles the girls always requested. Harriet had gone to finish dressing in her own room.

Maria's eyes fell on the armoire in the corner of the room, under which the ribbon box was hidden. How long it had been since she'd looked inside. She wondered whether Georgy might have concealed anything that might offer a clue to her secrecy and decided to look.

She waited until Julia had finished with Georgy and left to attend to Harriet, then went over to the wardrobe to retrieve the box.

'What are you doing, Muz?' said Georgy.

Something in Georgy's tone made Maria look over. She saw that her sister's face looked panicked at the sight of her holding the ribbon box.

'Oh, Muz, please don't,' Georgy begged, putting down the pot of cream she had been using. 'I... Well, isn't the box a bit childish now, anyhow?'

Maria felt stung. She didn't think the ribbon box childish at all.

'Why do you say so?' she said. 'Have you put something in there that you don't want me to see?'

'No! I mean... Well, yes, I suppose so.' There was a pause that Maria didn't try and fill. Eventually, Georgy continued, 'Only in that I meant to tell you about something but I haven't yet found the right moment.'

Finally, Maria was getting to the crux of what was perturbing her sister.

'And there's something to do with that in the box?'

'Yes.' Georgy looked abashed.

'Well, you will have to show me what it is.'

'Yes, I suppose I must. I concealed it under the lid.' Georgy was flushed. She turned away from the looking glass and came over to the bed.

Maria placed the box on the covers, careful not to get dust from it on her pristine evening gown. She lifted the lid and lowered it carefully. On the underside of the lid the paper was loose and under it was hidden a letter. She tried to look to see who it was addressed to, but Georgy snatched it out of her hands.

'Georgy! What is this all about? Who is that letter from?' Maria demanded.

Georgy swallowed; she clutched the letter and avoided Maria's eyes. Eventually, she took a deep breath, and when she spoke, her voice trembled.

'I'm sorry, Muz. It's not a story of which I'm proud. You see, I showed the ribbon box to the Prince of Orange one evening when he was here for dinner with some other officer friends.' Maria was shocked but didn't interrupt. 'It was late and everyone was wandering around the house so we could be quite free with each other without Mama getting suspicious.' Georgy was by now scarlet. 'I, well, he wanted to see my bedroom so I brought him up here. We got to talking about secrets and I wanted to share with him something that was special to me, so I told him about the ribbon box, and he asked to see it.'

Maria couldn't believe what she was hearing. To have a man in your bedroom was enough to ruin a woman's good name forever. But Georgy knew this and didn't need Maria to remind her. It was clear from the look on her sister's face that she realised she'd gone too far with the prince, so Maria tried to make light of it.

'Goodness!' She hoped she sounded more relaxed than she felt, for she was desperate to see what the letter said. 'Well, you'd better hope Mama never finds out; I doubt she'd ever let you out of her sight again. You would be the old maiden aunt to all our children, and serve you right!'

Georgy was hanging her head. 'I know it's shameful.'

'Oh, my love, shame is a harsh word. It was risky, yes. I

must say I'm surprised you showed him the box. It's special to *us*, Georgy, and now you've shown it to the prince it's rather spoilt, don't you think?'

'I'm sorry, Muz, I really am. It was just so thrilling to have him here, to have him in our bedroom.'

'What else happened? Come, now, you can have no more secrets from me.'

'Nothing beyond a kiss or two. It felt so special. We started to talk about what secrets we would put in the box and wrote down how we felt about each other.' She was looking at the box.

'You wrote notes, and put them in the box?'

'Yes.' Georgy was blushing furiously. 'They're sealed, you see, so we could only guess at what the other had written.'

Maria had to admit the idea was very romantic.

'I see, but the letter you're holding isn't one of those. That has an addressee.' Maria was eying the letter, but she couldn't see who it was addressed to. 'Georgy, who is that letter from? I'm guessing it was originally intended for me?'

Georgy was silent, but her eyes reached Maria's and pleaded for her to prise the secret out of her.

'I promised not to tell.'

'Promised who, exactly?'

Still nothing.

'Georgy, we have no secrets. We're sisters. If the letter refers to me or is for me, then hand it over this instant.' Maria tried to sound as fierce as she could.

Georgy suddenly relented.

'Dearest Muz, please don't be angry with me. I did it to

protect you from a man I believed to have only ill intentions towards you.'

'Who are you talking about? Give me the letter, Georgy.'

Finally, Georgy handed it over. The letter was indeed addressed to Maria, and in a hand she didn't recognise. The outside was worn, the corners dog-eared. It had probably been handled by several people before it came to be in the ribbon box. She broke the seal and opened out the page.

It was short, and unsigned.

Dearest Miss Muzzy,
If you feel in your heart the same
as I do about you, meet me at the
furthest west exit to the city, at
midnight this day next week, and let
us be together forever.

Maria stared at the letter, her heart pounding. She read it twice, not immediately sure of its meaning. She looked up at her sister.

'What can this mean? Who wrote this note?' she spluttered.

At first Georgy didn't respond, but then spoke in a very small voice which nonetheless seemed to echo around the room.

'You must know, Muz, the author of that letter is Lord Hay.'

Maria blinked, and felt her mouth fall softly open. She

didn't speak but looked down at the letter again.

'But – but when did he write it?' Maria finally stammered. 'Does he really mean…?'

Georgy sighed. She seemed much calmer now the secret was out, and she could see that Maria wasn't angry with her.

'I'm so sorry that I didn't give you the letter at the time it was passed to me. When I had the prince up here, he confessed that Lord Hay had given this letter to him to give to you after the Prince Regent's birthday ball.'

'So long ago! He must have thought I'd read it and not wished to go, or that he had offended me. When we spoke together last, he seemed so awkward and now it makes sense.'

'Indeed. It has pained me to keep this from you; I could see you were confused by his behaviour, but I wanted to protect you. Lord Hay wanted to elope with you, but the prince told me he didn't believe his motives were honourable. He might have gone through with the marriage, or he might not. He would have either brought you into a marriage without money and without the approval of your family or ruined your reputation forever.'

'Goodness!' was all that Maria could manage in response.

'I believe that's why the prince spoke to me of secrets, because he wanted to entrust me with this one, to protect you from Lord Hay.'

'He truly believed Lord Hay wasn't in love with me?'

Georgy looked uncomfortable. 'He said that while he was sure Lord Hay had great affection for you, he wasn't convinced that in such a short space of time his mind could have been made up to a lasting commitment.'

'It was rash of him, to be sure. The Prince of Orange was wise to say as much.'

Holding the letter limply in her hand, Maria felt a strange sense of relief that took her almost as much by surprise as finding out about the letter.

Lord Hay had wanted her. In fact, he had wanted her so much he'd been willing, if even for a short time, to risk everything to be with her. Eloping would have meant losing his position in the army as well as the favour of both their families, who no doubt would have refused the match. Running away together was no doubt a romantic notion, but the reality would have quickly soured their happiness. And yet he had wanted her that badly, if only for a brief time.

Georgy grasped Maria's hands. 'Dearest, please promise not to be angry with me, for I meant only to protect you.'

Maria met Georgy's eyes and smiled. 'I'm not angry with you, Georgy, just shocked at Lord Hay's actions. I was confused by his behaviour after the ball and believed he'd lost interest in me. Then General Barnes...' She tailed off, unsure of how to continue.

'Yes, the prince felt that the surprise proposal from the general provided him with the perfect means to intervene. He told Lord Hay that he would give you the letter when he felt the time was right, and report to him when he'd done so. When the prince heard what happened with General Barnes, he thought the situation could be used to show you were undecided, and therefore wouldn't run away with him. Of course, the real reason you didn't go to meet him was because—'

'Because I never knew about the letter.'

'Yes.'

'So for all these months, he has thought me sworn off him?'

'Yes, but hasn't he shown how inconstant he is? If he'd really loved you, he would have persevered, don't you think?'

It wasn't what Maria wanted to hear, but she knew Georgy was right.

'I doubt he ever truly loved me, not in a lasting or pure way. He acted out of lust to see if I would run away with him. It was all a game to him, a frivolous amusement.'

Georgy's response was warm. 'Yes, and it wouldn't have been at all amusing had you gone with him and then he didn't deign to marry you.'

Maria thought of what would have happened had she gone to meet him. She imagined the carriage jolting through the darkness, could almost sense being seated next to Lord Hay, quite alone and riding towards a new future. What an adventure that would have been! She imagined what might have taken place in the inn they would have stopped at. Such thoughts made her blush, distracting her from Georgy's next words.

'I'm so pleased you see my reasoning, Muz. I've so hated keeping this secret from you. At first, I wanted to burn the letter, but then I thought otherwise. I thought you might want one day to see proof of what Lord Hay was willing to ask of you.'

With an effort, Maria pulled herself back to the bedroom and concentrated on what Georgy was saying.

She replied, 'You were right, Georgy, and I am glad to know.'

Maria smiled at her sister to show there were truly no hard feelings between them and squeezed her hand. What Georgy had done couldn't have been easy, but she'd acted in Maria's best interests and Maria was quite sure she would have done the same for her sister had the roles been reversed.

Georgy put the letter in the box and went to close it, but Maria stopped her. Digging around inside, she found the exquisite ribbon with interwoven Brussels lace, the ribbon given to her by Lord Hay when they first met and that she'd worn on the night of Lady Greville's ball. Georgy looked worried; she recognised the ribbon and what it symbolised for Maria.

Maria held it out, admiring the skill of the handiwork. She smiled to herself; whatever had happened this was still a beautiful piece of ribbon that deserved to be worn. She would ask Julia to run it through her hair, flat across her crown and tucked behind her ears, as she had worn it all those months ago. Whatever happened that evening, she was pleased to wear it again.

Harriet, Georgy and Maria gathered outside the house, waiting for the carriage to take them across town. Maria felt a little sad that their mother had decided not to accompany them. She was nearing the time of her confinement and was now so broad she couldn't walk much further than the nearest sofa before collapsing in exhaustion.

'Have a wonderful time, my beauties, may you be the belles of the ball,' Lady Caroline had said. She was sitting up in bed, propped up on a pile of cushions. 'Have all sorts of adventures for me.'

Maria kissed her and grinned. They left the room in a flurry of muslin, ribbon and scent borrowed from their mother's dressing table.

The carriage was ready for them. Harriet got in first and positioned herself in the best seat, facing the horses, as was the custom for the eldest daughter.

'You look absolutely beautiful,' Capel said, making her smile, as he turned to help Georgy up and then Maria. Once Capel had seated himself next to Harriet, he knocked on the side of the carriage and it moved off.

Maria couldn't sit still. She fussed first with her dress and then her hair, until Georgy stopped her.

'You'll unsteady the ribbon!' she whispered.

Maria was more eager than ever to reach the ball. She wanted to see Lord Hay and for him to see that she had the lace ribbon in her hair again. The knowledge that he'd wanted to run away with her had shocked and pleased her in equal measure. He must have thought her appalled by his proposal. Now his behaviour since made sense.

How confused the situation had become! Now she was off to the event of the season with a chance to put things right. She was going to tell Lord Hay what had happened and finally close this chapter of her life forever.

Their carriage turned down on to the unpaved street where the Richmonds lived, the carriage bumping and jolting as it went.

'Only a family like the Richmonds could get away with living in this part of town,' Capel commented in an absent sort of way, 'but then I suppose their financial situation fits the district.'

Rather like ours, don't you think? thought Maria, but instead she said, 'The Duke of Wellington rather rudely calls it the Wash House, but he goes there often. He and the elder girls are very close.'

'Indeed, I should think so! They're as accomplished as all of you, and you all deserve to make the most of it before the war starts.' Capel leant forward to emphasise his next words. He was clearly in a pensive mood. 'Girls, everything is soon to change. Make the most of this evening. I want you to know, I am very proud of the beautiful young ladies you have become.'

Instinctively they all embraced, but before they could respond with more than mumbled words of thanks and love, the carriage driver called out and drew the horses to a halt. They had arrived at the ball.

CHAPTER XV

When the Music Stops

'This has indeed come upon us like a Thief in the Night — I am afraid our Great Hero must have been deceived for he has certainly been taken by surprise...'

Lady Caroline Capel to the Dowager Countess of Uxbridge

The Duke of Richmond's house was large but not particularly attractive. It had been built by a coachbuilder and the craftsman's old studio had been converted into a ballroom. It was about ten o'clock by the time the Capels arrived, and the house was lit by torchères standing sentinel at the ballroom's entrance. From the road, Maria could hear the hum of activity inside and see silhouettes through the windows.

They wove their way through the usual crowd of people and were greeted at the door by the elder Lennox girls, the Ladies Mary, Sarah and Georgiana. Their mother and father were with them. The Lennox sisters looked delightful in dresses that had clearly been made for the occasion, and their faces were shining with excitement. Maria couldn't help but feel a pang of jealousy that it was *their* mother throwing that evening's ball and not her own. If only they had a house big enough for an event such as this!

'Welcome, you all look wonderful!' Lady Mary said. 'There are many people here already and the dancing is soon to start.'

Lady Georgiana said to Maria as she passed, 'Lord Hay is inside, he and General Barnes have been avoiding each other again.' They grinned at each other, Maria somewhat sheepishly.

The ballroom was large, with high ceilings, the walls decorated with rose trellis wallpaper and lit by grand candelabra. There was even a mezzanine level for supper. Maria couldn't think of a more suitable place to hold such a grand ball and was mightily impressed, especially considering that the room had originally been designed to house coaches.

Maria decided she would like a drink before she spoke to Lord Hay. Now she was inside the ballroom she was less certain about what she wanted to say to him. She had rehearsed a few phrases in her head during the carriage ride but now they all seemed rather childish. She and Harriet took some punch, as Georgy was immediately whisked away to dance by the Prince of Orange. Harriet looked as worried as Maria felt. There could be only one subject on which she was ruminating.

'Is he here, Harriet?' Maria asked.

Harriet was biting her lip. She shook her head slowly.

'I'm not sure, there's such a crowd it's hard to see. If he is, I'm hoping I can avoid him.'

'It's hard to distinguish who is who when so many are in uniform. Perhaps you shall be able to miss him. I do hope so.'

'I too, although I do want to part on good terms, as war is so close.'

Maria didn't think it would be wise for them to meet but

decided Harriet could do without her opinion. Harriet let her heart rule her head these days, and Maria didn't want to lecture her, especially when her own conduct had been some way from innocent. She could see Harriet's gaze flickering around the room, searching each face in uniform, but then realised that she was doing the same in the hope of spotting Lord Hay.

The room was a haze of crimson uniforms. In the candlelight, medals stood proud on their owners' lapels and diamonds glittered on the necks and tiaras of the ladies. Above the music there was a happy chatter. Scent, that had been carefully applied during each lady's toilette, intermingled with cigar and candle smoke, creating a heady aroma.

People were enjoying themselves with a greater intensity than Maria had seen before. The evening seemed to hold real significance, not just for her but for every person there. Everyone seemed determined to make the most of this chance to be together before war separated them all again.

Finally, she spotted Lord Hay through the crowd, and taking a deep breath she nudged and twisted her way towards him. Her head started to thud and she felt uncommonly hot. She gulped down the last of her punch as she manoeuvred herself around pockets of friends and acquaintances wanting to engage her in conversation.

She thought Lord Hay must have seen her, but he was now forging a route into the next room. Perhaps he was avoiding her again. But Maria felt a steely determination to make this meeting happen, and she was going to do everything in her power to ensure it did.

She knew the Wash House well enough to know she could duck through a narrow passage to the left of the ballroom and cut Lord Hay off. After a moment's hesitation she disappeared down the corridor, surprising one or two servants along the way. Exiting near the front door, she finally came face to face with Lord Hay.

'Miss Maria, how do you do?' Although formal, Lord Hay didn't seem unfriendly, nor did he betray any notion that he'd been seeking to avoid her.

'Lord Hay, I'm glad to see you this evening. There's something I wish to speak about.'

Lord Hay broke into a rueful grin. 'Yes, isn't it exciting! I am beside myself to get started.'

'Get started?'

'With the war that is to come, of course.'

Maria felt her brows rise. 'Indeed?'

'Quite; it's such an opportunity to distinguish oneself.'

This was far from how Maria had envisioned the conversation beginning. There was a pause in which her mouth stayed open and no words came out, but it wasn't long however until she found her voice again.

'Indeed, there can be no doubt that you will, but surely you don't *wish* war upon us?'

There was another pause, more awkward than the last, as the look of childish excitement on Lord Hay's face slipped slightly.

'Why ever would I not?'

Maria could think of so many reasons, not least the death and destruction that would undoubtedly result from the coming conflict. That fate would be met by many of the men under Lord Hay's command and would be increasingly likely if Lord Hay's actions were as rash as his words intimated. His brazen disregard for the fate of his men disquieted her. Did he really not care for them at all? And what of his own life; did it mean so little to him that he would throw himself foolishly into the path of the enemy?

Yet now was not the moment to say all this. Maria wanted answers of a more personal nature, and this might be her only chance to get them. She could sense that Lord Hay, seeing the disapproval on her face, was about to defend himself.

'That isn't what I wanted to speak to you about,' she said quickly. 'You see, I now know about the letter. About the letter that you gave to the prince, to be given to me.'

In the end the words came out in a jumble, and she wasn't sure if what she said made sense, but at least it was done. She took a deep breath.

'The letter?' Lord Hay looked baffled, but slowly there dawned a look of comprehension on his face. 'Oh, *that* letter.'

To her surprise and shock, he laughed, throwing back his head theatrically. This wasn't the response Maria had been expecting, and she wasn't impressed. Her eyes narrowed.

'I didn't see the letter until this evening, as my sister felt it best to keep it from me,' she said.

Lord Hay's moment of mirth was over as quickly as it had come once he saw that Maria wasn't finding the subject as amusing as he was. Now he looked uncomfortable. Grinning sheepishly, he raised his hands as if the gesture would provide sufficient explanation.

'Well?' Maria demanded, feeling stronger by the minute. 'What do you have to say on the matter?'

There was another pause. 'Maria, you see the thing about that letter is... The thing is...' He was now looking excessively embarrassed. 'Well, anyway, it was so long ago, and you didn't reply, so what harm has been done?'

In many ways he was right, but that didn't stop Maria wanting to know more. The crowd thronged around them, getting ready for the next dance. They moved aside to let them pass. This was Maria's chance, and plucking up her courage she asked, 'Would you have gone through with it, Lord Hay? Did you truly want to run away with me?'

Lord Hay looked distinctly ruffled, his eyes darting. 'I can't answer you that, I'm afraid. It seems like a lifetime ago.'

'I wonder if you really loved me, then.'

Maria had said the words before she'd properly thought them through. It seemed rash to talk of love when whatever had between them was so clearly drawing to a close, but she had to get a measure of truth from him.

'I wonder, too.'

He had the grace to look directly at her and Maria saw the truth of the words in his eyes.

'So much has changed since that time.' She said it from the heart.

Lord Hay nodded in agreement and suddenly seemed shy and very young. 'It has, and looking back, it was perhaps rash on my part, and indeed I didn't treat you with the respect you deserve.'

Maria managed a small smile. She was finally seeing the real Lord Hay, and found she was not angry with him. If anything, she pitied his obsession with pleasure and fun at the expense of other people's lives and passions. In the end, she had been just another one of his games. When he had laughed at Maria bringing up the letter, she realised he really was still a child and not ready for matters of love, commitment or promises that shouldn't be broken.

She wondered if she would have acted as rashly as Lord Hay had she known about the letter at the time it was sent. She might have been so swept away by the idea of him loving her, and by the thrill of someone wanting to marry her. She might have gone to meet him. Despite her feelings for him, she knew that wouldn't have been enough to carry them through a life together. She felt sad but also stronger and wiser for knowing the truth.

Maria looked round the room. Really, they were only two parts in a much bigger, more important picture. She could almost taste the anticipation in the air, the anxiety, even excitement. In comparison, their ill-fated adventure seemed insignificant and trivial. Maria stood a little taller and made every effort to rise above the awkwardness hanging between them.

'Really, there's no harm done, Lord Hay. It was a flattering if unrealistic proposal.'

Lord Hay smiled back, looking relieved to have escaped their encounter unscathed. He had opened his mouth to reply when another gentleman joined them. He wasn't one of their usual circle, but he was certainly handsome; tall and dignified, with a moustache and fine, clear, confident eyes. With a rush of excitement Maria realised that this gentleman was the man who had helped her when she'd fallen at the review! She smiled at him warmly, but not knowing his name she didn't know how to greet him.

Lord Hay turned to the gentleman, surprised and perhaps a little relieved at the interruption, and said, 'Ah, Lord Fontanelle, how do you do? May I introduce you to Miss Maria Capel, who is a great favourite of ours here in Brussels. Miss Maria, this is Lord Fontanelle.'

Finally, Maria had the man's name. Lord Fontanelle smiled at the younger man's eagerness to impress, and turning towards Maria, took her hand and kissed it gently.

'Madam, I am your servant.' He spoke with the pleasing cadence of one who knew the English language as well as his own.

'Good evening, sir.'

Maria couldn't have been more pleased that Lord Fontanelle had joined them as it made her exit from Lord Hay suddenly simple and easy. It was obvious that Lord Fontanelle had come to ask her to dance.

And sure enough, Lord Fontanelle said, 'Might I be so bold as to request the pleasure of your company at the next dance?'

'I'd be delighted,' Maria said without hesitation.

Maria smiled sweetly to Lord Hay as she took Lord Fontanelle's arm and they walked away together. Lord Hay looked as though he was processing this surprising turn of events and found himself not entirely happy with the results.

As they waited for the dance ahead of them to finish, Maria and Lord Fontanelle smiled shyly at each other and watched the dancers spinning across the floor. Maria caught his scent, a peppery musk that was unlike anything she had smelt before.

'The orchestra is playing with extra feeling today, don't you think?' he said conversationally.

'I was just thinking the same thing. It's as though they know there won't be many balls left.'

The dance came to an end, the music changed and Lord Fontanelle gently took her gloved hand in his. Their dance was a waltz, much to Maria's pleasure. Indeed, it seemed they rarely danced anything but the waltz these days, and the music seemed to perfectly suit the drama and intensity of the moment.

As they took to the floor together, his arm at her waist and hers at his shoulder, Maria marvelled at how intimate dancing could be. Despite being virtual strangers, her body was so close to Lord Fontanelle's, his head turned to her cheek. As the music rose, they swept across the floor together and Maria's heart soared as her feet flew.

Lord Fontanelle was a superb dancer, light on his feet and with a rhythmic, easy movement. Maria thought herself a good dancer, too, but she found she was pushing herself to keep up with him, curving her back and extending her arms as they turned and spun and wheeled.

She had by this time danced with many of the men in the room, but none of those dances quite compared to this. There was something in the way that Lord Fontanelle held himself, the way his piercing bright eyes met hers, that gave her a thrill like never before. Dancing with Lord Hay was child's play in comparison.

Maria spotted Georgy across the floor, partnered of course with the Prince of Orange, looking as delightfully well matched as ever. The two sisters smiled happily at each other. Lord Fontanelle, spotting that Georgy was an acquaintance of Maria's, gave her a warm smile when they next rustled past each other.

As Georgy and the prince turned, Georgy mouthed over the prince's shoulder, 'Who is that?'

Maria only grinned as she was swept away again.

'Is that lady a friend of yours?' Lord Fontanelle asked. 'Or perhaps one of your sisters?'

'My sister, yes,' she replied.

Maria didn't want the music to stop, but in what felt like no time at all it had, and she and Lord Fontanelle were being swept along by the crowds surging towards the dining area.

'Shall we take a drink?' he said, holding her by the arm so they wouldn't be separated.

'Please, that would be lovely,' said Maria, intrigued to know more about this gentleman.

'I'm glad to see there's been no lasting damage from your fall. You dance very beautifully.'

Maria smiled at the memory and the compliment. 'Thank you, and yes, I am quite recovered, although I'm not sure my mother has forgiven me yet for making such a scene.'

'I certainly found it memorable; in good ways, I assure you.'

Maria recalled how Lord Fontanelle had brushed down her dress to remove the twigs and dirt. At the time it had seemed entirely appropriate but now it seemed suggestive of more. She couldn't help but smile.

They moved through the crowd together, passing people they both knew who greeted them cordially. They came across Harriet, and Maria introduced Lord Fontanelle, who made an elegant bow. Maria was pleased to see that Harriet seemed perfectly happy, apparently not having encountered Baron Trip, and the three chatted pleasantly together.

Then Lord Fontanelle looked across the ballroom and said, 'I do believe the man of the hour has finally put in an appearance.'

Following his gaze, Maria saw that the Duke of Wellington, accompanied by Baron Müffling, had finally arrived at the ball.

'Where has the duke been?' Maria wondered aloud. 'The Duchess of Richmond will be relieved. She must have thought he wasn't going to come.'

'I wonder at his coming at all,' Lord Fontanelle said.

'Why so?' asked Harriet.

'The rumours of Napoleon's advance are more than mere gossip, I'm sorry to say. I believe we are on the brink of a manoeuvre to meet his forces.'

Maria was intrigued. 'But how do you know that, Lord Fontanelle?'

'I have my sources,' he replied mysteriously.

'Well, he does look quite worried,' Maria observed, for although the duke was affecting his usual air of confidence and composure, he held himself stiffly and the lines around his pursed lips suggested concerns far removed from the trivial routines of the ballroom.

At that moment they saw Lady Georgiana Lennox go up to Wellington. They spoke for a few moments, after which Lady Georgiana curtseyed, the duke and Baron Müffling bowed, and she retreated. On seeing their group, she forced her way through the crowd to come close enough to speak.

'Why, it's true!' Lady Georgiana said, 'I just enquired of the duke about the rumours of Old Boney's advance from Paris, and he confirmed the army is to meet them en masse. We shall be going to war within days, if not hours!'

It ought not to have been a shock given all the talk of war in recent weeks, yet to hear it confirmed by the duke struck them dumb. Maria gaped and Lady Georgiana's wide chestnut eyes were filled with concern.

'Oh, whatever shall we do?' she said. 'I fear so for the men, but particularly my brother. I should be heartbroken if anything happens to him.'

'I'm sure Lord March will be well out of harm's way if he stays close to the Prince of Orange. They won't let anything happen to *him*,' Georgy said comfortingly, but Lady Georgiana was looking more panicked by the minute.

'I do hope you're right, but the duke looked so terribly concerned, more so than I've ever seen him.'

Lord Fontanelle turned to Maria. 'Madam, if you would excuse me, I must hear more about the situation.'

He made an elegant bow to each of them. Maria was pleased to be addressed as 'madam' again, but before she could say anything or curtsey in return, he'd moved away through the crowd.

'Who was that gentleman?' Lady Georgiana enquired. Maria explained about meeting Lord Fontanelle at the review and how he'd come across to her this evening when she'd been talking with Lord Hay. She also told her about Lord

Hay's disquieting enthusiasm for the battle to come, and Lady Georgiana nodded.

'Yes,' she said, 'I had a similar conversation with him on that very subject. It was very provoking.'

Despite the news that was sending shockwaves through the room, it seemed the evening was to progress as normal. Lady Georgiana was called away by her mother to help people to their seats for the dinner.

'Mama has arranged for me to sit next to the Duke of Wellington. What a thrill!' she said as she departed.

'Really,' exclaimed Maria after Lady Georgiana, 'that girl has all the luck!'

'She was born into the right family, that's for sure,' agreed Harriet. 'Come, let's find our seats; I hope we're close to each other.'

At dinner, the guests were more distracted from their food than Maria had ever seen them, and many plates were left untouched as everyone discussed the news of the battle to come. Maria was pleased to find that she'd been seated next to General Barnes.

'What annoys me most is the attitude of these young scamps,' he said, gesticulating down the table at the younger officers all around them. 'They're so anxious to dance off into battle and "prove themselves", with no knowledge of the horror, the guts, the blood and the suffering. They see war only as a game in which they want to show that they have the finest uniforms and the best horses.'

General Barnes must have seen something like agreement in Maria's expression, because he pressed on.

'Your young friend Lord Hay is a classic example of this. I know you care for him, but I worry his brashness will lead him and others into danger.'

Maria was touched by his concern but also recognised his irritation and perhaps a hint of jealousy towards his younger combatant.

Laying a hand on his arm she said, 'General Barnes, Lord Hay is no particular friend of mine. We would not be well matched in that regard.'

Barnes was surprised at her frankness. 'Is this a recent decision, or has the matter been settled for some time? I could see from the moment he laid his eyes on you in that little shop that he was interested.'

'I think perhaps in the heat of the moment he might have been, but I've since realised how badly suited we would be.' She felt a little awkward but pressed on. 'I know things were not supposed to work out between us, but I thank you for showing me the kind of man I want to be with one day.'

General Barnes was smiling warmly. He took her hand in a fatherly fashion.

'I appreciate that, Maria. I have felt for some time that it was right in the end that my proposal was unsuccessful, however hard it was at the time.'

'I suppose everything happens for a reason.'

'I wish you every happiness when you do decide to marry, Maria, and I hope you'll always think of me as a friend and confidant. For myself, I don't think that marriage would suit me. I'm wedded to my profession which, it would appear, is about to take up all my capabilities, so that is fortunate! Lord knows how long we'll be fighting Napoleon this time.'

'Then I wish you the very best of luck in your endeavours, and I am very pleased that we part as friends.'

When dinner was over, Maria and General Barnes stood to join the crowds filling the stairs that led to the dancing area. Despite the worry of impending war, Maria couldn't have been happier with the way the evening was turning out. It was as though Napoleon's return had forced her life into sharp focus. Gone were the months of uncertainty, frustration and anxiety.

Now she knew more of the true feelings of the men who had been circling her, in some shape or form, for months. She better understood their motivations and feelings towards her and felt a new clarity in her own thoughts too.

Her father's gambling debts and her lack of a dowry had cast a shadow over her and her sisters, but surely she could still make good a life for herself? Had she not proven that she was desirable? She'd had a man propose, and another want to run away with her, so surely it wasn't impossible that the right man would come along eventually? With the summer evening warm through the windows and dancing couples all around, anything seemed possible. She felt lighter than she had in months.

Ahead of Maria and General Barnes through the crowd was the Duke of Wellington, flanked by the Duchess of Richmond and Lady Charlotte Greville. Progress was slow, and no one was in much of a hurry. Maria was arm in arm with General Barnes, chatting happily, when they saw a commotion ahead of them. General Barnes stretched up on his toes to look over the heads of the crowd.

'What's happening over there?' Maria enquired. Her curiosity was piqued by the general's frown.

'It looks like Percy has arrived with a message for the duke. Here, come and look.'

Maria didn't know who 'Percy' was. To her surprise and delight, General Barnes pulled her over to him and hoisted her up easily, one hand either side of her waist. Held aloft in his arms, she enjoyed an excellent view of the scene before them.

An exhausted messenger in a mud-splattered uniform had just given a letter to the Duke of Wellington and was waiting while the duke gave orders to the officers clustering around him. She could see the letter clasped in the duke's hand. The Prince of Orange was with the duke and seemed very worried.

Something was wrong. The happy atmosphere in the room was shifting. Whatever information was in the letter spread through the duke's staff like a plague. As the officers began to push their way through the crowd, they brought a new sense of urgency to the room. Maria saw the Prince of Orange forcing his way out of the ballroom, speaking animatedly to the men trailing behind him, Lord March in their number.

'What can you see, Maria?' General Barnes said urgently. 'What's happened?'

CHAPTER XVI

The Last Hurrah

*'You may imagine the Electrical
Shocks of such intelligence — Most
of the Women in Floods of tears and
all the Military in an instant
collected round their respective
leaders and in less than 20 minutes
the room was cleared.'*

Lady Caroline Capel to the Dowager Countess of Uxbridge

General Barnes lowered Maria back to her feet and turned her to face him. She didn't know how to articulate what she had witnessed, the scene before her had been so confused. Something of this must have shown in her expression, because General Barnes spoke in a worried tone.

'Let's get closer, then we can find out what's going on.' He took her hand and they tried to move forward but were repeatedly jostled.

The music was still playing and the noise of the chattering guests had greatly increased, yet the crowd in front of them was growing thinner. As officers and civilians alike hurried away, they looked out for people they knew. Barnes stopped a young officer in the uniform of the 33rd.

'What news has been brought to Wellington?'

The man was no more senior than an ensign and looked

scared and excited in equal measure.

'It's old Boney, sir. He's over the border and only forty miles from here, at Charleroi. His troops are pouring over the Sambre. We are to mobilise and march to meet him at once. It's war!'

The man dashed off before General Barnes could question him further, and Maria was immediately reminded of Lord Hay.

'Damn!' exclaimed General Barnes. 'And from right under our noses!'

He turned to Maria and gripped her tightly by both arms. 'You must find your sisters and get yourselves back home. I'll go to my men and make them ready.'

'But when will you fight?'

'I imagine we'll leave as soon as it's light and begin once the day is established.'

'So soon! Can the French really be so near?'

'Apparently so. We can't lose any more time. We've dawdled here too long already.'

So, this could be their last moment together. General Barnes was already making to leave her, but she pulled him back.

'Then, dear Barnes, please go with my most ardent wishes for your safety, and for that of your men also. I'll be praying for you all.'

He smiled grimly and gripped her arm tightly.

'Thank you, Maria. It's your face I shall be fighting for on the battleground.'

Without hesitation, and to her great surprise, he caught

her up in his arms and gave her an ardent kiss on the lips. He released her and gave her a grim smile, but before Maria could say anything he'd turned and was weaving his way through the crowd. Within seconds he'd gone.

Maria looked round to see if anyone she knew had seen what had happened. Despite everything they'd said about just remaining friends, the general had kissed her! *Well*, she thought to herself, as she also pressed into the throng, *it's probably what I would have done, too, if I were heading into battle!*

She really ought to find Harriet or Georgy, but she didn't want to leave the ballroom, and on finding either of them she knew she would be made to go home. Not wanting to miss out on these last precious moments of peace, and wishing to soak up every second, Maria watched the men around her. Some looked excited, others panicked, still more were comforting their loved ones; sisters, mothers, lovers. They pulled away, leaving the women weeping and comforting each other.

She walked slowly round the room, sure now that her sisters would have thought her already on her way home, observing as if through a lens the surreal scenes unfolding before her.

She saw that some gentlemen had decided to make the most of their final hours of freedom and snatch a few last dances with their favoured ladies. The emotion etched on their faces as they danced across the floor moved her to tears. The couples clutched each other more passionately than would usually have been considered proper, occasionally missing steps in the process. The band played on nobly, adding to the drama with each swell and lull, and with such a small number of dancers on the floor the effect was as eerie as it was beautiful.

Turning a corner, she saw a lady and an officer embracing passionately, partially concealed from the main hall. They didn't notice her coming upon them, and she hastened to leave them to their goodbye. Wiping away her tears, she spotted Lord Hay. He had seen her, too, and was making his way over. All past humour forgotten, he now looked deadly serious.

'Well, Maria, it is time,' he said, most solemnly.

'Lord Hay, please be careful. We would all be devastated if anything were to happen to you.'

A young lady rushed past, knocking into them, her face contorted with tears. They turned back to each other.

Looking directly at her, Lord Hay replied quickly, 'You remember my horse, Miss Muzzy, who I named after you? In a few hours I shall be riding her into battle. I can think of no better companion.'

Maria could feel the weight of more tears behind her eyes and blinked rapidly. She didn't want to cry in front of Lord Hay. He continued, and his words caused her surprise, and made it even harder to keep from crying.

'Remember, I shall fall in the first action and I shall fall on Miss Muzzy. If I have time to speak I shall send her to you, and you must always keep her.'

'How can you be so sure of your fate, Lord Hay?' she managed to say.

'It's my destiny to die young, and before my time.'

'I'll still pray for your safety,' the tears were falling now.

He seemed so sure, and so sad. The rushing about in the ballroom was a blur around them. Maria bent her head and carefully unpinned the ribbon he had given her from its place across her crown. She held it out.

'You may not remember, but you gave me this ribbon the day we first met.'

'Of course I remember,' said Lord Hay, although he seemed mightily surprised to see it. 'How sweet of you to keep it all this time.'

Before Maria had a chance to be embarrassed about keeping the ribbon and wearing it that evening, she said quickly, 'Will you take it, as a charm to bring you good luck?'

'Miss Maria, it would be an honour to wear it. With this and Miss Muzzy, perhaps my fate shall be different.'

He pushed back the sleeve of his dress coat and Maria wrapped the ribbon around his wrist and fastened it securely.

'Thank you.'

They smiled at each other and moved instinctively to clasp hands. Maria knew then that they were parting as friends. As she moved away at last, she suddenly felt incredibly tired. Her feet and back ached, and she wished she were in the carriage with her sisters on the way home. It was a long walk back from this part of town to the Parc Royal but perhaps some fresh air would revive her flagging spirits.

Seeing her friends depart and not knowing if she would see them again gave her a leaden sense of worry and filled her heart with woe. How would they cope over the next few days? What if Napoleon broke through and looted Brussels? What would happen to their family, her friends, the servants?

What had she been doing, waiting around at the ball when she should be with her family? They would surely be worried about her. She looked round with renewed vigour, checking that none of her family remained in the ballroom.

There were several people still in the hall, although the majority had now left. The Duchess of Richmond was at the door, imploring her guests to stay a little longer, but it was time to go home. Luckily, Maria knew the way. She would be quite safe.

She dodged the duchess, not wanting to be kept inside a moment longer. As she left the house, someone called after her.

'Miss Capel, do stop. Might I escort you?'

She turned and saw Lord Fontanelle. He had clearly run to catch her up as he was a little out of breath.

'Are you walking home? If you're alone, I would be honoured to accompany you.'

'Thank you, my lord, but I don't want to put you to any inconvenience. It's quite a walk from here to the Rue Ducale.'

'Why, I am headed that way myself, as I'm staying with the Marquis d'Assche. I'm sure your father would prefer you had an escort rather than walking alone. Shall we?'

Before Maria could pause for thought, Lord Fontanelle had offered his arm and she had taken it. She looked up at his elegant face with its piercing, confident eyes and nodded, and they headed off down the dark street together.

PART III

JUNE 1815

CHAPTER XVII
The Beginning

'...we first heard the distant Cannonading which approached for some time, and awful as it was, every breath was hushed to listen the better.'

Lady Caroline Capel to the Dowager Countess of Uxbridge

Maria and Lord Fontanelle walked in silence for a time, listening to the sounds of the night swirling around them. This part of the city had no lighting, so their way was lit only by the glow of the moon and the candles glimmering from inside the houses they passed. Every now and again a carriage would rush past, driving up dust as it sped into the city, carrying anxious passengers back to their homes.

Maria suddenly became conscious of her hair. It must look a sight after she had pulled the ribbon out of it. She smoothed the sides of her coiffure as she tried to subtly ascertain the damage. She wanted to look up at Lord Fontanelle but felt shy, unsure of the etiquette of the moment. Maria knew she really ought to instigate some conversation, but she was still savouring the calm of the street after the chaos of the ballroom, and the silence between them felt friendly rather than awkward.

Lord Fontanelle was walking with a slow, deliberate gait,

as though he too wanted to soak up the moment. They were walking a little closer to each other than was strictly necessary, but there was a chill to the air that made her glad of their closeness.

After a while Lord Fontanelle broke the easy silence.

'I don't wonder at our reverie this evening. What an extraordinary turn of events. I never would have believed Napoleon's advance could have been so quick.'

Maria was keen to know more about this gentleman and his reasons for being in Brussels but was embarrassed to ask in case he was French. She still couldn't place his accent. However, it was as though Lord Fontanelle had read her mind.

'I suppose you're curious to know which side I am on?' he said.

Maria smiled and couldn't resist a joke. 'Well, indeed; should I be running to the nearest house and begging for help?'

He smiled too and gave her a gentle nudge as they turned around a corner and headed into the main part of town.

'My family are indeed originally from France, but we've had a complicated relationship with our mother country, and for some years have resided in Switzerland.'

'Do you mind my asking what happened to make your family leave? Were they followers of Bonaparte?'

Lord Fontanelle looked a little offended, his brow crinkling before his good manners could correct the impulse.

'You think I am one of those Bonapartists who cling to that madman? If I were, would I have been invited to the ball this evening?'

Maria had clearly hit on a sensitive subject, but she felt she could uphold her side of the argument.

'I meant only that it must be odd, with war about to start against your own nation, that you are here with the Allied side and not with the French,' she said.

Lord Fontanelle considered her statement. At any rate his expression softened slightly.

'It is indeed a perplexing moment,' he said, 'but I don't identify Bonaparte and his men as part of the France I know and love. I shall rejoice when the true France, one led by the king, is restored again.'

'Do you like the king, my lord? I've heard such contrary stories that it's hard to see him in a positive light.'

Lord Fontanelle stopped and turned towards her. His face was in darkness, but she could tell, or rather sense, that he was smiling.

'Miss Maria, might you call me Marius? As it's just you and I, walking as equals? Let's not stand on ceremony.'

She nodded, remembering uneasily the same agreement she had once enjoyed with Lord Hay and where that had led her.

As they moved off again, Marius told her of his dislike for the bloated, corpulent king, cowering in Ghent while the men of other nations tore each other to shreds to bring down the would-be usurper, Napoleon. He spoke of his father, who'd been a member of the convention that had decided the fate of the last king of France, Louis XVI, the king who had been sent to his death by guillotine.

Maria had gasped at this, saying, 'Your father was on that very council?'

'Indeed,' Marius said ruefully. 'Those were dark times. I was but a boy and understood very little of what was going on around me.'

'Pray, how did your father vote?'

'For the death of the king, I am ashamed to say. He and my grandfather were supporters of Napoleon. After the monarchy was re-established, we were labelled enemies of the state, but by this time we had safely made it to Switzerland. That's when we changed our name to Fontanelle, my mother's title.'

'But you say, despite your family's connection with the empire, you do not love Napoleon?'

'I could no more easily love Napoleon than love the devil. I wish for peace in Europe, and that will never be achieved with that tyrant running loose about these lands.'

There was such bitterness in his voice that Maria believed him. His story thrilled her. She'd met many interesting people in Brussels, but never anyone who'd had such close dealings with the Revolution in France. His telling of the horrors of that time, and of the family friends and members he had lost, kept her enthralled. The Revolution was a subject of fear and revulsion to Maria and her family. Her parents always talked of it with a shudder, even all these years after the guillotine had stopped falling in the Place de la Révolution.

Maria hadn't noticed much of the journey at all. Without conscious thought her tired feet had carried her through the streets of the city she had come to love. She had taken in little of their surroundings. Marius steered her in the right direction when necessary, by gently nudging her elbow and nodding in the direction of travel.

They had taken a roundabout route, past the cathedral and back up to the Place Royale, the large, cobbled square flanked by the impressive courthouse and the Palais du Coudenberg. She wondered if Marius had chosen that path so their conversation could be drawn out for longer, but as they gained on the Place Royale all such thoughts were pushed from her mind by the sight before her.

Maria gasped. There were hundreds, perhaps thousands, of soldiers lying on the cobbles, sound asleep. They lay in their uniforms in rows, as though in a dormitory. They were ready for battle; kit bags lay neatly at their sides. The pattern of their prone bodies was as bizarre as it was moving. The men barely stirred, although soft snores and rustles could be heard on the slight breeze that swept through the square.

'They mustn't have to leave until dawn, so they're catching up on their rest while they can,' whispered Marius, as though even one raised voice might rouse the men from their slumber. He looked at Maria and must have seen what a shock the sight was for her, for he smiled reassuringly.

'Here they are safe, Maria. We must all pray that as many as possible return in the state we see them in now.'

Marius took her gently by the hand, smiling encouragingly. Quietly, they picked their way through the lines of sleeping soldiers, careful not to accidently trip and wake them. A few times Maria caught sight of a soldier lying with his eyes wide open, looking up at the stars. One had his arms clasped about him, his lips moving in silent prayer. What thoughts were keeping him from sleep, Maria could only imagine. Slowly, they passed through the Royal Palace, serene in the moonlight, before heading left down the Rue Ducale towards Maria's home.

'What poor manners,' Marius said. 'I have been regaling you with stories of my sordid family history and asked not a word of your own people. Now I feel I must relinquish you back to your home, otherwise what would your family say? But I should like to hear your story, perhaps at a more suitable time.'

'Really, there is little of note to report.'

'Come, now, the house of Essex is not a mere trifle in English society, or so I am led to believe.'

'You seem well read on my family history!'

They had by now reached the entrance to the Capel residence.

'I was lucky enough to meet your father when we both dined with the Duke of Wellington the other day.'

Maria was surprised but pleased to hear this. 'What a coincidence! That must have been an interesting evening. Do you know the duke well?'

'Our paths have crossed over the years, and more so recently.'

Maria's interest was piqued, but Marius clearly didn't want to elaborate.

'I suppose I should be bidding you goodnight before your papa comes out to see where you have got to,' he said.

'Yes; goodnight, Marius. Thank you for the company, and the conversation.' She was not quite ready for them to part so she added, 'What will you do with yourself over the coming days?'

'I have an errand. I was given a letter of great importance

to take to Antwerp. I must leave as soon as I can, but I shall return to Brussels in a few days.'

'It was kind of you to walk me all the way home when you have such a task ahead of you.'

Maria thought back to the ball and Lord Fontanelle leaving her as soon as it was clear Napoleon had made his move.

'Can I assume your errand has something to do with the current situation? Is it a letter from the duke?'

'I couldn't possibly say,' he said, but his eyes twinkled and told her everything she needed to know. She wondered what his connection to the duke really was. Was he some kind of spy?

'Will the journey be very perilous?'

'Nothing in comparison to the battle to come. I'm sure I won't come to any harm. It helps I speak enough languages to get by comfortably.' Marius took her hand and kissed it again. His eyes met hers again; they were both smiling. 'I must go, but I hope we meet again.'

'I, too. Good luck with your journey.'

'Keep yourself and your family safe. If you need to, make haste for Antwerp and get word to me that you are there. The Marquis d'Assche will be able to assist you.'

With that, he turned and walked down the side street leading off the Rue Ducale. Maria could not believe they'd lived so close to each other for so long.

Maria paused in the entrance hall. The house was quiet. She slipped off her shoes, wincing as her stockinged feet made contact with the floor, and padded up the stairs. She made it to the landing but then saw the door to her mother's room was open. Lady Caroline came out to meet her.

'Maria, wherever have you been? I've been so worried.'
Indeed, she looked more upset than angry. 'Tonight of all
nights you shouldn't have been out alone.'

'I'm sorry, Mama, I truly am. In the confusion I lost you
all, and then a new friend accompanied me home. He was the
perfect gentleman.'

'Who was this?'

'His name is Lord Fontanelle. He met Papa the other day
at dinner with the Duke of Wellington.'

This mollified Lady Caroline. 'Be that as it may, you are
not to walk out without a chaperone, you know that. Anyhow,
I'm just glad you're safe. Luckily your father is not back yet.'

'Will you tell him?'

'No, I think not, now off to bed with you.'

'Yes, Mama, goodnight.'

She kissed her mother and went to open the door to her
bedroom, but her mother called back. 'And what did you
think of this Lord Fontanelle?'

Maria barely knew herself. The last hour had passed in such
a blur. 'He was quite different from all the other gentlemen
friends I have made, but I can't quite put my finger on why.'

Her mother smiled with what Maria thought was a
knowing look and returned to her bed.

On entering her room, Maria saw that far from being
asleep both Georgy and Harriet were sitting on the window
seat, fully clothed, and the room was brightly lit with candles.

'Maria!' exclaimed Georgy.

'Wherever have you been?' Harriet looked concerned and
a little cross, but mostly eager to hear her sister's answer. 'Come,

now, you must immediately tell us what adventures you've had!' Harriet looked more positive and animated than Maria had seen her in a long while, although her face was still pale.

'Yes, don't keep us waiting a moment longer!' Georgy's hands were outstretched. Maria went to sit with them.

Really, there was nothing more thrilling than sharing the stories of your adventures with those you loved, and nothing could beat the company of sisters for dissecting a night like the one they'd just experienced. Maria told her tale, starting with her conversation with Lord Hay and her giving him back the Brussels ribbon; moving on to General Barnes and their kiss; and ending with her dance with Lord Fontanelle, who had been so kind and commanding, and who had walked her all the way home, past the sleeping soldiers in the square.

This brought the reality of the situation home with a crash; there was to be a war, and there was to be death, and their situation was far from secure. Her sisters let her finish and didn't interrupt save for a few exclamations.

Georgy looked glum and Harriet had tears in her eyes.

'Did you see Baron Trip before he rejoined his regiment?' Maria asked quietly, taking her sister's hand.

'Yes,' she said, 'but it was not a sweet parting. But I think it's the only closure on the matter I'll ever get.'

Maria could see her sister's pain through her composure. She had finally made peace with what had happened with Baron Trip. She wished that Harriet could have had the kind of reconciliation that she herself had enjoyed that evening, but it wasn't to be.

Maria turned next to Georgy. 'And you, my dearest; I see

you got to dance one last time with the Prince of Orange?'

'Yes, and it was wonderful, it was perfect. And now he is gone, and I don't know if he'll survive the battle.' Georgy was crying too, now, tears dripping on to her clasped hands. Maria had never seen her cheery sister look so forlorn.

How cruel and twisted love's thorns could be. Between the three sisters they had experienced it all. They had loved, they had been kept apart, they had loved mistakenly, they had been saved from ruin. Yet perhaps, with the coming battle, it was as well that none of the romances they had experienced had come to fruition. Who knew which of the men they loved would return from the battlefield, and in what state?

Georgy wiped her eyes with her handkerchief. 'Whatever will become of us, Muz?'

The ball was over and the war was about to begin. In the fray would be all the men they had met and danced with, the men with whom they had shared kisses and kept secrets. The men who had proposed, the men who wanted to run away with them and the men who had broken their hearts.

Also making their way to the battlefield was their uncle, and the brothers, sons and husbands of their friends in Brussels. The only certainty was that the women were going to be left behind, with little knowledge of the conflict that would be taking place on their doorstep until it was all over. How would they bear it?

'At least we have no brothers fighting,' Maria said into the sad silence that descended between them.

'But what of Uncle Uxbridge?' Georgy asked. No one had an answer to the question.

Their uncle would no doubt be at the very front of the fray. That was how he'd always fought, leading his men from the front, charging at the enemy with little regard for his own life. It was practically a death wish.

The sisters slipped into silence, but they didn't want to sleep. Harriet was resting her head on the wall by the window seat, her eyes half closed and her mind far away. Georgy was pacing the floor, her arms wrapped round her body, eyes darting across the room, unable to settle or find peace. Maria was still, seated next to Harriet with her hands in her lap. She wished, irrationally, to have Lord Hay's ribbon back so she could run it through her fingers, as she had secretly done when she couldn't sleep and wanted to be close to him.

Dawn arrived, unbidden and unwelcome. Maria didn't think she'd ever seen such a colourless morning. Their bedroom wasn't well situated to hear or see what was happening in the street, so they changed into day clothes, sleepily helping each other with stays and bodices, and moved to the sitting room on the first floor that overlooked the park. It was now five thirty in the morning and the rising sun lit the room softly with a creamy glow.

They found their mother and father already looking out of the sash window, which had been raised to let in the noise of the soldiers in the park. Maria joined them and saw soldiers in the park huddled around small fires, standing in groups, drinking tea from steaming cups, cleaning their muskets and packing away their possessions. Some looked relaxed, even nonchalant; others looked anxious and dejected, their heads bowed.

'What a sight,' Lady Caroline sighed, her palms flat against the pane of the window. 'To think our safety is in the hands of these men.'

Capel had a hand on Lady Caroline's lower back. 'They're the best, my dear. Wellington will see them through, and Blücher too will do his part. No Frenchmen will breach the gates of the city if they can help it.'

Together they turned to their daughters.

'Goodness, didn't you sleep?' said Lady Caroline.

Before they could reply a bugle sounded, loud enough to cut through the noise in the park and carry through the open window. The men stopped in their tracks; hands froze, conversations halted and all heads turned towards the noise. There was a second's pause, before the men scrambled into action. They pulled their pack bags on to their backs and stamped out the fires.

'They're on the move!' said Capel.

Slowly the men got into line and began to move off in formation, the rhythmic stomping of their boots muffled against the sun-bleached ground. It was an affecting sight. Maria looked to her mother and saw tears falling down her cheeks, a handkerchief forgotten in her hands.

Before long, the park was empty and silent, quiet and peaceful. The soldiers had left behind the kit that wouldn't be of use on the battlefield. Piles of it had been unceremoniously abandoned. But Maria felt left behind too, and she was sure her family felt the same way.

CHAPTER XVIII

Waiting and Wondering

'You would have been much surprised by Maria's heroism — I really never saw anything to equal it, except Lord Ux:, she certainly has shewn Paget blood.'

Georgy Capel to the Dowager Countess of Uxbridge

Maria wanted to go outside and see things for herself. 'May we take a walk?' she asked, looking to her mother for permission.

'You may go; but be back for breakfast.'

They left their parents standing at the window and went downstairs to fetch shawls, as the morning had yet to turn warm. They left the house and walked around the edge of the park towards the Royal Palace. There was an eerie calm about them that seemed to hang like smog over the streets, condensing on street corners. It was as though they were wading through the fears and excitement of the men they had just watched leave.

They saw a few people heading in the direction of the ramparts, from which Maria guessed they might get a view of the battlefield developing. Those who passed them walked by quickly, looking anxious. No carriages were to be seen as they walked the length of the far side of the park, past the Duke of

Wellington's residence. The house itself appeared to be empty. The duke must have already ridden off to lead his army.

'It's uncanny with the men gone,' said Georgy. 'Shall we go back and join the others?'

'I want to discuss something with you both first,' said Maria. For in those restless hours before dawn Maria had thought of how they could be useful in the coming days.

Although not medically trained, she was sure they could help the men returning from the battlefield. The soldiers would need care, aid, kind words. Messages would need sending, and the doctors and nurses would surely wish for assistance too. As soon as the thought had come to her, Maria knew she wanted to do everything in her power to help, and she was sure her sisters would feel the same way.

She was right on that score.

'I've been thinking something similar,' Harriet nodded. 'We should of course try and do our bit. But do you think Papa will let us?'

'If we reassure him that we will stay together and look out for each other, I think we can convince him,' said Maria.

Georgy said, 'We should certainly do it. It's daunting, but also exciting to be involved.'

On their return to the house, they saw the servants rushing from room to room, their arms full of things. Packing boxes had been brought down from the attic and laid out in the front hall. Maria looked at her sisters in disgust, knowing immediately what had been decided in their absence.

Maria marched upstairs to confront her mother. She found her in her bedroom, giving instructions to Julia, who was folding her mistress's dresses into a trunk. Lady Caroline had one hand on her bump while the other massaged her back. Before Maria could say anything, her mother spoke.

'Maria, I can't speak to you at the moment; I'm too busy and I'm too tired.'

'But Mama, I don't want to leave. I want to stay and help.'

'Go and see your father, he'll explain. But we're leaving and that's the end of the matter.'

As Maria went downstairs to find her father, she thought back to the year before, when they'd been told they had to leave London. Then, too, the move had been presented to them as a fait accompli. But Maria was older now, she had made a life for herself in Brussels, she loved the city and wouldn't leave without putting up a fight.

'Papa, may I speak to you?'

Mr Capel was in his study, rustling through papers at his desk. The parrot was perched on one of his favourite spots on the library shelves. The bird looked down with an earnest expression in his eyes, and showed his contentment by whistling and clicking his tongue. He had always been fond of Maria.

'Ah, Maria, will you help me catch this wretched thing? Algernon is insisting we take him with us to Antwerp.'

'Papa, I don't want to go to Antwerp. I want to stay here.'

Her father didn't look up from his papers. 'Don't be ridiculous, we're leaving tomorrow. Please go and help your mother pack.'

'I'll help her pack, but I'm staying here.'

Her father deigned to lift his head. 'You can't stay here,

Maria, who would stay with you? In any case, it isn't safe. The Duke of Wellington himself told me we might have to leave. I've been making plans for weeks.'

'Then you should have told us of your plans before now.'

'I don't need to inform you of my every decision, Maria. Please do as you are told.' Capel seemed more tired than angry, but Maria's face was already hot, and she felt her voice rise and tremble.

'I'm not a child any longer, Father, and you can't treat me so!'

'You are my child, Maria, and I shall treat you however I please.'

They stood across from each other with the desk between them. Just then, there was a distant but unmistakable *boom*, powerful enough to make the thin windowpanes in the library rattle. Even the curtains swayed with the force of the blast.

'Do you hear that, Father? We are at war! We *can't* leave now. What of the men who will soon return injured? They're sure to be in need of assistance.'

'They'll be assisted by doctors and nurses, not by ladies such as yourself. You have no place here.'

'I have, and I shall make myself useful! Why should I not? Why should I not help? You're running away again, just like you did in London, and dragging us with you!'

Instantly, she knew she'd gone too far. Capel looked furious.

'What can you know of such matters?' he said.

'I know more than you think. We all know we're penniless and that your gambling is the cause.'

Maria had never spoken to her father like this before. She had to admit it was rather liberating. She felt the balance between them shifting. Capel took a turn around the room to calm himself before replying. He was obviously angry at her but there was a deeper emotion there, too, one that looked to Maria like shame. He looked at her with that odd mixed expression.

'I didn't realise you knew so much about our problems. I can't deny I am the cause of them. I'm not proud of it. Indeed, we had to leave London because of my debts. But this occasion is different.'

'So you haven't been gambling?'

He clearly didn't want to give her a straight answer. 'The question of my gambling has no bearing on our decision to leave Brussels, Maria, they are two separate matters.'

'But, Papa, we have a home here, one we can afford. We have friends here, male friends who want to support us and who don't mind our lack of money. Why would we leave when they need us? And what would our friends in England think, should we abandon them in their hour of need?'

These points seemed to resonate with Capel. He looked down at the papers on his desk, his brow furrowed, clearly thrown. Maria, her heart jumping, was thrilled her words had made such an impact, and allowed a moment of calm to settle between them.

'Maria, I'm trying to do what's right for our family. Think of your mother; in her condition it isn't right that she should stay here.'

'A perilous journey to Antwerp is hardly what Mama needs

right now. Let us at least stay for a few more days until more is known. Please, Papa. Let us *help*.'

Mr Capel looked her full in the face. 'You're sure this is what you want to do? You don't know what sights you'll see.'

'I'm sure.'

'Let me talk to your mother and we'll consider the matter.'

'Thank you, Papa.'

She made to leave, but as she reached the door she turned and said, 'You know, Papa, your gambling has caused so much trouble for our family. We love you, and always will, but it's time to put a stop to it. You only have to ask, and we will help you in any way we can.'

She left before he could answer.

❧❧

Maria spent the next few hours working with her sisters to decide how best they could help the wounded when they began to arrive. They sought out their plainest and most practical clothes and put on their stoutest boots. They tied up and pinned back their hair.

They went to ask the cook to prepare extra food. They were delighted to discover the staff had already gotten started; the kitchen was flooded with the warm and comforting smell of baking bread.

While they were in the kitchen their mother burst in with news.

'The battle is being fought at a tiny hamlet called Quatre Bras, very close to here, I believe, although I've never heard of the place myself.'

They rushed to the library to consult a map of the area. Quatre Bras did indeed seem perilously close to Brussels, the letters of their names almost touching.

'Do we really know nothing more?' asked Maria.

Her mother shook her head.

'I wonder how long we'll have to wait before we hear anything,' said Georgy. 'They must have been fighting for hours already.'

'Have you spoken to Papa?' Maria asked her mother.

Lady Caroline frowned at her daughter. 'Yes, I have. He's rather shaken by what you said. I didn't know you all knew so much.'

'We've known for months, Mother. But did he say we could stay?'

'Yes, you've somehow convinced him, for now. We are to pack, and to be ready to leave quickly if we need to, but yes, we can stay for now.'

'Oh, thank you, Mama!' Maria kissed her. Her mother smiled grimly and kissed her back.

They could still hear the cannonading that had so shocked Maria a few hours earlier. Like rolls of thunder, the crashing folds of noise gathered in intensity and intent before falling away again. As time passed, the sisters ceased to mention it, nor did they comment on its increasing ferocity.

As they readied to leave the house their father joined them. He had been at the Literary Club to see what news could be found. He looked grim, with grey puffy circles under his eyes. Maria felt awkward; this being the first time they had seen each other since their argument earlier that day, but she was also burning with curiosity to know what he might have discovered.

'Girls,' he said, 'the news is not what we'd hoped for. The Prussians have been savagely attacked at Ligny, thousands of men have been lost. They have had to retreat. The English and Dutch armies at Quatre Bras have also seen heavy action. I believe the plan is for the duke to retreat also, so that Bonaparte can't drive a wedge between our army and Blücher's.'

'They will retreat? Will that mean they're even nearer to Brussels?' asked Georgy.

As if in response to these words, the sounds of cannonading got louder.

'The duke has no choice; he must keep the two armies near each other. He has a solid knowledge of the area, I hear, and will no doubt have an idea of where best to make a stand. We are only at the beginning; it'll take some time to move the armies.'

'Have you heard of any injuries?' asked Georgy.

'Nothing yet; it might be some time before we hear anything.'

Far from keeping Napoleon's armies away from Brussels, the Duke of Wellington was actively bringing them closer to their door. They had to trust he knew what he was doing. What scared Maria was how powerless they were and how much their fate rested in the hands of others.

The cook came to remind them it was time for lunch. It was surreal how the day could continue as normal despite the extraordinary events happening so close by.

As they all left the library, Capel pulled Maria aside. They looked at each other, and Maria was pleased to see that her father no longer seemed angry with her.

'Papa, I'm sorry if I spoke out of turn earlier, but I meant every word.'

'I'm glad you said what you did. It wasn't easy to hear, and I still believe we ought to leave for Antwerp, but I'm resigned to staying here a few more days – unless we get a warning from the duke or one of his men.'

'Oh, Papa, thank you. And we can help?'

'Yes, you can, and Georgy and Harriet too, if they wish.'

'Thank you, Papa.' They embraced.

～～

Lady Caroline was sitting in the drawing room after supper that evening, writing another letter to her mother. First, she wanted to thank her for sending over money so quickly. She had hidden the notes in her drawers, and Julia had promised only she would attend to Lady Caroline's room to ensure they remained safe.

It was enough, so that if they had to leave for Antwerp, they would be able to afford the cost of transport and lodgings, as demand had caused the price of both to rise exorbitantly. She was greatly relieved she had followed her instincts and asked her mother for help, and that they had a safety net should they need one.

Lady Caroline knew there was every chance the battle would have been won or lost before the Dowager Lady Uxbridge received this next letter, but she also wanted to give her own account of what was happening.

To an English Ear unaccustomed to such things, the cannonading of a real battle is awful beyond description, and to have one's friends walk out of a ball and straight into battle, is a sensation far beyond description...

As she wrote, her family gathered in the room around her. No one had any intention of retiring early. Capel called for coffee to be brought, but Lady Caroline was far from tired.

She felt sick with worry for her brother and the danger he must be in at that very moment. He had always been her favourite and he had made them all so proud, despite the mess he had made of his personal life. Now she kept thinking of the shot, cannon or sword that could at that very hour be cutting into him. She prayed that Lord Uxbridge's rank might keep him safe, but also knew there was every chance he would throw himself into the firing line at the first opportunity.

Thoughts of General Barnes were also on her mind, and her quill shook on the page. A battle on this scale, with so many thousands of soldiers across hundreds of miles, would surely take days to conclude. When would they hear word that he was safe?

Despite her best efforts, her feelings for General Barnes had grown from a platonic friendship into something more. She knew by the way he looked at her that he felt the same. If she had been less loyal to her husband, she would have willingly fallen into the arms of such a warm-hearted bedfellow. But she knew she would never stray from Capel. Despite his faults and failings, her husband had been a constant and kind companion for all their years together. Yet Lady Caroline still feared for the safe return of General Barnes.

She lifted her eyes from the page and let them linger on her husband, who was drinking a small glass of port. She found it curious that when so many men had left their families to fight, Capel was happy to remain at home and wait for news. Deep inside, she felt a little embarrassed that he wasn't fighting and that part of her ached for General Barnes all the more.

As the injured had yet to return from Quatre Bras, the Capels worked together that evening, sorting through clothes, blankets and provisions to be distributed the following day. Then a letter was delivered by one of the servants. Capel ripped it open and read the contents. He signed heavily.

'There has been a general action, as we suspected – but thank God the cavalry has not yet been engaged.'

They all sighed in relief. Lord Uxbridge was safe, for now.

'General Barnes has been in the fray and has distinguished himself most gallantly. He has had two horses shot from under him and rallied a corps of Belgians who had been about to turn tail.'

The girls cheered in relief. Lady Caroline grinned and wiped her eyes hurriedly.

'What miraculous news that everyone is safe, and that the cavalry wasn't needed!' she said.

'They are safe, for now. Though Lord only knows what they have faced since this was written. It is dated some hours ago. I'll go to the club to see what more I can discover. Don't wait up.'

'Before you go, I wanted to ask you something. And the girls, too.' Lady Caroline was looking a little flushed. 'I wondered what you thought about asking General Barnes to be godfather to the baby, when it arrives?'

Capel was clearly taken aback but said, 'If you wish it, my dear. If Barnes survives the battle, then we shall ask him.'

There was a pessimistic note in Capel's voice, and they all knew he was doubtful that General Barnes would make it through.

'I suppose,' Maria said, 'it's rather irregular to have a man who proposed to you become godfather to your little brother or sister, but I'm pleased he'll be a regular feature in our family. He's a good man.'

'That he is,' her father said, but Maria noticed the look of concern on his face. 'Now, I'll be off. Try and get some rest, won't you?' he said to Lady Caroline. He kissed her on the cheek, handed her the letter and left the room.

Lady Caroline immediately re-read its contents.

'Who is the letter from?' Maria asked.

'I don't recognise the hand. It's rather a scrawl but seems to be "M. Fontanelle".'

'Fontanelle!' Maria couldn't believe it. Lord Fontanelle was sending letters to her father!

'Is this the same man who walked you home from the ball?' Her mother's memory was as good as ever.

'Yes, it is. Goodness, what a surprise.'

'Well, he is clearly a useful fellow, and a kind one too for writing to your papa with what he knows.'

Georgy could clearly not wait any longer, asking 'Mama, is there any word of the Prince of Orange?'

Lady Caroline handed her the letter. Georgy scanned it and exclaimed, 'Indeed, yes! Lord Fontanelle writes that the prince has been fighting all day, and in the same shirt he wore to the ball, but that he is not injured!' Georgy laughed with relief. 'Thank the Lord! He'll be so pleased to have distinguished himself.'

They all shared in her joy, for it was indeed good news and even better to see Georgy smile for the first time since the Duchess's ball the previous day. So much had happened since then, it seemed like a lifetime.

'And tomorrow we shall begin our work,' said Maria, with an optimism in her voice that didn't quite reach her heart. 'Mama, how do you think we could be the most useful?'

'There are always ways one can help, often in the small things. Carrying messages, helping the wounded. The blankets and things you have gathered so far are a good start. But we'll have little idea of what these men really need until we go and meet them.'

'But Mama,' said Harriet, putting her arm around her mother, 'you shan't be going anywhere in your condition. You must stay here and rest. Send us out, and we shall return regularly with reports.'

Lady Caroline smiled at their concern. They were quite right, of course, but how she would have loved to join them in their endeavours. She would be of little practical help, but she must warn her daughters of the horrors they would no doubt witness in the days to come.

Before they all left the room to go to bed she said, 'Girls, war is a terrible, messy business. It will be a test for you just as much as the men on the battlefield. You will need to be brave, and you will need to be strong. You'll see things that will shock and appal you.'

'We want to do what we can, Mother,' Harriet said, taking Maria and Georgy by the hand.

'We want to help. We want to be a part of it,' said Maria, and Georgy nodded, too.

Lady Caroline felt a rush of pride in her earnest, confident daughters, and drew them close.

CHAPTER XIX
Homefront Heroism

'My dearest Grandmama how can I describe all the horrors of a Hospital Station — which Brussels is — the streets crowded with wounded wretches and with waggons filled with dead and dying.'

Georgy Capel to the Dowager Countess of Uxbridge

Maria was exhausted by the day's uncertainties and fell asleep much sooner than she'd expected. Yet she slept fitfully, and her dreams were filled with the horrors of the battlefield. Soldiers ran at the enemy, their bayonets not raised but tied across their arms so they couldn't fight. Maria watched but could do nothing to help the men, frozen as she was in restless slumber. Then she was back in Brussels and the sisters were cowering as their father charged the cavalry with bloodlust in his eyes, Lord Uxbridge's broken body lying on the ground.

Maria's eyes flew open, and she found herself tangled in her sheets. *It was just a dream*, she told herself, pulling the covers off with difficulty and taking a gulp of water from the glass on the table beside her. *Papa isn't even going into battle.* Georgy, lying beside her, looked to be asleep, yet when

Maria whispered her name, she turned to her straight away, eyes wet and wide open.

'You've been dreaming, Maria,' Georgy said. 'I can tell by the look on your face.'

As they prepared for the day ahead Maria's hands began to shake. She couldn't help but feel that she was heading downstairs to bad news.

'Do you have the feeling, Georgy, that something terrible has happened?'

Georgy turned and clasped Maria's hand reassuringly.

'Muzzy, I'm sure all is well. I don't think we shall hear any bad news just yet; you'll see.'

Maria tried to steady her nerves as they headed downstairs together.

On opening the door to the breakfast room, they saw Lady Caroline in tears and Capel looking grim.

'What is it?' Maria demanded of her father, before they had taken their seats.

'Sadly, the question is rather, who is it,' he said, 'and I'm afraid the answer is there have been two fatalities of people we know, and one of them is the young Lord Hay.'

Maria's eyes widened in shock. She stared at her father.

'Lord Hay is dead? Truly?'

'Sadly so. The story is a sensational one.'

The next thing Maria knew, she was sitting, and her father was holding her hands and smiling kindly at her in a way he never had before. He took a deep breath.

'I'm sorry to have to be the one to tell you this, my dear Muzzy, and despite my reservations as to the character of the boy, of course I'm very sorry he's been killed.'

Everything was a blur, and deep down inside a tiny scream of pain began to sound a shrill melody.

'What happened, Papa?' she managed to say.

Her mother who spoke first. 'I really don't think now is the time, John.' She was dabbing her eyes with a handkerchief.

'I'd like to know the full story,' Maria beseeched.

There was a pause as Capel considered her request. He said to Lady Caroline, 'My dear, she'll find out soon enough. Perhaps you ought to go and lie down.'

Lady Caroline left the room gladly, and Capel turned to the girls.

'Lord Hay was killed in action yesterday, although we've only now had word of it. He was on horseback and was shot by a Frenchman who mistook him for a more senior officer.'

Maria took in this information blankly, barely registering the words. Georgy's eyes darted to her sister.

'Was he riding Miss Muzzy?' Georgy said.

'Who?' said Capel.

'His horse, he named his horse after me,' Maria said numbly.

'I'm sorry, I don't know about that. I'm afraid there's more. Lord Hay was not the only fatality yesterday. The Duke of Brunswick has also been killed. He was rallying his troops and received as many as seven shots to the stomach. He was carried off the field by his men, but he couldn't be saved.'

The Duke of Brunswick, the glamorous and beloved leader of the Brunswickers, whom they had seen at the ball on the fifteenth, now dead. Lord Hay dead, too. It hardly seemed possible that Maria and Georgy had seen both these men only two nights before, that they had spoken to them; Georgy had danced with the Duke of Brunswick, Maria had made peace with Lord Hay. Now neither man would dance or flirt or kiss or laugh again.

Maria felt dazed. She held the cup of tea Georgy had brought her but didn't take a sip. It was as though someone else had been told that Lord Hay was dead, and she was merely an observer of that person's shock and grief. In any case, how could it really be that a man she had once thought herself in love with was dead? In her mind's eye she saw the 'other' Maria's reaction. That version of herself wept and wailed, but somehow that person's grief wasn't her own.

Lord Hay would play no further part in her life. His life had been cut short, as he had foretold. How had he known that such a fate awaited him? No doubt he had been rash, taking risks that others would not have.

Did Maria respect him for that, or did she think it a waste of a life that could have been led more prudently, more respectfully of the potential he'd been blessed with? Her questions would never be answered. The man she had kissed so passionately was dead, and he had died wearing the ribbon she herself had wrapped around his wrist.

What a void there was in her now, and although her heart thudded in her chest, she felt the cold like a blanket around her. No, surely that grief did not and could not belong to her. So she didn't weep or wail just at that moment, but took a sip of the tea. She noticed that her hand trembled as she held the cup and wondered at what point the pain would engulf her.

The breakfast room had been silent for a long while, but Maria hadn't registered it. Capel was scratching out a letter and Georgy was sitting quietly next to Maria.

'Muz,' she said softly after a while, 'can I do anything?'

Turning, Maria took her outstretched hand and squeezed it.

'Truly, Georgy, I am well. It's a shock, is all, despite his own prediction.' Her voice caught a little, her throat thick. 'Let's make ourselves useful, as Mama suggested.'

'I imagine the wounded will have begun to arrive by now,' said Georgy.

'Well,' Maria said, pushing her chair back from the table and feeling the room sway, 'we had better go and see how we can be of assistance.'

Their father looked up from his letter. The crease between his brows was particularly pronounced.

'Girls, are you prepared for what you are about to see? War is no picnic.'

'We know, Papa.'

'Then do what you can for these men. When you can do no more, come home.'

He stood, and kissed them each on the cheek. He gripped Maria's arm before she moved out of the room, and the girls departed, filled with a grim sense of purpose.

They met Harriet in the hall. She was taking off her hat and looked determined.

'I have been out to see what's needed most. Such horrible sights, my dears, and worse is on the way. Wagons are making their way from the battlefield, each filled with men desperately in need of attention. The hospital is quickly filling up. Soon they will be laid out on the streets.'

'What do they need? What can we do?'

'Supplies. Let's head towards the hospital with what we have to see how best it can be distributed.'

They went to the kitchen and loaded baskets with bread, cheeses, bottles of brandy and water flavoured with cherry. Then the three sisters staggered away from the house towards the hospital. Looking back, Maria saw Louisa's face at the window. She had been deemed too young to go into town with them, and tears of disappointment rolled down her face. Although Maria was sad to go without her, she was glad not to have the responsibility of keeping an eye on her little sister.

There was no need to haul their baskets all the way to the hospital, for as soon as they came upon the Place Royale, they saw it teeming with injured men. Horses pulled in wagons full of stricken bodies, some stirring, some still. Once they were lowered to the ground, most of the men didn't move. Only a few were able to stagger away to the quieter patches of ground in the shade of the buildings that bordered the square. A confusing cacophony of shouts, cries and orders reverberated off the palace walls. Natural pathways were being forged through the growing number of groaning men by more carts, and others arrived on horseback.

Looking to her left, Maria saw a soldier lying on the ground, half his face blown off and bloody. Another had a filthy wound in his stomach the size of a dinner plate. They both moaned in agony, and the sound was horrific. She had never heard anything like it. Turning right, she saw a man lying silent, every inch of him covered in blood and dirt. His eyes were vacant.

Maria's heart quickened and she felt faint. She took a deep breath and forced herself not to look away. To bear witness to this was the least she could do when these men had given so much, but the smell of them and the sight of their wounds was like nothing she had ever experienced before. It was somewhere between burnt meat, sweat and gunpowder.

How could she even begin to help? She felt powerless and overwhelmed.

'Don't be afraid,' Harriet said to Maria. 'We can do much to assist these men.'

After a few minutes Maria's vision and purpose began to clear. She would start with the smallest jobs, the ones the medical men were too busy for, and she would begin with the man lying nearest to her.

And so they began.

First, they set out the food and drink they had brought, rationing it out and distributing it to those in need. Maria was reminded of her journey through this square with Marius, only two nights before, and how peaceful the men had looked in their slumber. Now they were again lying prone on the ground, but this time crying out in pain and fear.

Others still lay as though in sleep, but dirty, bruised and mutilated. From these men Maria averted her eyes. *You can do nothing to help these sleeping men*, she told herself practically, *best keep yourself busy with those you can.*

Before long, seeing they were eager to help, the doctors and nurses working in the square began to send them on errands. They dashed off to the hospital to fetch bandages, or to the local apothecary to beg some particular medicine that was desperately needed.

Maria felt a profound compassion for each man she knelt beside and what he had been through. On other men's orders they had been sent into the fray, straight into the heart of the battle. Now they were abandoned, at the mercy of the few left in the city to help them.

The hours flew by. Maria was called to sit with one soldier who was shouting for his mother. His leg had been badly smashed. It looked grossly diminished under his trouser leg, as though the bones had been crushed by an elephant's foot.

Has he been run over by a cannon? she wondered. Blood had seeped through the fabric and dried in a dark mess. The boy looked younger even than herself, and Maria took his hand firmly, relieved at any rate that he had the strength to grip back.

Suddenly unsure what to say, she stammered, 'Goodness, what a commotion. Don't cry now, you are in safe hands.' She vowed not to leave his side until he was seen to. She shouted, 'Please send help urgently, this man requires a doctor!'

She turned back to the boy. His eyes were closing so she gave his hand a shake.

'Hey there, don't sleep now. Tell me your name.'

'Harry, m'lady,' he murmured.

'Well, Harry, this is a fine turnout, for I have some cherry water here for you. Let me fetch it from my bag.'

The boy was so terrified he wouldn't let go of her hand. His grip was vice-like.

'Don't leave me, please. I'm scared.'

'Of course, Harry. But you're off the battlefield now and can be treated by the doctor.'

The boy was crying, fat, unashamed tears of pain creating rivulets through his blackened face.

'Don't send me back there, don't send me back to the battle.'

'No one is sending you anywhere but to the doctor.' Maria found she too was crying.

It was raining now, unnaturally large drops of rain. The sky was a deadened grey, darkening with each moment. Finally, a doctor came across them and arranged for the boy to be taken away on a stretcher to the hospital. When they lifted him, he screamed so shrilly Maria felt her heart wrench.

His hand went limp in hers. She knew she wouldn't forget the sound of that scream until the day she died. She had no time to wish Harry good luck or goodbye, for the orderlies took him away as soon as he was aloft.

She was left kneeling in the bloodied dirt of the square, her hands shaking and her eyes full of tears. But a few minutes later she hauled herself upright, brushed down her dress and turned to the next man in need.

Being able to help practically had given her a sense of purpose that she found exhilarating. To wait, helpless, in the house would have been insufferable.

The hours passed with little time to dwell on the injustice of the injuries Maria saw around her. The sisters took a short break to drink some water and stretch their aching backs, sheltering in the entrance hall of one of the houses opposite the palace. Rain was falling steadily.

'The weather has changed so quickly,' Maria mused aloud, looking across to the men in the square. 'It's only been a few days since we were at the ball in our summer best.'

'One of the doctors told me that rainstorms often accompany great battles like this,' Harriet answered her. 'It's caused by the heat rising from the cannon and shot.'

'How extraordinary.'

'It seems to be getting worse. This doesn't bode well for those spending the night on the battlefield. We must do what we can to get these men under cover before the light fades.'

Maria sighed. It was time to rejoin the fray.

They all wondered how the battle was unfolding, only miles from where they were fighting their much smaller battle against the injuries they saw around them. In those moments Maria allowed the thought of Lord Hay to slip into the edges of her mind, just a little, and felt the grief circling around and burrowing down into her chest. She didn't allow it anywhere near the surface and found it quite easy to push away again when she saw another wagonload of injured men arrive in the square.

Many more women were now helping in the streets; Dutch, Belgian and English mingled together. Maria saw her worry reflected in their eyes. Some questioned the injured men, asking for news of a particular regiment or an individual – their brother, uncle or husband. Maria resisted this temptation and focused solely on the work that needed to be done. She heard snippets of conversation that pricked her ears: 'Wellington', 'yes, killed', and even once 'the prince', but she didn't allow it to distract her from whatever task she was carrying out.

In the afternoon their mother sent one of the maids to bring them home for some food and respite. Their parents had no new information about the battle, so after they'd eaten a hurried meal the three sisters went to the Duke of Richmond's house to visit the Lennox girls and see if they knew anything more.

The rain had stopped for a while and so they found the ladies Mary, Sarah and Georgiana hard at work in the garden, sitting on blankets, ripping up tablecloths and rolling the strips into bandages. Their other activity was scraping pieces of fabric with a sharp tool and collecting the soft lint that came away into small piles; they explained that the lint was used to dress wounds. Delighted to see their friends at work, the Capel sisters put on aprons and set about assisting them.

While they worked, they spoke of the news coming in from the front. As Maria had suspected, the Lennoxes were better informed than her own family, as Lord March and their other brother Lord George were fighting.

As Lord March was an aide-de-camp to the Prince of Orange, Georgy was able to ask if they'd heard anything of the prince.

'We haven't heard a thing, I'm afraid, but I'm trying to reassure myself that in the circumstances no news is good news,' said Lady Georgiana.

Lady Mary said, 'They say tomorrow will be the deciding engagement, but the losses have been colossal already. I worry so for March and George, I can't bear to think of them in harm's way.'

Knowing that Lady Sarah would be most anxious about General Maitland, who was still a great favourite of hers, Maria asked after him.

'As far as I know he is alive and uninjured.' Lady Sarah had dark circles under her eyes but was clearly making an effort to keep her spirits up, 'I pray for him and for my brothers constantly, but who knows how this hell will play out.'

Lady Sarah turned to Maria and squeezed her hand. 'We are all so sad about Lord Hay. It hardly seems possible, although of course he always professed he was destined for such an end.'

'He spoke to you of his belief?'

Lady Georgiana nodded her pretty head in agreement. 'It could almost be poetic. He spoke to me in a similar way at the ball and vexed me so by his enthusiasm for battle. Now I wished we had parted with kinder words.' She was close to tears.

They heard footsteps coming down the path. Looking up, Maria saw Lord William Pitt Lennox coming towards them. His sisters leapt up to greet him.

Lord William's recent injury meant he couldn't accompany his commanding officer into battle, and no doubt he felt he was missing out. Maria liked the fellow, but his close friendship with Lord Hay brought his loss into sharp focus, and she wasn't yet ready to face it.

Lord William greeted the group. 'How good to see you hard at work. Sarah, Mary, Georgiana, you do our mother credit. She has barely stopped weeping about Hay and Brunswick.'

'We are pleased to do our bit, brother,' Lady Georgiana replied. 'Is there any word of March and George?'

'I've been to the battlefield to see what is about and I tell you, to see cannon firing and bullets whizzing about your head is really something to behold!'

'You must tell us everything!' they cried and dragged him down on to the grass to tell them in more detail what he had seen.

'Well, the fighting is taking place about ten miles closer to Brussels than yesterday, just past the Forêt de Soignes.'

They all exclaimed at once, 'Truly!', 'How awful!', 'So close to Brussels; whatever shall we do if they break through?'

'It is indeed a terrible business. I'm afraid the death count is already very high, and on all sides. Blücher has had a severe lashing. They are falling back to the area around the Haye Sainte, but manoeuvring the armies is proving a damn hard business after all this rain, and the rye fields are making it near impossible to see the enemy.'

Lord William picked absently at some lint on the grass. 'I feel wretched at not being able to do my bit, particularly after hearing about James.' He caught Maria's eye. As the others began to talk amongst themselves, he spoke quietly to her. 'Pray, might I have a private word?'

She nodded and they walked a little way from the group, along garden paths bordered with roses. Lord William was hesitant, but eventually stopped on the path and turned towards her.

'I think you ought to know something about Lord Hay.'

Maria had known this would be the subject of their conversation and waited patiently for him to continue.

'It's about a young woman he told me about before he left on the sixteenth. As you know, he was sure he was to die *gloriously* in battle.' Lord William spoke these words with a pronounced bitterness. 'So, he entrusted to me some special articles in case what he predicted came true. For his mother and father, his sword and sash, and for a young lady with whom he said he was in love, a gold chain.'

Maria felt cold despite the warmth of the late afternoon sun. Something about Lord William's expression told her the young lady to whom he was referring was not herself.

'Who is this lady?'

'She lives in England; I don't believe you know her.'

'He has been in love with her all this time, all the time he has been in Brussels?'

Lord William looked suitably awkward. 'I believe so. I wanted to tell you, so you knew the truth of the matter. I hope you don't think me out of turn, but I didn't want you to hear some rumour of it in the months to come.'

Maria wasn't sure she would have ever chosen to know this piece of information but appreciated Lord William's frankness. It couldn't have been easy for him.

'Thank you for telling me. Will you go to the lady in question and give her this trinket?'

'In time, yes, but for now my place is here. It will be good for her to have a keepsake of him, I like to think.'

Maria felt a little jealous of this unknown lady in England, but before she could think of a suitable response, Lord William spoke again.

'There was something else that Lord Hay mentioned to me only hours before he died. It was, in fact, one of the last things he said to me before we were parted. He said that he had promised his horse, Miss Muzzy, to you, and that I ought to make sure you got her.'

This was yet another surprise. 'He really meant for me to have her? I didn't think he was being serious.'

'He was adamant. It seems he really knew he wouldn't be coming back.'

'Did he say anything else about me?'

'I'm afraid not.'

'But I'm guessing Miss Muzzy didn't make it back from the battlefield?'

'It's too early to say, but I would be surprised if she does.'

She nodded and her throat felt hot and constricted. The grief was threatening to break through the walls guarding her heart, the protection crumbling.

She managed to blurt out, 'He was a great friend to you, I'm sure you will miss him very much.'

'Aye, he was my best friend and comrade. I know he liked the dash and danger of life, but he was my true and constant companion.'

'I hope that's how he'll be remembered.'

The sound of cannonading could again be heard from the south. The next stage of the battle had begun. They both turned instinctively towards the noise, a reminder that their shared grief was only a tiny part of the battle unfolding outside the city limits.

CHAPTER XX

For Glory

'The horrors of that night are not to be forgot — The very Elements conspired to make it gloomy — For the rain and darkness and wind were frightfull.'

Lady Caroline Capel to the Dowager Countess of Uxbridge

Maria went back to the group without Lord William, who wanted to return to the battlefield. The ladies asked about her conversation with him, but Maria shook her head; she wasn't yet ready to recount it, so they turned back to their work, and Maria was glad to have something to focus on while she reflected on what Lord William had told her.

She sat a little apart from the others, a large pair of scissors in one hand and a sheet in the other, focusing on cutting bandage after bandage and the feel of the fabric on her skin. She was soon surrounded by neat piles of rolled bandages ready to be taken back to the square and given to the nurses. The spirals of fabric reminded her of the ribbon box, and the letter from Lord Hay hidden inside it.

The sky darkened again and drops of rain once more began to fall. No sooner had they got themselves and their work indoors than one of the maids from the Capel house arrived in the family carriage to tell the girls their papa wanted them home. The day was done, with no further news from the battlefield, and the weather had fully turned against them. The Capels bundled into the carriage and were driven across town.

By the time they arrived at the Parc Royal the weather had worsened again to great rolls and claps of thunder. The sky, having mixed with smoke from the battlefield, had become a thick mottled grey. Periodic flashes of lightning threw the street into stark relief. *How will the men sleep in such rain?* Maria thought, feeling guilty as she sought sanctuary in the warmth and comfort of their home.

That evening, they were told that Lord Uxbridge had distinguished himself against Marshal Ney's men and had got into a bad scrape with a contingent of French lancers. Reading between the lines of what their father would tell them, it sounded like a bloody and violent clash, but thankfully their uncle had survived unscathed. Lady Caroline looked white and strained as Capel recounted the news. It had been a lucky escape.

'How quickly could they get to us, Papa, if the French break through now?' Harriet asked, looking anxious.

'We're still some miles from the battle. If there is a surrender, we'll know in good time.'

'But what about the retreat?' asked Harriet.

'It's a strategy. Wellington is said to be concentrating his forces in the area around a small village called Waterloo. This is so Blücher's troops can make it back to join them tomorrow.'

'What news of Blücher?' Maria asked.

'At Ligny, the day before yesterday, he was trapped under

his dead horse for several hours, and was ridden over by the French cavalry, yet still refused to die!'

Maria laughed in relief. 'So the Prussians are not routed?'

Capel smiled grimly. 'It would take more than that to finish old Blücher and his men.'

It was dizzying to think that mere months before the great general had stood in their parlour in Dover and shook hands with them all. They had been in awe of him then, and now Blücher had again proved himself a hero. Maria prayed the Prussians would return in time to join Wellington; surely the Allies could not defeat Napoleon unless united?

After supper, Lady Caroline ordered them all upstairs and to bed, but although Maria and Georgy were exhausted from the activities of the day neither could sleep. They watched raindrops race each other down the windowpanes as they sat up for hours, talking, wrapped in thick rugs and warming their hands on cups of hot milk from the kitchen.

In the safety of their room, Maria finally felt she was able to speak about Lord Hay.

'It doesn't seem possible that he really is gone,' she said.

'I suppose there could have been a mistake. There must be hundreds of men presumed dead, who in fact are alive but lying wounded somewhere where they can't find help.'

'It's surely a strange reality we're living in where that thought provides some comfort, don't you think? I can't imagine what horrors the men on the battlefield are currently enduring. No, I believe Lord Hay is dead. Even the story of his final drama fits his personality perfectly, and that's not all, for I have more to tell you.'

Maria confided to Georgy what Lord William had told her in the rose garden at the Wash House.

If Georgy was shocked, she hid it well, saying only, 'Who knew such a young man could already be carrying so many secrets? I don't like to speak ill of the dead, but perhaps you and this lady in England are better off for pursuing a life without having to fight each other for Lord Hay's affections.'

'I think you might be right,' Maria sighed. She rested her head against the windowpane and looked out into the nothingness of the darkness, listening to the howl of the wind and the drumming of the rain as it fell in torrents.

'I don't know if we'll ever discover the fate of Miss Muzzy, but it was a fine thought that Lord Hay wanted to give her to me.'

Eventually they slept. They were jerked awake hours later by the sounds of movement from the street. The hour was barely decent, but they headed downstairs anyway. They were keen to return to the square to help, but Lady Caroline insisted they remain at home until they knew more about the outcome of the battle. If they needed to leave for Antwerp, she wanted to have all the children together and ready to depart.

At about half past eleven the thunderous sound of cannon began again. They all immediately abandoned the cups of tea they were drinking and headed into the street. Those in the houses around them were doing the same. Of course, outside the noise was even louder; to Maria, it seemed like the battle was on their very doorstep. People crowded together on the street, sharing snippets of information and comforting those who had received bad news in the night.

'Mama, please, we won't go far, but we must go to help,' beseeched Maria. Lady Caroline looked uncertain.

'How about this,' said Harriet, 'if we stay in the square, you'll know where to send Julia should we have to leave?' Her suggestion was so sensible that Lady Caroline agreed, and Maria, Georgy and Harriet once more headed out to help the wounded.

A few hours into their work they were asked to go to the hospital to get more supplies. Harriet agreed to stay in the square in case Julia came to fetch them.

As Maria and Georgy walked through the town, a colossal, ear-splitting cacophony was suddenly upon them. Around two dozen horses and their riders were charging towards them on the narrow street, completely out of control. The sound of hooves on the cobbles was thunderous, the horses were whinnying in terror. The men were wild, riding as hard as they could, shouting to each other as they tried to get control of their chargers.

Maria and Georgy leapt to one side to escape injury. The horses galloped past them and off into town. Maria couldn't be sure whether the riders were friend or foe, but they were wearing boots and breeches not unlike those of the Hussars. Were they retreating? Was the battle over? There was panic on the street now, people were clinging to each other and running down the side streets to find a place of safety.

'Good heavens! Are we overrun?' shrieked Georgy hysterically.

Maria didn't know what to say. She lowered her hands from her ears and stared at the large cloud of dust the horses had left behind. Was this the beginning of defeat? Were they to be overrun by the French? She grabbed Georgy's hand and they dashed off towards home, which happened to be in the direction the soldiers had been travelling.

Before they got very far, they saw what they recognised as General Barnes's carriage. It had been overturned by the charging cavalry, and supervising its recovery was one of his staff officers.

'What's happening? Have the French broken through?' enquired Maria. The ringing in her ears made her words into a shrill imitation of her normal voice. She felt a little hysterical herself.

'Those damn fellows!' spat the staff officer. 'They're lucky no one's been killed.'

'Is this it, is everyone retreating?'

'No, no, for God's sake, don't say that or you'll have everyone running. They looked like one of the Hanoverian regiments to me, the Duke of Cumberland's Hussars, perhaps. They've abandoned the battle. Wellington always knew they'd be unreliable, and he's been proved right. The devils! We shall wring their necks for this cowardice!'

Maria felt quite sick at the thought of whole regiments retreating from the battle. Although the staff officer seemed sure this was a one-off, what if he was mistaken and this regiment led to others abandoning the battlefield? It was so hard to know what news was accurate as the information changed so quickly and couldn't be depended on. What if Napoleon was winning and his armies were, as they stood there, making their way up the road to the city?

Unable to feign bravery any longer, the sisters ran the rest of the way home. On their arrival, they bolted the door behind them and sped off to find their parents, who reassured them they'd heard no news of any mass retreat. It really did seem possible that the Cumberland Hussars had panicked and fled the battle alone. There was no further news to share of friends or family.

After the immediate fear brought on by the deserting Hussars had passed, Georgy and Maria returned to the square to spend the rest of the day tending to the wounded. Maria had by now become somewhat used to the distressing scenes before her, and the sight of one broken or mangled limb began to merge with the next.

She became hardened to the cries of the younger men, and lingered less over the older and calmer soldiers, who were used to the chaos of a field hospital. Most stoically accepted a hot drink or piece of bread, before encouraging her to move on to the next poor soul.

'Be a dear, see to Benjamin. Never mind me, it's only a scratch.'

'No, no, you see Corporal Trench over there, with the eye bandage? Take this to him, he needs it more than I.'

Maria was profoundly touched by the care the men showed one another.

Hours later, with the day done, she collapsed into bed, her feet throbbing, the room spinning. Within minutes she was asleep.

The next morning Maria again woke early. She was groggy and her body ached horribly. As she turned over, her back cracked painfully. Georgy was still breathing heavily.

Maria's mind fluttered briefly to Lord Fontanelle. She'd barely had time to think of anything other than the battle and their work over the last few days, but thoughts of him had tapped her on the shoulder several times, and she wondered again what business he had been attending to in Antwerp and whether he was back in Brussels yet.

She didn't want to get out of bed and face the day. She didn't want to know the outcome of the battle, or the fate of the men who were fighting it. She pulled the covers up to her chin and tried to go back to sleep. She could hear birds chirping in the trees outside their window. At least they sounded hopeful.

Suddenly the door flew open, causing both girls to jump up with shouts of alarm. It was their mother, barrelling in with great enthusiasm despite her size, followed closely by Harriet, Louisa and their father.

'My loves! We are saved! Napoleon has been thrashed and the French are in retreat. We have victory!'

CHAPTER XXI
Alive and Kicking

'...the news reached us early of the total defeat and retreat of the French; personal safety was secured, but what horror was it accompanied with!... No paper would hold the anecdotes that reach one's ears every moment.'

Lady Caroline Capel to the Dowager Countess of Uxbridge

Such were the shouts and cries of jubilation that soon all the members of the family joined their early morning revelry. Harriet and Lady Caroline cried as they embraced. The younger Capels bounced up and down on the bed. Algernon was whooping with glee. Maria couldn't stop grinning. She hugged her father, who wrapped his arms tightly around her. He broke their embrace, held her at arm's length and addressed his three eldest daughters.

'I am so proud of the way you have conducted yourselves these last few days, my dears. You are a credit to your mother and I.'

Maria's grin grew wider. 'Is everyone we know safe?'

'Yes, we believe so,' her mother replied.

Two fat droplets of relief rolled down Maria's face.

After a raucous breakfast, so unlike the sombre affairs of the past few days, they decided to walk through the park to see what further news could be discovered. They were not the only ones to settle on this course of action. They had rarely seen the park so crowded with people; English, Prussian, Belgian and Dutch all intermingled, cheerily greeting even those they didn't know and exclaiming the good news. From the centre of the park they could see a crowd gathering outside Wellington's headquarters.

'It looks like they've been there for a long while. Is the duke back from the front already?' asked Lady Caroline.

'Ah, I see Creevey is here, what a stroke of luck,' said Capel, spotting someone in the crowd. 'He's always the best for news.' He flagged the man down. 'I say, Creevey, how do you do?'

Mr Creevey saw them and came over. He touched his hat to the ladies and shook Capel's hand.

'How good to see you all. What a fine and memorable morning we have here.'

'Mr Creevey, have you been in to see the duke?' Lady Caroline enquired.

'I have indeed, madam; he gave me the honour of a short audience. The duke was working on his dispatch to send to Lord Bathurst in London. It was clear he hadn't yet rested; he was in the same clothes he wore on the battlefield, his face still smeared with dirt.'

'What did he say about the battle?' asked Capel.

'He was very grave. The losses have been colossal, as high as thirty thousand men on our side alone.'

'Thirty thousand!' Lady Caroline exclaimed in horror.

Maria could barely visualise such a number. She thought back to the review, some seven thousand strong, and tried to multiply it in her mind.

'Indeed,' continued Mr Creevey, 'the horrors are not to be imagined. We don't yet know the number of French lost, but around the same figure would be a good guess. It will be months before we know the true number. The duke said to me, "It has been a damned serious business." The two forces, ours against Napoleon's, were so evenly matched. Victory hung in the balance, and could have swung either way, if truth be told.'

The Capels tried to take this in. Maria was heartily glad they hadn't known until now the truth of how close they had come to defeat.

'I firmly believe the thing couldn't have been done without Wellington,' Mr Creevey said. 'His presence rallied the troops and keep the Allied regiments in line.'

'Except those we saw deserting!' Maria exclaimed, and she told Mr Creevey about what she and Georgy had seen.

Mr Creevey nodded. 'Aye, you are right, they were the Cumberland Hussars. They claimed they were being pursued by the French but very few believe their story. I've been told the regiment is to be disbanded, having shown such cowardice.'

'Well, Wellington is certainly a hero to us all, the saviour of Europe!' said Lady Caroline with feeling. 'Now we can breathe easily again.'

'I too rejoice that your family may grow and prosper with Europe at peace,' said Mr Creevey, glancing at her rounded belly.

'You don't believe that Napoleon will be able to gather his forces again?' asked Maria.

'It's impossible. His army is destroyed, and he's being hunted down as we speak; perhaps they've already caught up with him. Another abdication is unavoidable. This time, I hope we find a more secure place of exile for him than Elba.'

They all nodded in agreement. 'I certainly hope so,' said Georgy.

'By the way, they're calling it the Battle of Waterloo, which has a rather nice ring to it, don't you think?'

They thanked Mr Creevey for his time and valuable intelligence, and decided to go to General Barnes's residence to see what could be found out about him. Aside from knowing him to be alive, they knew nothing of his condition and Maria was eager to see for herself how he was. Lady Caroline insisted on going with them, despite her obvious fatigue, so their papa joined them too.

On entering the house, they saw the same staff officer who had attended General Barnes's carriage the day before. He shook hands with them.

'The general has been badly wounded but will heal. He was led back to Brussels on horseback yesterday evening, and is very weak,' he said grimly.

'May we see him?' enquired Lady Caroline.

'Yes, but only for a short time, madam, if you please. He tires easily.'

As they entered General Barnes's room, Maria realised she had never seen a man in bed who wasn't a member of her family. It was an odd thought that this sight would have been completely normal to her by now had she accepted his marriage proposal. The idea made her blush.

General Barnes was propped up in bed, with official documents and papers spread across the sheets. She was glad to see him in one piece, although his face was ashen, and stubble peppered his usually clean-shaven face. He was clearly in a lot of pain and winced as he turned to greet them and shook each of their hands.

'A few broken ribs not a bad trade-off for peace, eh?!' he exclaimed cheerfully.

Maria thought the general was probably putting a brave face on the matter and wondered how much internal damage he had sustained. She sat at his bedside while Lady Caroline slowly lowered herself down on to a chair on the other side of the bed, helped by her papa.

Maria smiled at General Barnes warmly.

'Dear friend,' he said to her, 'how glad I am to see your happy face again.'

'Oh, how I worried for you, General Barnes! You can't imagine the agonies we've been through waiting for news of you.'

'Aye, and it was quite warranted, to be sure. It was a fight and a half, the likes of which I've never seen before and never wish to again. But how tired you look, Maria. Have you been slaving away, ensuring the injured are fed and watered?'

'I only hoped to do my bit, however small.'

'I'm sure our boys will be mightily grateful for your efforts.'

They talked gently to General Barnes about his experience, the pride he felt for the way his men had behaved, and his injuries, about which he was vague and non-committal.

'Oh, this is nothing,' he said, 'I shall be right as rain in no time.'

He was already beginning to tire, slumping back on his cushions. Maria leant forward to do what she could to make him more comfortable.

'Before we go, there is something we wanted to ask you,' said Lady Caroline. She looked up to Capel who nodded. 'We were hoping you would do us the honour of becoming godfather to our next arrival. Nothing would bring us more joy in the midst of all this loss and suffering.'

Maria could think of no greater tribute to a man who had been so committed to the happiness of their family.

Barnes smiled warmly. 'The honour would be all mine,' he said, managing a bow despite being propped up in bed. He gasped involuntarily at the pain this caused, his hand clasping his ribs. 'What a lovely thing. I am thrilled, honestly.' His voice sounded faint.

'I think it's time we said our goodbyes,' said Lady Caroline.

They rose to leave. General Barnes didn't try to make them stay. When he turned to Lady Caroline, he said warmly, 'Thank you so very much. You've made me so happy, and I hope I can be a useful godfather to the little one.'

Maria left the room feeling the happiest she had for days. They walked back together, talking excitedly. Lady Caroline was tiring as they reached the park, so Maria, Georgy and Harriet left their parents to rest awhile on a bench and continued back to the house.

On their arrival, they were delighted to find the Ladies Sarah and Georgiana Lennox, and Lord March, waiting for them in the downstairs drawing room. Georgy lit up at the sight of Lord March.

'Have you any news?' she asked immediately.

'Yes, indeed we have,' said Lady Sarah. 'We have been sitting here like pixies ready to pounce on you the second you arrived. We have much to tell you.'

Harriet called for tea and explained that they'd been visiting General Barnes. 'Tell us your news, and then we can tell you about our visit.'

It was Lady Georgiana who spoke. 'We've heard that your uncle, Lord Uxbridge, has excelled himself most brilliantly. However...' She paused, clearly unsure how to proceed.

Her brother took up the story. 'I'm afraid we have some bad news to impart, but not the worst, so please don't alarm yourselves too much.'

'What is it?' Harriet said quickly.

'I'm sorry to tell you that Lord Uxbridge's leg has had to be amputated.'

The sisters gasped.

Lord March told them the whole story. Maria was glad their mother wasn't there to hear the details, as Lord March gave them a much bloodier account of Lord Uxbridge's gallantry than perhaps they would otherwise have received.

Their uncle had been in command of a staggering number of cavalrymen, some thirteen thousand soldiers and more than forty guns. In the early afternoon he had led a spectacular charge of the Household and Union Brigade against the French, rescuing General Picton's division, who were heavily outnumbered and falling fast. This charge was gloriously successful and resulted in the French scattering in disarray.

Yet, as Lord March told them, cavalry in such numbers are

notoriously hard to control and could gallop for miles into enemy lines. This is what had happaned and the cavalry had been heavily cut up by a French counterattack. Lord March described the battle in vivid terms, having been there himself, relating the sounds, the smell of gunpowder and the screams of injured men being ridden over by horses. Hearing the details made Maria shudder but she wanted to hear what it had really been like to be there and experience it first-hand.

Lord March pressed on, hungrily munching the biscuits that had been brought in with the tea and spraying crumbs all over the floor as he gesticulated.

'Uxbridge continued to lead smaller charges for the rest of the day and had several horses shot from under him. However, during one of the final actions yesterday afternoon, as Sir Hussey Vivian's brigade were going down to the charge, his leg was hit.'

Maria was reminded of the poor boy she had comforted on that first awful morning when they'd helped the wounded in the Place Royale.

'He had found another horse and was next to the Duke of Wellington. It was terrible luck, one of the last shots of the day. It just missed the duke's horse, Copenhagen, and smashed instead into Uxbridge's right leg. They were able to hold him in the saddle and eventually get him back to headquarters at Waterloo. There, they decided the leg would have to be removed.'

The looks of horror on the faces of the Capel sisters must have been only too evident. Lady Sarah put a hand on her brother's shoulder to stop him from continuing the tale. He nodded and took the opportunity to help himself to another biscuit.

'I know it's a shock, but the rest of the story is marvellous, I promise, and March's telling will do it justice,' Lady Sarah said.

Maria was feeling quite sick. She looked across at Harriet and Georgy, who were ashen faced but determined to hear him out.

'Well, let me tell you,' Lord March continued, 'I've never heard of anyone acting better in the circumstances, and I've seen a fair few amputations in my time. It was Wellington's doctor who did it, Hume; a capital man. He removed the leg as quickly as he was able, but there was no laudanum to hand or anything like it. Your uncle never uttered a sound throughout the entire procedure, he was as cool as they come. Lieutenant Wildman told me Uxbridge said, "I've had a pretty long run. I have been a beau these forty-seven years, and it wouldn't be fair to cut the young men out any longer." Can you imagine?!'

Despite their horror, the Capel girls smiled on hearing their uncle's words, for it sounded so like him.

'Gosh, I couldn't be prouder of him,' said Georgy. 'To think he went through such an operation and didn't make a squeak.'

'He is already on the road to recovery, but of course his convalescence will be long, and his military days are now behind him,' said Lady Georgiana.

'I suppose *that woman* will want to come here to attend to him,' Harriet said rather primly.

'Well, I imagine so, as she is his wife,' said Lord March firmly.

'Mama may not allow her in the house, but I suppose she will have to see her,' said Harriet.

Georgy clearly decided it was time to change the subject and asked what she was evidently bursting to know.

'Lord March, what can you tell us about your adventures with the Prince of Orange? He is alive? I feel sure I would have heard had he been killed.'

'Indeed he is, Georgy, alive and kicking, although he has been injured and quite seriously so. The prince was riding Vexey, his favourite horse you know, when he was hit by musketry fire. He dismounted and I helped him off the field to a place of safety.'

'Thank God he's safe!' said Georgy.

'He is lucky, aye, as are we all. None more so than the Duke of Wellington, who put himself in the line of fire countless times. We owe the victory to him.'

Just then, they heard the front door open and close. Their parents were back from the park and would need to be told what had happened to Lord Uxbridge. Maria didn't want to be the one to break the news to their mother. Looking towards her sisters, she could tell they felt the same way.

Lord March stood and said calmly, 'Don't worry, I shall tell your parents,' just as they entered the drawing room.

CHAPTER XXII

Into the Dark

'Many interesting things have occurred lately my dear Grandmama; we are told that frequently good proceeds from evil...'

Georgy Capel to the Dowager Countess of Uxbridge

It was late and Maria knew they ought not to be venturing out on to the streets of Brussels, busy as they were with displaced soldiers and stragglers from the battle, but the lure of the night was too strong. Georgy, too, had a glint in her eye, and before they could doubt themselves and their mission, they left their bedroom, Maria clutching the ribbon box. They tiptoed downstairs and were soon out on the streets, the wind surprisingly cool after the enclosed warmth of their home.

'Let's go to the ramparts,' Maria whispered. She tucked the box under one arm, took Georgy's hand, and together they crept off into the night.

The moonlight cast a surreal glow over the streets of Brussels. Luckily for them the city's slumber was broken only by a few stray drunks and small knots of men moving about as though on official business. No one stopped or spoke to them. Maria felt invincible as they stole through the streets she knew like the back of her hand.

It seemed to take them no time at all to reach the ramparts of the city, overlooking the battlefield in the far distance. It was too dark to make out much more than the shape of burnt-out buildings and abandoned wagons that would be scars on the landscape for many weeks to come.

Maria tried not to think about the number of bodies that still lay on the battlefield. She remembered Mr Creevey telling them that thirty thousand had died on their side alone. The thought weighed heavily on her.

Maria leant into the battlements and felt the acrid smell of gunpowder burn her nostrils. Looking down at the ribbon box, she thought of all the childish jokes and secrets they had scrawled on slips of paper and secreted inside. She felt a knot in her throat, not just for those hopes and dreams she'd held for Lord Hay, but for all the hopes of their childhood, now so far behind her.

'Are you sure you want to do this?' she asked Georgy, who nodded.

So they sat on the stone parapet, the wind whistling around them, and slowly went through the box. Maria re-read the letter from General Barnes asking to visit her and signed with a dot, and the one from Lord Hay asking her to elope with him. Georgy read the letter from the Prince of Orange that he had written when she had brought him up to their room. Maria was curious to know what that letter said, but sensed Georgy would want to keep it private. Georgy smiled sadly as she read the prince's words, and tears dripped steadily on to the page until she wiped them away from her eyes.

She sighed as she folded the letter back up.

'You know,' she said, 'I think I finally believe that nothing will come of my time with the prince, and that it's for the best.'

Maria was relieved to hear her sister say it, but it was sad to hear nonetheless.

When they had finished opening the wax seals on the other slips of paper and reading their contents, some so old their childish hand in faded pencil could barely be read, Georgy took some matches out of her pocket.

'Well, here we go,' she said, handing the box over.

Maria lit a match, and taking the letter from Lord Hay she carefully set one corner alight. The paper glowed and curled, and as the last of it was burning she let go. It floated up on the wind and over the ramparts into the night.

Georgy was already lighting the letter from the Prince of Orange. Her tears flowed freely.

Slowly they burnt all the letters and slips of paper in the box until all that was left were the rolls of ribbon. Maria did not want to spoil the ribbons, they seemed to have so much life in them still. She took the box and indicated to Georgy that they could tip them over the edge. Georgy smiled; she clearly liked the idea.

Before she could change her mind, Maria spilled the contents out into the night. The ribbons rose and twisted in the breeze. For a second or two they appeared suspended in the air, spot lit by the moon.

The two sisters watched in silence as the ribbons danced gracefully, and then began slowly to fall to the ground. They both leant forward to watch the descent, but before long the streams of colour were swallowed by darkness. Maria knew that by dawn the ribbons would have disappeared, gathered up by those who walked to the battlefield searching for trinkets and valuables. She wondered who might pick them up and hoped it would be a little girl or a mother, or a young man who would give them to his lover. *Let these ribbons give pleasure*, she thought, *as they have done for us*.

CHAPTER XXIII

Finding Peace

*'Brussells looks very dismal indeed
to us who have seen it in such gaiety,
the Park quite deserted, nothing but
wounded men wandering about.'*

Georgy Capel to the Dowager Countess of Uxbridge

A full week had passed since victory had been declared and Napoleon's armies shattered. The French troops taken prisoner by the Prussians, rumoured to number some eight thousand, had long since been marched down the main road to Brussels and sent home. There were to be no prisoners of war; peace was desired above all things and by both sides.

In the town the bodies of the men who hadn't survived the ministrations of the doctors in Brussels had been left in piles outside people's houses – a gruesome sight. From the ramparts some three thousand bodies could be seen lying exposed on the battleground, waiting to be buried.

Hundreds of dead horses lay in the streets. In a terrible state after the fighting, most had been put out of their misery with a well-aimed bullet. Maria had never discovered the fate of the horse named after her but hoped she had not suffered.

Brussels was a changed place from the city the British had

so enjoyed over the past year. Streets that had once been filled with busy and prosperous people were now filled with injured soldiers.

The locals went out of their way to help those in need, seeing the English and Scots in particular as their saviours, but not everyone could be helped in time. Wounds and injuries were prone to infection that often proved fatal. The injured lay in the streets and the boulevards of the park, encamped in the Grand Place where the guilds had once been filled with bustling businessmen.

Most of the English had left or were making plans to do so. Many were travelling to Spa, a town to the east of Brussels famed for its mineral-rich waters, where the 'season' was beginning. Most were keen to leave the fields of war and its brutal realities far behind them.

There had been a rather thrilling chase to track down Napoleon after he'd fled the battle, and he'd got as far as Paris before he was caught. The Capels had heard the previous day that he had abdicated for the second time in only a year, despite tens of thousands of soldiers remaining loyal to him.

'Well, my dear, shall we depart? The carriage is ready.' Capel peered around the door to his wife's rooms but could see she was still seated at her looking glass, fiddling with her dress, now pulled tight over her expectant stomach.

'Have the children gone already?'

'Yes, the carriage has left. I must say, I don't know if I approve of them going to see the battlefield when everything is still so fresh.'

Lady Caroline grimaced at the double meaning of that last

word. 'I just need a few more moments, John. I'll meet you downstairs.'

Capel left her, and Lady Caroline sighed. Although she wanted to visit her brother, on this occasion she would rather have stayed at home. She had hoped she could use the impending arrival of the baby as an excuse, but there were no signs of her labour starting yet. Sadly, she always tended to go late and this time was no exception.

She had already been to visit her brother and seen his stump. She had wept, sickened by the sight of his amputation, but insisted that she remain by his side as the bandages were changed. Afterwards she had retched in the corridor outside his room.

Luckily no sign of fever presented itself. Lord Uxbridge was recovering from the injury as well as anyone could have dreamed, without a word of complaint or protestation. He was already getting fidgety and tiring of the multiple beds that had been set out for him to move between on crutches.

'I reckon I still have a little fight in me, don't you think Caro?' he asked her playfully one day.

Of course, as soon as Lady Caroline had heard that her brother had been so seriously injured, she knew that Lady Uxbridge would make the crossing from England to be with her husband. It was only natural that she should want to attend to him personally, although this rattled Lady Caroline, who would have much preferred to do it herself.

Lady Uxbridge's arrival in Brussels put her in a difficult situation, for she had barely seen her since the elopement, and they had certainly not spoken on those occasions. Now Lady

Caroline was going to have to bury her reservations and make polite conversation.

Sitting at her looking glass, she put on her favourite coral necklace and pearl earrings. She wore an elegant light summer pelisse of periwinkle blue, but she felt uncomfortable and flustered. She so wanted to look her best. There was a gentle knock on the door to her dressing room, as her husband entreated her again to join him. Lady Caroline heaved herself upright and headed to the door. She hoped her children were having a better day.

∽◦∾

Maria, Georgy and Harriet were in the family's carriage. It had taken them past the Namur Gate and they were now heading towards the Forêt de Soignes, whose massive beech trees spread for miles outside the town. Maria soaked all of this in as she watched the goings-on out of the carriage window.

In some ways, normal life was returning for those living in Brussels. She saw traders on the road and families going about their daily business. Sadly, everyone seemed to be becoming somewhat immune to the sight of corpses and dead horses piled in the streets.

When Maria had first seen a heap of bodies, the day after she and Georgy had burnt the letters in the ribbon box, she had wept and shook. It had been monstrous. Now when she saw a dead soldier she felt only a deadened sort of sickness before turning her eyes away. The smell, however, was not something she thought she would ever get used to.

When the battle had ended the jubilation had surpassed

anything Maria had ever experienced. The celebration of Napoleon's abdication a year previously paled in comparison. She still felt a rush of emotion when she recalled the moment they had finally heard that victory had been achieved. Yet when they had learnt how many had been lost, their elation had been immediately tempered.

She understood now what it took for men to reach peace on behalf of two warring nations, and what was the real human cost. The knowledge filled her with awe and disgust, and she vowed never to favour war or profess its advantages. Despite this, she wanted to see more of what had taken place on those killing fields so close to the city she had grown to love dearly, and where she had known so much happiness.

She had pestered her mother and father every day since the battle had ended for permission to go to Waterloo and see the field of battle for herself. She and her sisters were by no means the only ones making the journey. As soon as the smoke and fog of the battlefield had faded and the blood had dried on the streets, carriages had begun to make the journey to the village of Waterloo. While many went to gawp, others came to pay their respects and seek answers about those who had not returned.

Maria's motivations were not so clear-cut. Part of her wanted to see the area where Lord Hay had been cut down, yet at the same time she didn't want to acknowledge his loss. Lord Hay's disappearance from her life still felt surreal and otherworldly. Would seeing the battlefield bring home the reality that he was dead?

At first, Lady Caroline had refused to let her daughters go.

'None of you is to set foot on that battlefield, and that is final,' Lady Caroline had said sternly, as she watched her daughters scraping lint in the back garden. It was an occupation they now undertook daily, as so many wounds still needed tending to.

'But, Mama, we have seen so much already. Will you really deny us the chance to see the place where the most important battle of our generation was won?'

Maria thought this a strong argument. Lady Caroline looked unmoved, but Maria pushed her advantage.

'When we are mothers ourselves, and even grandmothers, do you really want us to have to admit that we were so close and yet didn't see it, and so can't tell others what it was like? Or even to have to lie?'

Lady Caroline eventually relented, and so it was that a few days later the three eldest sisters were permitted to go to Waterloo. Maria strongly suspected her father's hand in convincing her. Maria had noticed that he'd been treating his three eldest daughters with newfound respect since the battle.

He had also been home more often in the evenings, spending less time at the Literary Club. Maria reflected on the cross words they had exchanged that day in the library, and on her warning about his gambling. To Maria's great pleasure he appeared to have taken this to heart. She saw how happy this made her mother, also, and how content her parents were in each other's company again. It made her heart swell.

The beech trees whipped past the window, blurring her view, as the carriage made its way through the forest. This had been the place Lord Hay had wanted to meet Maria when he wrote all those months ago. What a place of significance it would have been had she acted on the letter! If she had run away with him, she would now be a widow, mere months after marrying.

In the week since the battle there'd been more time to reflect on Lord Hay and what might have happened in another version of her story. She had, in the end, succumbed to many a night of tears, weeping silently into her pillow, or going for walks in the garden alone so she could give way to sorrow on the seats between the rose bushes. She was just one of thousands of women across Brussels suffering in the same way, feeling the injustice and energy of grief, like a raw, open wound.

Maria missed seeing Lord Hay, she missed chatting and laughing with him. Now he would never visit them again, never ask her to dance with him, never kiss her. Had she been foolish to let him slip through her fingers? But then, of course, there was the other woman to consider.

Had Maria known about her, she surely would have behaved differently. This lady would perhaps have heard by now the fate of her beau, so many miles away. Maria wondered how she was coping in England, with such little news of the battle, and was glad for the thousandth time that she was in the thick of it here in Brussels.

The carriage jolted over a rock on the path and Maria was shaken from her heavy-hearted thoughts. Georgy took her hand and squeezed it, smiling warmly at her. Sweet Georgy, who had provided such comfort and security to Maria in the past week. Georgy, who had not been nearly so keen to come to the battlefield, as she was scared to see the bodies and blood close-up, but had come anyway, to support her sisters. Georgy, who had not seen the Prince of Orange since the battle, busy as he was with his wounds and his duties and was trying her hardest not to let it upset her.

The bond between the three sisters had undoubtedly been strengthened by their shared suffering, and Maria would not have wished to be making this journey with anyone but her two best friends. She returned Georgy's smile and glanced over at Harriet.

If only her eldest sister could be the happy, confident young lady who had arrived in Brussels just over a year ago. Harriet, seated opposite them, was pale and pinched. Their father had told them Baron Trip survived the battle, but he hadn't contacted Harriet and she didn't speak of him.

Maria thought of the many balls they'd attended in the months preceding the battle, how men and dresses, hats and ribbons had been all that occupied their thoughts. How far away that life seemed now. Looking at her sisters, she knew they felt it, too. The brave new world they were stepping into was quite changed from the heady days before the battle, when they had lived in blissful ignorance of how war could scar not only landscapes, but people. Now they were to face it in the flesh, and their education would be complete.

The carriage stopped and the coachman helped each of them out. Looking down so as not to miss her footing, Maria saw pieces of shot, fabric and something that looked like bone on the ground near her feet. She stumbled, but the coachman had her arm and held her steady. Looking across the skyline, she took in all that was before her, a hand shielding her eyes from the sun.

The landscape before them had been all but destroyed by fire, cannon and shot. Farmhouses and gardens were burnt black, the trunk of a tree shattered into pieces. Everywhere they looked were mounds of bodies as well as loosely covered graves. Dead horses lay strewn across the ground. Crows and ravens hopped and flapped about, their squarks the only sounds they could distinguish over the rush of the wind.

Some colours were distinct: the unmistakable red of an English uniform, or the blue of the French. They could make out abandoned clothing, cloth caps, splinters and cannon shot, but much was disguised by thick, congealed mud.

The stink of dirt, blood and sweat, and something worse that reminded Maria of a butcher's shop, was so intense that Harriet and Georgy put their handkerchiefs to their faces. Maria resisted the temptation. Although she too felt nauseous, she wanted to see, feel and smell it all, to remember this sight for the rest of her life.

She had never felt sadder, yet more proud at the same time. Proud of these men who had died so that she could stand there now in safety, with her sisters, and survey the scene as though it was already a page in history. Tears welled and ran down her face, and she let them.

Their papa had warned them that a great number of men had not yet been retrieved from the battlefield.

'They're doing what they can,' he had reassured them, 'but the numbers are far greater than anyone could have prepared for.'

They watched as medical men and nurses went from body to body to see if any lives could be saved. Some were being removed on stretchers. Maria's eyes followed these men, and she prayed they could be spared from making the ultimate sacrifice. There had been far too much of that; the evidence was all around.

They had walked a little way and now returned to the carriage. The coachman handed them down the baskets of food and bottles of cherry water they'd brought with them from the kitchen. As they headed off, intent on finding those they could attend to, Maria turned to her sisters.

'One day, our children and grandchildren will ask about what happened here in these fields, and we shall be able to say we did our bit and saw it all.'

Soon the church bells from the nearby village tolled, calling the evening Angelus. As the sisters went about their work, they whispered the prayer under their breath.

CHAPTER XXIV

Finding Home

*'I am enjoying quiet and security
in a very beautiful spot, after scenes
such as I never expected to witness.'*

Lady Caroline to the Dowager Countess of Uxbridge

Back at the house, the girls saw their parents had returned from their trip to visit Lord and Lady Uxbridge. Entering the drawing room, Maria was pleased to see that her mother looked better than she had for days. Had the meeting with Lady Uxbridge gone that well? Lady Caroline was smiling as the three sisters entered the room.

'My dears, we have a visitor.'

Maria looked round to see what was pleasing her mother so and gasped in surprise, for standing there in the room was Lord Fontanelle, his arms clasped behind his back. He smiled.

'Good afternoon, ladies,' he said. He turned to Maria and added, 'Miss Maria, it's a pleasure to see you again.'

Maria blushed, suddenly worried that her father, at least, did not know Lord Fontanelle had walked her back from the Duchess of Richmond's ball.

Luckily Lady Caroline said, 'Lord Fontanelle has most kindly come to call. I've already explained to your father how you became acquainted.'

'Yes, it appears Lord Fontanelle has made himself useful not only to myself over the last few weeks.' Capel turned to him and continued, 'I thank you very much for keeping me abreast of the situation with your letters. It was most generous of you.'

Lord Fontanelle inclined his head. 'It was my pleasure, I wanted to make sure you knew the lines of communication were open in case you needed to leave, to make sure you were all safe.' His eyes returned to Maria's.

'Do come and meet my other daughters,' Capel said.

Maria could sense Harriet and Georgy looking at her, eyes wide. They each dropped into a curtsey as Capel introduced them.

'I'm so glad to meet you all,' Lord Fontanelle said. 'It has indeed been a most challenging time, but from what your parents have been telling me, you ladies have done a splendid job of caring for the wounded.'

'We did what we could, enough to understand how much was given and lost,' said Harriet.

The parrot came flying in through the open window and landed on the fireplace with a clatter, knocking over the ornaments and framed miniatures that were propped up there.

'Heavens!' shrieked Lady Caroline in alarm, as the girls laughed.

'What a beautiful creature,' said Lord Fontanelle.

'I don't know,' said Maria shyly, 'we find he is rather aggressive towards visitors.'

'I shall have to keep my distance then,' Lord Fontanelle replied cheerfully, and took the opportunity to stand a fraction closer to Maria. To everyone's great surprise, the parrot, squawking loudly, flew over to Lord Fontanelle. The man didn't flinch, but bravely held out his arm. To their delight the bird landed on it with surprising grace, and immediately settled down to clean his feathers as though they were old friends.

'Goodness!' was all Maria could say.

'Well, I think you are the first male guest we've had who the parrot has approved of, that must count for something!' said Georgy, laughing.

'I suppose we shall have to keep him, then,' Lady Caroline sighed. 'But when we eventually return to England, he will *not* be coming with us.'

'You are to stay in Brussels for now?'

Did Maria detect a hopeful note in Lord Fontanelle's tone?

'For the present,' Lady Caroline answered, her eyes darting to Maria.

'How did you find the battlefield?' It was Capel who spoke, and Maria who answered.

'Incredibly moving. A sight I'm sure none of us will ever forget.'

There was a natural lull in the conversation, before Lord Fontanelle surprised them all again with his next words, which he directed to Capel.

'Sir, might I prevail upon your kindness and have the honour of taking a short walk around your charming garden with Miss Maria? We won't go far.'

Maria was surprised but pleased and looked to her father for his response. For once she didn't feel embarrassed and her cheeks didn't betray her. It seemed the most natural thing in the world for Lord Fontanelle to want to see her alone. Capel looked taken aback but didn't hesitate in giving his consent.

'Why, of course; I'm sure Muzzy would be delighted.' His eyes twinkled as he said to Maria, 'Go and enjoy yourself, my dear, but perhaps it would be best to leave the parrot here.'

Walking around the garden in the bright summer sunlight was a blissful balm after the scarred landscape at Waterloo. Lord Fontanelle seemed to be in a reflective mood. Neither said anything for a while; each enjoying the experience of being alone together again.

Finally, Lord Fontanelle remarked, 'How different life is from when we last walked together. I think then I was plagued by what had happened to me in France, and what was about to take place. I hope I didn't distress you in any way.'

She stopped and turned to him. 'Not in the slightest. It was a most illuminating meeting and opened my eyes to much of what had happened in France that had been kept from me. I only hope you didn't think me an ignorant child for not knowing more.'

'Nothing could be further from the truth.'

They had not carried on walking. Maria felt no awkwardness when looking up into Marius's warm and comforting eyes, and felt sure that all was well between them and would be for quite some time.

Marius looked down at her and said, 'I hope your heart has not been left behind on the battlefield.'

'No, I was lucky to escape that plight.'

'Maria, might I call on you again? I feel we have so much to learn about each other.'

Maria found herself saying, 'Yes, of course, I would like that very much, Marius.'

He smiled in response. Her brain hadn't fully engaged with what Lord Fontanelle intended by his words, but Maria knew it was what she wanted. It was enough that he wanted to see her again and that she wanted the same.

'I am so pleased that you shall be calling Brussels your home for a while longer,' he said.

'I'm in no hurry to leave. I feel I have so much yet to enjoy here, and I've come to love the city.'

Lord Fontanelle opened his mouth to reply but suddenly there was a loud squawk, and the parrot came flying towards them again, making them jump and laugh. The bird soared over their heads and settled on the branch of a nearby tree. As Maria turned back, she found Lord Fontanelle closer than before, his hand at her elbow.

She felt hot and happy as she raised her face to his and their lips met. How sweet was the embrace! All her senses were suspended in the moment. They broke apart, beaming sheepishly at each other.

'We should probably get you back to your family before they begin to think we have eloped,' Lord Fontanelle said.

Maria, giddy with pleasure, smiled at the irony in his words.

But it was sometime later when they finally made it back to the house, by now arm in arm. The parrot had settled himself on Lord Fontanelle's shoulder. The light of the summer evening had dimmed around them, making the path glow softly, the trees rustling gently and the scent of roses heady in the air.

All adventures must have an ending, and Maria felt sure she was at last on the path that had been laid out just for her. Brussels had taken her on quite the journey, and now she had found her own slice of happiness. Lord Fontanelle took Maria's hand in his, and the trio of man, woman and parrot slowly walked back through the garden towards the house to begin their next chapter.

Afterword

The majority of *The Belles of Waterloo* is recounted exactly as it happened over two hundred years ago, with a few adjustments that are in keeping with the period and, I hope, add to the enjoyment of the story. Luckily, the letters sent to the Dowager Countess of Uxbridge in England by the eldest Capel sisters and their mother were published in 1955. They have become an invaluable source not just for me, but for countless historians of this period. Here I will detail how the lives of each of the main characters played out in real life.

Capel's gambling addiction and the impact on the family, including the reason they had to leave London, is exact. General Barnes proposed to Maria in March 1815 and also became a confidant to Harriet. Lady Charlotte Greville did reportedly say to Lady Caroline, 'Which of your daughters is General Barnes to marry? Or is he to marry *them all*?' General Barnes never did marry but held various senior military positions in Ceylon (now Sri Lanka) and India before moving into politics.

Lord Hay died on the battlefield on 16 June 1815, and did leave his horse, who was called Miss Muzzy, to Maria. The words he spoke to her at the ball are recounted verbatim: 'Remember, I shall fall in the first action and I shall fall on Miss Muzzy. If I have time to speak I shall send her to you, and you must always keep her.' These words were recorded by Lady Caroline in a letter to her mother dated 18 June 1815. While the romance between Lord Hay and Maria is invented, he was a constant friend to the family and did leave mementoes for an admirer back in England for Lord William Pitt Lennox to pass on.

Maria and Lord Fontanelle met at the Duchess of Richmond's ball and readers will be pleased to know that they did marry, but not until 1821. The reason for the delay is not known. Maria became the Marquise d'Espinassy de Fontanelle and lived until 1856. Their son, Alfred, fought in the Crimean War and lost an arm in the Siege of Sevastopol. Maria's younger sister, Louisa, a peripheral character in the book, married Lord Fontanelle's brother, Count Auguste, in 1827.

The attachment between Georgy and the Prince of Orange is suggested in the letters, but not explicit. Georgy married an Englishman in the same year Maria married. She was widowed and married again in 1831, living a further four years.

The romance between Harriet and Baron Trip was real, and the letters discovered by Mr Capel in Chapter IX are verbatim extracts. Mr Capel and Baron Trip's duel did take place, although it happened later than in the book, in April 1815.

The fate of Baron Trip is a sad one. He survived Waterloo but was clearly a troubled soul, as he took his own life in 1816, causing Harriet fresh heartbreak. She, however, married the following year, although sadly she died in childbirth eighteen months later.

Lord Uxbridge's life, adventures and injuries are all recounted truthfully.

Exactly a month after Waterloo, Lady Caroline gave birth to a girl, Priscilla, and General Barnes became her godfather. Unhappily, the child died in September 1815, causing the family great pain. She was buried just outside Waterloo, at the same site as the officers who fell during the battle.

After this, the Capel family moved to the town of Lausanne, on the shores of Lake Geneva in Switzerland, as even the house where they lived in Brussels had become too expensive. Possibly this is where Maria and Lord Fontanelle met again, as he was brought up in Switzerland.

Lady Caroline and Capel did not go on to have any more children, Capel dying only four years after Waterloo. In total Lady Caroline had thirteen children, as one other daughter had died young, in 1794. Lady Caroline saw all three of her sons marry into noble families and four of her daughters marry during their time in Switzerland. She outlived not only her husband but three of her daughters, including Harriet and Georgy, dying in 1847.

Acknowledgements

It's been such a pleasure to have *Belles* published, made all the better for having worked with so many talented people. Firstly I thank Jennifer Potter who gave me invaluable early feedback as part of the Royal Literary Fund Writing Fellows scheme. Jane Branfield, Archivist at Stratfield Saye, has always encouraged my writing endeavours and read the earliest draft with great kindness. A few years down the line Alice Boggis-Rolfe did the same and boosted my confidence just at the right moment. My thanks to you both. I also thank Rory Muir who kindly helped me with some historical accuracies during the final edits.

I have so enjoyed working with the team at Unicorn Publishing Group again and would like to particularly thank Lord Strathcarron, Ryan Gearing, Felicity Price-Smith, Lauren Tanner and Vivian Head. My thanks also go to Dea and Matthew at Fiction Feedback. It's not always been easy to juggle editing with looking after a new-born, so I thank you all for your patience. Thea Mason provided the author's image, a happy memory of one of the many summer's days spent in her excellent company.

Several people contributed financially to the book's production, for which they are owed a special thank you. They are John Chatfeild-Roberts, Sir Lawrence Clarke, Alan Cooper, Chris and Vicki Crossland, Richard Foster, Joanna Jensen, Christopher and Clare McCann, Jane Williams, and the 'Belles of Burrington' – Pollyanna, Imogen and

Arabella. One further very generous sponsor shall remain anonymous, but I hope they enjoy the tour of Apsley House, for which I thank Josephine Oxley, Keeper of the Wellington Collection.

To Suzanne and Faye, thank you for keeping the house running smoothly so I could ensconce myself in the office. So many of my friends checked in on me regularly, I'm afraid too many to note here, but I am so grateful.

Finally, the biggest thanks of all must go to my husband, Charlie, who has supported me from day one and especially through a series of gruelling final edits as my pregnancy progressed. It turns out he is also a whizz with Photoshop and catches more typos than anyone I've ever met, so I think we make a good team.

February 2022, Dorset